W9-BMM-707

"My mama's dead, Miss Sam. I ain't got nobody."

Samantha put her arms around the little girl. "It's okay, honey. You're going to come home with Joe and me." She held her tight and rested her head against Corey's hair.

Corey looked past Samantha to Joe.

Sam couldn't see Corey's expession, but Joe could. And her thoughts were instantly visible to him. Mixed with her genuine misery was a challenge. *I've got her now. See if you can top this, buster.*

Joe told himself she was just a little girl.

He told himself she was a little girl whose life had been tough and sad.

He told himself that he and Sam were making a *big* mistake.

JANET DAILEY
AWARD
WINNER

Praise for *Iron Lace*

"A fascinating historical tale of the tangled race relations and complex history of Louisiana...this is a page-turner."

—*New Orleans Times-Picayune*

"Intricate, seductive and a darned good read."

—*Publishers Weekly*

"Emilie Richards has penned a riveting masterpiece of forbidden love, revenge and moral consequences that ricochets through several generations."

—*Romance Forever*

EMILIE RICHARDS

THE TROUBLE WITH JOE

MIRA BOOKS

ISBN 1-55166-279-5

THE TROUBLE WITH JOE

Copyright © 1994 by Emilie Richards McGee.

All rights reserved. Except for use in any review, the reproduction or utilization of this work in whole or in part in any form by any electronic, mechanical or other means, now known or hereafter invented, including xerography, photocopying and recording, or in any information storage or retrieval system, is forbidden without the written permission of the publisher, MIRA Books, 225 Duncan Mill Road, Don Mills, Ontario, Canada M3B 3K9.

All characters in this book have no existence outside the imagination of the author and have no relation whatsoever to anyone bearing the same name or names. They are not even distantly inspired by any individual known or unknown to the author, and all incidents are pure invention.

MIRA and the star colophon are trademarks of MIRA Books.

Printed in U.S.A.

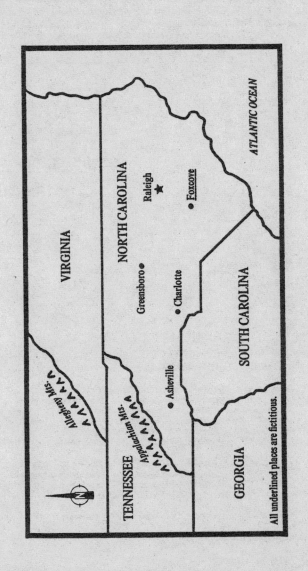

All underlined places are fictitious.

Prologue

Nothing was hotter than a summer day in Sadler County, North Carolina. And even if the calendar said it wasn't quite summer, the mercury on Sadler County thermometers hadn't been informed.

In the worst part of the afternoon Joseph Giovanelli stood in the heart of a grove of pines and felt waves of heat shimmer over his body. His white shirt was already wet, and an interior voice reminded him that he would have to change before he returned to school.

He wasn't sure where he would find the vitality to go back at all. He had come home for something he had left behind, a list of new students who would be attending the high school in the fall. Due to a colleague's absence, the task of assigning the students to home rooms had fallen to Joe. That wasn't unusual. Historically rush jobs fell to the first in command. And as principal of Sadler High, the buck always stopped at Joe's wide-open door.

He hadn't minded the extra work. He had done it last night, finishing after midnight. These days he relished working late. He had always been an active man, happiest when he was busy. Now there was a manic quality to that activity; he was as aware of it as everybody else. But work

was the only thing that made Joe feel alive. And if a man
didn't feel alive at least some of the time, he might as well
be dead.

Overhead a crow cawed his displeasure at Joe's presence
in the woods. Joe told himself that the crow was right. He
needed to get back; he did not need quiet woods or dis-
quieting contemplation. Despite that, something urged him
forward. His feet passed down a well-traveled path, one he
had lined with wood chips from the trees he had been
forced to take down when landscaping near the house.

He had made good use of the rest of the wood, too. One
hundred yards down the path he stopped in front of a small
log cabin whose wide shadow stretched to the calm blue
of a one-acre lake.

There were ducks swimming near the shore, and at Joe's
approach a goose, like a white-feathered watchdog, honked
a warning. But the warning was drowned out by voices in
Joe's head, the voices he had come to hear.

Joe, you know you're crazy, don't you? Nobody, but no-
body, builds a playhouse for children they don't even have
yet. Not before they finish the house they've got to live in
every day. There's no floor in our dining room and not a
cabinet in the kitchen. I'm tired of cooking from cardboard
boxes. Let me repeat... Joe, put me down! No, I will not
be a party to this. Not here. I don't care if the playhouse
has walls, Joe. There aren't any doors. Yes, I know it's
getting dark. Yes. Oh, Joe, you idiot! You wonderful idiot!

He stared at the cabin and saw the ghosts of two people
with their lives stretching in front of them, good lives,
happy lives. He saw his wife, Samantha, as clearly as if
she were really standing there, as clearly as he had this
morning when he watched her drive off to her job at Foxcove Elementary School. Blond, reserved Sam, with the
china-doll complexion and the lake blue eyes. Eyes that hid
so well the passion only Joe had known.

Sweat poured down his back and beaded his forehead. There were other ghosts here, too. Ghosts of children who would never run along this path or play in this cabin. Ghosts of grandchildren who would never know the beauty of this lake, the peace of piney North Carolina forests.

He couldn't hear their voices or their laughter. He had never heard them and never would.

In the stillness the crow cawed again, as if he had followed this strange upright animal to ask what he planned to do next.

"I plan to go back to work," Joe whispered. "What in the hell else is there to do?"

He turned his back on the cabin, on the lake and on a lifetime of dreams.

When the crow cawed again, there was no one there to hear it.

1

Roses faded. Roses wilted. But to Samantha Giovanelli's knowledge, roses never turned into something else entirely. Not unless they had a little help.

Or a little helper.

Sam had walked by her desk three times that afternoon and never noticed that flawless white rosebuds had turned into wilting yellow dandelions. Now she could ignore it no longer. Long stems had been exchanged for those just long enough to fit into a child's grubby fist. And the delicate white porcelain vase that had been delivered with the roses had a sizable chip in the rim.

Sam supposed she was lucky the vase wasn't leaking water all over the papers piled on the desk, papers collected after a year of teaching twenty-six first graders how to read, 'rite and resist clobbering each other. In three years as an educator she had learned to appreciate the smallest things—and people. Now as she rummaged through her wastebasket she told herself that the dandelions were a symbol of what the year had meant to one little girl. They were a sign that Sam had succeeded in an impossible task: civilizing Corey Haskins.

Not that the task was finished.

At the bottom of the wastebasket, piled high with papers, used-up workbooks, melted crayons and lumps of clay were six formerly perfect rosebuds. The stems were crushed and the petals bruised. Sam lifted them carefully—although care at this stage was a sign of terminal optimism—and trimmed the stems to two inches with blunt-end scissors from her desk drawer. Then she filled the sink on the other side of the room and immersed the flowers in the cool water.

If she couldn't have a bouquet, at least she could have a corsage.

"Sortin' your trash now, Sammy? If we were all as organized as you, this school would run like a four-legged dog in a three-legged race."

Sam turned off the water and weighted the ends of the stems with a rock so the roses wouldn't float to the top. She flashed a smile at Polly, the first-grade teacher from a room down the hall who was standing in the doorway. "A four-legged dog in a three-legged race?"

"Think about it," Polly drawled. She wandered into the room at the same speed as her words. As always, Polly seemed in need of a jump start. "You did know your trash was higgledy-piggledy all over the floor?"

"I know." Sam dried her hands and headed for the wastebasket again. She began to stuff the trash inside.

"And you do know that this is the last day of classes, and you're supposed to be doin' flip-flops up and down the corridor?"

"Anybody who could do flip-flops in this heat deserves a gold medal."

"Mind tellin' me what you're doin'?"

"Did you see the man from Allen's Florist in the hall earlier?"

"Yep, I did."

"Well, Joe sent me roses. Six gorgeous white roses."

"Joe can put his sneakers under my bed just any old time he chooses."

Sam laughed. Polly was ambling toward fifty, and along the way had picked up an extra pound for every single year. Her hair was bottle red and her clothes most suitable for a church rummage sale. But Harlan, her husband of thirty good years, still thought she was the most wonderful woman in Sadler County, and so did their eight children. Sam didn't have a thing to worry about.

"So why do you have the world's poorest excuse for dandelions in this vase if Joe sent you roses?" Polly ran her finger over the chipped rim and shook her head. "Next question's why you have this vase at all?"

Samantha finished the trash and began to straighten her desk. "It was minus the chip when the roses came in it. Apparently one of my students decided that dandelions would look better and switched them sometime after class. Probably when I was up at the office. Then she threw the roses in the trash and covered them up well. I just found them."

"She." Polly hadn't missed the pronoun that eliminated fully half of Sam's classroom. "Corey?"

"Probably," Sam admitted.

"I'da chained that little gal in the closet if she was put in my class this year."

"Sure you would have." More often than not when Sam walked by Polly's classroom door, some child was settled in Polly's ample lap or arms receiving either a dose of TLC or the gentlest of reprimands. She was Miss Pollywolly Doodle to all the first graders, and she would no more raise her voice or hand to a child than she would take up running or go on a diet.

"Why do you suppose she did it?" Polly asked.

"I guess Corey wanted me to remember her."

"Like anybody here could ever forget her."

Sam couldn't argue. Corey was unforgettable. She lifted the framed class photo from her desk and her eyes went right to Corey in the back row. Corey was shorter than most of the other children, but the photographer had taken one look at her and relegated her to the back, where her clothes would be covered by the heads of other children.

The maneuver had been only partially successful. There had been no way to hide Corey's chopped-up blond hair and scratched-up face. Sam had tenderly washed that little face herself, but Corey had been mauled by an alley cat— she had probably tormented the poor thing—and under the usual dirt had been railroad-track scars that showed clearly in the picture.

"What will she do this summer?" Sam asked.

Polly took the photograph from Sam's hands and set it firmly back on the desk. "Now, you listen here, Sammy. First off, that little girl is now a second grader. By the grace of God, maybe, but still a second grader. She's somebody else's problem now, because she sure can't be yours anymore. There's nothing you can do. She's got a mama, and the county says her mama is fit to raise her."

"Does a fit mother send a child to school in filthy bedroom slippers?"

"You know we can't take a kid away from her mama just because she's poor."

Poverty wasn't the issue, and Sam and Polly both knew it. There had been other poor children in Sam's classroom; Sadler County, North Carolina was full of poor people. But most of the time their kids were clean. Those kids came to school with something in their stomachs, even if it wasn't Sam's idea of good nutrition. And the parents showed up for teacher conferences, or took the time to fill out forms so that their children could receive free lunches.

Corey's mother could learn a lesson from any of them. There were people all over the world who longed des-

perately for a child; Sam knew that all too well. And then
there were people like Verna Haskins who had a child and
cursed the day that child had been born.

"I know I can't be her teacher forever," Sam said. "But
it's hard to let go."

"Better learn."

"Do you know how many phone calls I got this year
about Corey?" Sam forced a smile. "Thirty-two. I kept
track. All from angry parents wanting to know what I was
going to do about her. You'd think I'd be doing those flip-
flops you were talking about."

"While you're at it, don't forget the time old Ray Flynn
tried to have her put in a class for the disturbed and you
threatened to quit your job over it."

"If Joe wasn't the high school principal, Dr. Ray would
have forced me out."

"Yep. Joe can make things tough on folks who go after
what's his, that's for sure."

"Is that right?"

The deep voice from the doorway caused both women
to turn. Sam felt the impact of her husband's presence just
as she always did. It started somewhere deep inside, curled
and crept through her until she was smiling.

And hoping that he would do the same.

"What are you doing here?" she asked.

"I just came to see how you managed on your last day."

"I'm headin' out." Polly started toward the door. She
patted Joe on the cheek as she passed. He took her hand
and gave it a courtly kiss before she vanished down the
hall.

Sam didn't move. There had been a time when she
wouldn't have had to. Joe would have strolled over, lifted
her off her feet and whirled her around the room. But the
Joe lounging in the doorway was a different man. So many
things had changed in the past six months.

"I got the roses," she said. "They were beautiful. I was so surprised."

"*Were* beautiful?"

"Well, there was a tiny accident. I'll be wearing them on my dress at the party tomorrow."

He pushed away from the doorjamb and came over to the desk. She rose on tiptoe to kiss his cheek. His arms closed around her and she rested against him.

"How was your day?" he asked.

Questions behind a question. She knew what he really wanted to know. Was the last day of school particularly hard this year? Was it painful to leave the children behind? Was she going to make it through the summer without the sound of childish laughter?

"All right," she said. "How about yours?"

"The seniors trashed the lawn and poured ball bearings in the hallways. Sometime this week somebody spelled out Dean Lambert Sucks on the football field. In herbicide. The grass died today."

"That's it?"

"If we're lucky."

She slipped her arms around his waist. Joe had a quarterback's physique—long muscular legs, trim hips and waist and broad, broad shoulders. He looked equally good in a suit or bathing trunks, but he looked his very best in nothing at all.

She leaned back so she could see his face. His features were striking and strong, straight off the steamship from northern Italy, with only a Slovenian grandmother to dare reconfigure the Giovanelli gene pool. His hair was shining black and his eyes as dark as his most secret thoughts. When he smiled his face came alive. Or it had once upon a time.

"Thanks for taking the time to come over here," she said.

"It was either this or chopping out sod on the field. I thought Lambert should chop, since he's the one who enrages the kids."

"Al wouldn't know what side of a hoe went where."

"Actually, he's got all the juniors who still owe detention hours doing it."

"Great. That way he can be sure the same thing will happen next year when *they're* seniors." Reluctantly she moved away. They couldn't stand in each other's arms all afternoon, no matter how good it felt. "I've still got next week to finish cleaning the room. Do you have to go back to school, or can you come home with me?"

"I'll follow you back."

She was so surprised that for a moment she didn't know what to say. "Well, fine," she said at last. "Maybe it'll be cooler there."

"Don't count on it."

"We can stand under the ceiling fans and drink iced tea."

"Do you need help with those?" He nodded toward two cardboard boxes beside the door.

"Just a few little things to keep me busy this summer. Some new textbooks to look over. The workbooks the board's decided we'll be using next year. Some music to learn, since the music teacher's been cut to half-time and now we'll be teaching music as well as everything else in the classroom."

"Overworked and underpaid."

"The definition of a teacher," they finished together.

"I'll get the boxes," he said. "Do you need to stop by the office?"

She nodded. "I'll meet you in the parking lot."

He started toward the door.

"Joe?"

He looked over his shoulder.

"The roses were the loveliest thing to happen to me in a long time."

His smile was brief and lopsided. But it was a smile. Hope stirred inside her. He had been gone a full minute before she collected herself and started for the office.

Joe fit both boxes in the trunk of his car. It was an American sports car, shiny black and low slung with more horsepower than the North Carolina blacktop could handle. He had bought it six months ago without consulting Sam. When he'd brought it home she had said all the right things, but her expression had told him what she really thought.

He didn't know what had possessed him to buy a car that every boy in the high school would sell his soul for. He had seen it in the lot, a visible symbol of everything masculine and powerful, and he had signed the papers that afternoon. The psychology behind that decision was perhaps best left unexplored.

Killer—Sam's name for the car—bounced when he slammed the trunk. Joe had parked under a magnolia tree in full bloom, and a welcome breeze waltzed the scent through the air. A piano tinkled through an open door to the cafeteria, and children's voices sounded from the playground on the other side of the school. He leaned against the car and crossed his arms. Despite the sensory attractions even the short wait made him restless.

He scanned the school yard for something to look at. A squirrel attempted the leap from one tree to another and managed admirably. A mockingbird squawked at the intruder, then made a faulty dive bomb when the squirrel didn't take the hint. Just beyond the school grounds a car pulled from its parking place and drove down the empty street.

Joe tapped his foot and drummed his fingers against his arms. Pressure built inside him. He was so seldom idle that now he felt as if someone had tied him, hand and foot. He thought of a million things he needed to be doing, and wished he could do them simultaneously.

Suddenly a small figure crawled from behind one bush to another under the windows of the classroom closest to the parking lot. The landscaping was overgrown, and there was almost no room between the flourishing juniper and holly and the brick wall. At first Joe wondered if he had fantasized the child as an antidote to unaccustomed inactivity. He took off his sunglasses and squinted at the bush where he thought the child had gone. Nothing moved, but there was the tiniest scrap of red visible between one evergreen branch and another.

He started forward.

"Joe?"

He held his finger to his lips, but Sam, coming toward him from the other side of the building with a loaded box topped with a vase of wobbling dandelions, didn't see.

"Joe, grab this vase, will you, before it falls?"

He abandoned hide-and-seek and went to meet Sam. Twenty-five yards from the car he took the box and let her carry the vase.

"There's a kid hiding in the bushes over by the sixth-grade classrooms," he told her.

"Why?"

"Who knows? It's been a while since I was a kid."

"I don't see anybody."

"This kid knows how to hide, you've got to give her that."

"Her?"

"I caught a flash."

"What exactly did you see?"

"Blond hair. Red shirt."

"Corey." Sam set the vase on Killer's hood and started toward the bushes. "Corey," she called, "come on out and meet Mr. Joe. You're going to get all scratched up back there.''

There was no telltale rustle. "Corey?" She moved closer, but not quickly. Joe guessed that Corey was easy to spook. Sam would know from experience.

"Come on, Corey," she said softly. "Nobody's mad at you. We just don't want you to get hurt. That's no place to play."

There was a flash of red at the far end of the row, three classrooms and more than two dozen scratchy evergreens away. Sam straightened. Joe turned his head just in time to see a little girl dressed in a long-sleeved shirt and corduroy pants—too worn to be appropriate any time of year—crawl out from behind the last bush. She stood and stared at him. Even from a distance he detected suspicion in the dark eyes that took up half the child's face. Then she turned and made a run for the sidewalk in front of the school. She disappeared around the corner before Sam could say anything else.

"So that's Corey." Joe went to stand beside her.

"That *was* Corey. I'm sorry. I've talked about her so much I wanted you to meet her."

He stuffed his hands into his pockets. "After all the stories I've heard, I can wait until high school before I'm forced to get to know her."

She smiled, but he saw the tinge of sadness in her eyes. "You just might like her, Joe. The two of you have some things in common."

"Yeah?"

"You both love me."

He wanted to touch her hair, to tell her that Corey obviously had exquisite taste, but instead he shifted his weight to his heels, not quite moving away from her. "What else?"

"Neither of you has the slightest idea how to cope with your feelings."

He stared at her. The remark was so unlike Sam that for a moment he was at a loss for words. "What brought that on?" he asked at last.

She looked away. The breeze lifted a lock of her long blond hair and blew it against her cheek. He had always loved her best like this, when something unexpected ruffled her calm exterior. Now he wanted to tuck the hair back in place—almost as much as he wanted to insist she take back her words.

"I'm sorry." She didn't elaborate.

"So it has been a tough day," he said.

"Yes."

"I know you hate to say goodbye to your kids."

"Not *my* kids, Joe." She sighed. "I really am sorry. It's just that it's hardest of all saying goodbye to Corey. She has such potential. Her IQ is so high Dr. Ray went back and hand-graded the test after the results came in. Nobody but me believed she could be that smart."

"You're going to have a Corey every year in every class."

"And is it that easy for you to stay distant? It never used to be."

"You learn."

"You know what? I hope I don't. I hope my aptitude for cutting myself off from people is so low the psychologists have to hand-grade my results, just to be sure."

She had managed a smile, but he couldn't make himself smile back.

"I guess I need to get out of the sun," she said. "Let's go home and have that iced tea. I'll make something special for dinner tonight. How about your mother's manicotti?"

He looked at his watch. "No dinner for me. I've got Kiwanis tonight."

She searched his face. "Is it really important? We haven't had a night together in a long time." She moved a little closer. "We could test out the pond and see if it's warm enough for swimming. And if it's not..."

He knew the rest of the sentence. They could keep each other warm.

"I'm sorry, but I promised to give a report, so I can't skip." He looked at his watch again, as if it might help something. Anything. "And I hate to say it, but I didn't realize it was getting as late as it is. I'm not even going to have time to go home first. I've still got some work to do at school before the meeting."

"Can't it keep?"

"I wish." But he didn't, because he didn't want to go home anymore. He wanted to be busy. He wanted to do a thousand things at once.

"Why, Joe?"

He pretended he didn't understand. "Why what?"

"Why did you come here this afternoon?"

"I came to see how your day had gone."

"I think the part that's already finished is going to be the best part of it." She started toward her car, parked several rows from his.

"This is always a busy time of year," he said.

"Which makes it the same as every other time."

He caught up with her. "We've got all day tomorrow."

She stopped. "We have a houseful of people coming for our housewarming."

"We'll find some time alone."

"No, we probably won't." She stopped beside Killer and got the vase she had left on the hood. The dandelions had shriveled in the sun until they were nothing more than stems.

"Go home and get some rest." Joe leaned over and kissed her cheek. For one moment he was close enough for anything, for kissing or shaking or sobbing in her arms. Then he pulled away. "I'll try to get home early."

She didn't answer. She just turned and walked away.

2

Sometimes the silver-lining theory of human existence had merit. Sam and Joe's house was a perfect example. One hundred years before, it had been a general store, weathered wood and flapping tin roof, with a wide front porch where customers could practice spitting tobacco or watermelon seeds into the ragtag bushes below. From those days of relative prosperity it had fallen onto harder times. The proprietors had departed with the advent of the automobile. There hadn't been a need for a store on Old Scoggins Road when everyone could go into Foxcove for a wider variety of merchandise.

Over the years the store had been used sporadically as a community center, then a storage barn for hay. Most recently it hadn't been used for anything except marking the halfway point for anyone looking for the Insleys, residents of a prosperous farm just a half mile farther south.

Turner Insley, the owner, hadn't seen much need for tearing down the store. It was too far away from anything to be a danger. If it collapsed in the dead of night, chances were good that no one would be nearby to notice. Tearing it down cost good money, and there was always a better use for that. Over the years the store had grown a little more dilapidated, a little sorrier, but nobody had minded much.

Not until Joe Giovanelli.

One afternoon Joe had been driving past the store on his way to see Turner about his youngest granddaughter. Nesta Insley was the most vivacious, flirtatious sophomore in a school of close competitors. Southern charm was common enough to be ho-hum in Sadler County, but one flutter of Nesta's eyelashes and Rhett would have abandoned Scarlett. Nesta had successfully wrapped every male teacher around her pert little fingers, but Joe had been immune. Behind Nesta's vitality and charm he had seen a scared little girl who was cheating her way through school and life in general. Since her parents had claimed to be too busy to meet with him, Joe had been on his way to explain the situation to Turner.

He'd been a hundred yards past the store when he had applied his brakes and backed up to stop in front of it. In nearly a hundred years no one had seen the store's potential. But Joe had looked at the old building with the rusting tin and the sagging porch and called it home.

Conducting himself like the professional he was, Joe had waited until he and Turner had come to an understanding about Nesta. Turner was no fool; all he'd needed was Joe's professional opinion of his granddaughter and a few observations of his own. He had assured Joe that Nesta would be taken in hand. They had agreed on tighter curfews, supervised study hours and attention to weekly progress reports. Turner's word was still law in his family. If he told his son and daughter-in-law to shape up, they would.

Then the two men had gotten down to real estate. No, Turner didn't need the store, and he didn't need the land around it. There was a nice spring down behind the store, so he couldn't let the land go for nothing. No, sir, not for nothing. On the other hand, all he had to sell was the land, because nobody in his right mind wanted the store. Tearing it down was an expensive proposition. Yes, sir, a mighty expensive one, which was why it was still standing.

So they had bargained for the land. And after the two men had shaken hands on six acres, Joe had told Turner that he planned to renovate the store and make it his home. Turner had seen him out, laughing all the way to the car.

Sam had been the next hurdle. Now as Sam neared the store-turned-home she remembered the first time Joe had brought her here.

He had been sheepish, which for Joe meant that he was only half as cocky as usual. He had promised her a drive in the country. Their apartment in town was cramped, and getting out for the afternoon had seemed like a good idea. They had driven south, and Sam had assumed their destination was a lake near the county border. When Joe had turned onto Old Scoggins she had been mildly curious. When Joe had stopped in front of the store and suggested they take a walk she'd been curious.

When Joe had told her he had bought the store and land she had been furious.

It had taken a full month for Joe to persuade her they could turn the store into a home. Joe wasn't an easy man to say no to. He was domineering and brash. As a senior in high school the verbal score on his SATs had been high enough to garner scholarship offers at three different colleges. Polly always said that when Joe was fired up he could wear a body down so completely they'd do just about anything to make him go away.

But Sam had remained firm. She and Joe were opposites in many ways, but she was no less stubborn when something really mattered to her. Living in the store mattered. She hadn't been able to imagine that even fifty years of hard work would turn it into a home. Joe had looked at the store and surrounding land and seen a paradise. She had looked at it and seen heartbreak.

In the end, both of them had been right.

Today as she turned into the dogwood-shaded driveway, sunshine glinted off shiny tin and fresh white paint. Ivy and petunias spilled out of bright red window boxes flanked by spruce green shutters. A porch swing and three oak rocking chairs with blue calico cushions waited patiently on the front porch for someone to while away the evening sunset, and a hummingbird darted over the trumpet vine that screened one trellised end.

The scene was idyllic. There was enough sun to grow flowers and enough old trees to provide summertime shade. Red brick framed the flower beds and crisscrossed a walkway to the porch. The grass was soft and green, perfect for barefooted children to romp over. There were no children, but there was a bevy of kittens. Tinkerbelle, an aging calico who was old enough to know better, had presented Sam and Joe with her first and only litter just a month before.

Despite the kittens, despite Tink's greeting rubbed lovingly against Sam's leg, despite the cheery petunias and the newly flowering roses, Sam felt an oppressive loneliness.

A glass of iced tea, a shower and a change into soft knit white shorts and crop top did little to improve her mood. She picked at a muffin and tried the afternoon newspaper, but neither held her attention.

Finally, with the kittens frolicking at her heels, she started toward the pond. On its shore she reassured Attila, the watchgoose who had never learned to tell the difference between friend and enemy. The sun was dropping too slowly to suit her, but she settled on the soft grass at the pond's edge and watched its slow descent. There was no reason to go back to the house, no business there that couldn't wait.

The night she had first met Joe had been a little like this

one. It had been late spring, but hot, anyway, so hot that she had spent the day drifting from one air-conditioned room or vehicle to another. Until she had met Joe, her life had consisted of nothing but slow, graceful passage from one comfortably colorless moment to the next.

Now, despite all the problems that confronted them, she remembered that night. And, despite everything, she smiled.

"Oh, Samantha, not the red tonight. It's too bright and too low cut. I'll never understand why you bought something so unsuitable." Kathryn Whitehurst surveyed her daughter as she spoke, assessing her hair, her tasteful makeup, as well as the dress in question.

Samantha watched her mother silently tick off the details of her appearance. The red, a muted watermelon shade, was perfect with her pale blond hair and alabaster skin, and the sweetheart neckline just highlighted the subtle swell of her breasts. But it wasn't worth an argument. Kathryn had rigid standards for everything, but particularly appearance. As long as Samantha conformed, she and Kathryn could pretend they were the perfect mother and daughter. Samantha could be the flawless pearl bracelet to her mother's flawless double-strand choker.

"I'll wear the blue dress you bought me in New York," Samantha said.

"Well, hurry." Kathryn's tone implied that changing was Samantha's idea entirely. "Your father will be here in a few minutes, and you know how he hates to wait."

"I'll just be a minute."

In her room Samantha tossed the red dress onto her bed and found the blue in the back of her closet. It was the insipid hue of a cloudy sky, and once it was on and she surveyed the effect, she scolded herself for giving in to Kathryn's whims. She was twenty-one today, and she still couldn't stand up to her mother—or her father, for that matter. In fact, after twenty-one years of doing exactly what was expected of her, she couldn't stand up to anyone. She was a well-bred child turning into a well-bred woman. She had nothing but a well-bred future to look forward to.

Back in the living room she watched her mother's expression darken. The red silk flowed under her fingers as she held it out in apology. "The blue dress needed cleaning. I'd forgotten. But I softened this with the Hermès scarf you gave me. Don't you think it's better?" She smiled, encouraging her mother to compromise, too.

"I think you look very nice." Fischer Whitehurst came through the door just in time to hear her. "Imagine. You're twenty-one today." He didn't hold out his arms for a hug, but to his credit he didn't extend his hand, either. He just smiled—distant, reserved, eternally polite Fischer Whitehurst who, of Samantha's two parents, was slightly the colder.

"Our reservation is for seven. We'll have to hurry." Kathryn turned toward the door. "There's still time to change your mind, Samantha. We could eat at the club if you'd rather."

"Oh, let's try La Scala," Samantha said, looking toward her father for support. "I'm really in the mood for something different."

He held out his arm. "It's your birthday."

It was her birthday, a momentous one, and because it was, she had dutifully agreed to let her parents celebrate it with her. They had offered a party, something tasteful— and abysmally oversize—at their country club, with a band, champagne and a midnight supper buffet. She had countered with a plea for a small family dinner at a new restaurant in Georgetown.

Kathryn rarely set foot in Washington. Chevy Chase was already too close to the sprawling, brawling heartbeat of

the nation. She still longed for her childhood home in
proper suburban Charlotte, as she had for every day of the
thirty years of her marriage. She could pretend she was still
living in the genteel South if she didn't have to get too
close to the purpose of Chevy Chase's existence: Washington, D.C., the city where her bank-president husband over-
saw a financial empire that had weathered two hundred
years of political wars and rain-forest summers.

Now Kathryn gathered her jacket and tightened her lips
into a line. She was obviously unhappy about Samantha's
choice, but she would go, because it was expected.

Samantha was touched by the route their driver took to
get to La Scala. Melwin, the friend and confidant who pi-
loted her father's limo, drove past national monuments lit
by floodlights and along the Potomac where falling cherry
blossoms littered the ground like drifts of snow. The route
he'd chosen added twenty minutes to the trip, but she
shushed her father when he tried to complain. Samantha
knew the trip was Mel's present to her, and she was en-
chanted.

She and Mel had made this trip before—often, in fact—
throughout the lonely years of her childhood and adoles-
cence. To her parents Mel was simply an employee, a
poorly educated but trustworthy nobody. To her he was the
grandfather she'd never known, the fantasy caring uncle
who brought her silly gifts or tickled her under her chin.

Mel had always done what he could to brighten her life.
In his second week of employment he had taken one look
at her long face and promised a treat if she would smile.
Her dancing lessons had mysteriously slipped away that
day—her parents had never known—in favor of a drive like
this one. Melwin had told her stories about the city he
loved, and in the process brought history to life for her.

That trip had been the first of many. Through the years
they had eaten ice-cream cones at shabby neighborhood

groceries, fed pigeons—and the occasional vagrant—in downtown parks, watched fireworks on the mall and traced tear-stained fingers over the name of Melwin's son on the Vietnam memorial.

Now Mel was trying to teach her something again.

By the time they arrived at La Scala, Samantha felt renewed. By Mel's subtle rebellion, his carefully plotted course, he had reminded her that she could have a different, more colorful future. She was officially an adult. Their trips to Washington no longer had to be secret, nor did her thoughts and feelings. She could be the woman she wanted; she could be free if she gathered a little courage.

He winked at her as she got out of the limo, and she winked back. Mel was retiring soon to go live with a daughter in California. She was going to miss him.

"I'll have a drink," she said, after the maître d'—who obviously recognized her father's name—had settled them at the nicest table in the house. The restaurant was subdued by her standards, but wildly frenetic by her parents'. Roman pillars flanked the cavernous marble-paved room, and despite the use of wooden beams and dark Oriental carpets, laughter and high-volume Puccini echoed off every surface. The cuisine was Mediterranean, with an emphasis on herbs, olive oil and garlic. The air itself was a fragrant enticement to eat heartily, to experiment and savor.

"Champagne?" her father asked. "Dubonnet on the rocks?"

"Bourbon. Straight." She didn't look at her mother. "Make it a double."

A male voice responded. "Only our best bourbon. We age it in casks Davy Crockett nailed together right before he left for the Alamo."

She looked in her mother's direction and saw a man looming larger than life at her side. He was dressed in black with a pleated white shirt that was so bright against his olive skin it almost hurt her eyes. He smiled at her, as if he understood exactly what kind of statement she had been trying to make. Something warm and liquid curled lazily inside her.

For a moment she couldn't respond. He was long and lean, and he stood like a man so confident in his own powers that serving others was nothing more than a small, thoughtful gift of himself.

"Make it a triple," she said.

He laughed, and the sound sparkled through her bloodstream, like the bubbles of the champagne she had refused. "Only if you promise to let me drive," he said in a low, distinctly dangerous voice.

Her mother made a small, distressed sound. There was a clear line between the server and the served, as clear to Kathryn as the difference between Chevy Chase and inner-city Washington. She spit out her own order and her husband's without asking his preference, then she waved the man away. "I don't know where you heard about this restaurant, Samantha." She massaged her forehead, as if she could erase the past few moments. "But it's really not our kind of place."

Samantha sat back. She felt alive; she felt daring. She felt bratty. "I don't think *we* have a kind of place. This is *my* kind of place. You have *your* kind of place. I was in the mood to share." She smiled her sweetest, most innocent smile. "Loosen up, Mother."

By the time she was halfway through her bourbon, her parents were speaking only to one another. Since she found she preferred it that way—and wondered why she had never realized it—she was free to sweep the room with her gaze in search of Joe. He had introduced himself with impressive flair when he returned with their drinks, and rattled off a history of La Scala, along with a varied list of special appetizers. He hadn't deigned to look at anyone but Samantha during his entire recitation.

She hadn't known that white bean soup with anise-spiced sausage could sound like an aphrodisiac, but it had, coming from Joe's lips. Words like calamari, risotto and tortellini had taken on the cadences of poetry. She had wanted to dance to them, twirl her Hermès scarf in wild gypsy abandon from a vacant tabletop as he regaled her with phrases like Provenąl bouillabaisse and Casablanca couscous.

"Samantha, you're making a fool of yourself over that waiter!"

She noted the way her mother hissed her name and wondered if this was new, or if she was just aware of it now because of the fire of fine Kentucky bourbon and a stranger named Joe in her bloodstream.

"How can I be making a fool of myself?" she asked. "I'm sitting here listening to you and Daddy talk."

"You're watching everything that man does!"

"Well, he's a gorgeous male animal, and any woman worthy of the name would do exactly what I'm doing.' She smiled lazily. "Watch him yourself, Mother. It's better than aerobics."

"I think you'd better stop at one drink, Samantha," her father said.

"I think I need another."

She had several, each time smiling more seductively at Joe as she gave her order. His eyes were midnight velvet, a dark caress against her bare arms and throat and the hint of flesh just under her primly tied scarf. His teeth were a white slash against his skin, and they flashed only for her—and often. She was deeply in love before the salad and desperately in love by the time the bones of her oregano-scented lamb had been whisked away.

Her wrist and the side of her breast tingled where he had brushed them as he delivered her salad. Her heart sped unevenly because he had stood beside her, close, so very, very close, when he had taken the same salad away.

"I'd like dessert," she said when her father prepared to signal for the check.

"Your behavior has been disgraceful." Kathryn pushed her chair back, as if she might leave before they paid.

"I am having dessert." She pronounced the words slowly. She was immediately impressed with her own vocabulary. Her statement seemed to hang in the air, like the words of a comic-strip character. She tried another. "I am having a life, too." She liked the sound of that one. "My own life. I am twenty-one today."

Her father put his hand on hers. It was an uncharacteristic gesture, and there was no affection in it. She knew he was upset, and somehow, that pleased her. "Come on home now, Samantha. We'll talk about this tomorrow."

"Tomorrow it won't be my birthday." She leaned toward him and found that the room shifted subtly. "Today *is* my birthday," she said gravely. "I've been good for twenty-one years, and it's been such a burden."

His voice grew even colder. "You've had too much to drink. We're going home."

"You're going home. I'm staying for dessert."

"Just how are you planning to get back?"

"In a taxi." She considered. "Or I might not come back." She shrugged. "I don't have to, do I? Amazing. I really don't have to."

"*We'll* take a taxi." Her father stood and signaled Joe. "We'll leave the car here for you. But I'm telling Melwin not to let you leave unless it's with him. Do you understand? You can stay here and make eyes at that..." He stopped himself, possibly just on the verge of an ethnic slur.

"Nice young man?" She narrowed her eyes. "Take this." She fumbled with her scarf and threw it clumsily to her mother. "And tell Melwin I might be very, very late. I might eat two desserts. Maybe even three."

Joe arrived at the table. "I'm sorry. Is there a problem?"

Her father thrust a credit card at him. "Take this, add your tip and whatever else she orders to the bill. If the card doesn't come back with my daughter before midnight tonight, I'll have you fired and investigated. Do I make myself clear?"

Samantha watched Joe's expression freeze. She was horrified, but before she could find the right words, Joe was towering over her father.

Joe found the right words with no problem.

Her father turned white, as if the suggestion for what he should do with his credit card had been meant literally. The rest of the exchange was a bourbon haze in Samantha's head. The maître d' arrived; the maître d' left with her parents, apologizing profusely as he went. The maître d' returned before she could form the words to apologize to Joe, who still looked frozen with rage. The maître d' told Joe to gather his things and never darken the front door again.

She began to cry.

"Come on, sweetheart." She looked up and Joe was bending over her. "You're coming with me."

It was the best idea of the night. She wondered why she hadn't thought of it herself. Her tears stopped immediately. "I've led a very repressed life," she said.

His face unfroze, inch by inch. In a moment he was howling with laughter. He put his arm around her and helped her stand. She leaned against him and realized that she fit as if she had been measured for this position by a master tailor. "I don't think I'll be very good at sex," she confided. "I'm too upper class. You know, saltpeter in the boarding-school food. Too many perfect marble statues of

David in Rome and Paris. A real man probably looks deficient.''

He hugged her more tightly. "You're going to have some morning tomorrow. What's your name?"

"Samantha. Samantha Whitehurst."

"Yeah, I know the last part."

They were outside, and she didn't know exactly why and how. She only remembered a sea of shocked and fascinated faces, parting, as if by Moses' command. "I think I love you, Joe."

"I had the bartender water your drinks, Sam. Not a one of them was a double. You've only had three drinks tonight. That's all."

"Would you kiss me?"

He stopped in the shadows just outside the welcoming glare of La Scala's floodlights. Around the corner traffic roared down Wisconsin Avenue, and not too far in the distance she saw Melwin standing beside the family limousine.

"Is that the three drinks talking?" he asked.

She remembered that she had thought his voice was dangerous. Now it was even more so. "No."

"Are you slumming tonight? Because I know who your father is. I was told in no uncertain terms back there, just before Gino fired me."

"Slumming?" The word had no meaning.

"Why do you want me to kiss you?"

"Because..." She looked up at him, and suddenly the world stopped spinning. She rested her hands against his shoulders. They were broad, and as solid as the earth. "For twenty-one years I've done what everyone else wanted me to. For the next twenty-one I'm doing what I want."

"What if I tell you that for the next twenty-one years you're doing what you want...with me?"

She didn't answer. She didn't have time to. He brushed her lips with his, as if giving her time to change her mind.

He was warm, and his scent was as provocatively male as his smile. Her lips parted immediately, pleading for more. He pressed against her with the same passion that had been building in her all night.

She wasn't frightened, and she wasn't repressed. She wasn't even herself. The woman who kissed Joe back had never been to boarding school and never seen a statue. She was the woman inside Samantha who had known, from her first glimpse of Joe Giovanelli, that she had found the man for her.

3

"There won't be enough food. I could roast a steer and twenty suckling pigs, and there wouldn't be enough food." Sam fussed over the dining room table, which groaned under the weight of casseroles she had made and frozen over the past month and platters heaped with deli meat and cheese.

North Carolina sunshine lit even the darkest corners of the room and bounced off brightly colored balloons and streamers. Last night Sam had stored everything precious and fragile in closets and locked the laundry-room cupboard and medicine cabinet. The house was ready for a family party.

Joe lounged in the doorway. "Mama's bringing a turkey, a vat of spaghetti and ten pies."

"You didn't tell me that."

"*She* didn't tell me that. But I know my mother. And everybody else in the family will bring food, too."

"It still won't be enough."

"You've never understood. It's always enough. It's just that the Giovanellis eat everything in sight. It's a custom. You put out too much food, we eat too much food. It's simple."

She stood back from the table and pretended to study it, but she studied Joe from the corner of her eye instead. He wore dark shorts and a madras sport shirt unbuttoned at the neck. His black hair hung straight and sleek over his forehead, and her fingers itched to brush it back. Not because she didn't like the effect, but because she wanted to touch him, yearned with everything inside her to touch him with that kind of casual we'll-always-be-married confidence that until six months ago she wouldn't have thought twice about.

"I wish my parents could have come," she said. "It would have been good for them. Rose always sets my mother on her ear. By the time she leaves one of these gatherings, Mother acts almost human."

"They'll come when they can."

"Maybe for the Fourth or Labor Day. They should be back from Europe by then. Maybe we should have another party."

He didn't respond. Joe, who lived for parties, for family gatherings, for excuses to celebrate, remained silent.

"And maybe we shouldn't." She felt her shoulders slump in defeat. "Maybe we shouldn't even have this one."

"Don't start, Sam." His voice was so restrained it seemed charged with emotion.

She was immediately contrite, but there was no point in apology. Both of them knew there was more that she hadn't said. "I'm going to change."

Their bedroom at the head of the stairs was large, filled with plants and faded antique quilts. A king-size bed loomed from a corner, an altar to sex that had once been so perfect Sam had half expected to die in Joe's arms. Now she avoided the bed as she gathered her clothes, just as she avoided thinking about what had just passed between them in the dining room. She was learning to avoid everything except the moment. Yesterday's retreat into memory had only made Joe's late arrival home last night that much harder to bear. Thoughts of the future were too painful to consider.

She heard the first horn honking as she stepped out of the shower. Some of Joe's family lived more than four hours away, so she knew they must have left home at dawn. By the time she started downstairs again wearing the new dress she'd bought for the occasion, the house was filling up with people.

She greeted Joe's brothers and sisters, his nieces and nephews and occasional cousin as she pushed her way into the kitchen where Rose, Joe's mother, was already holding court.

"I brought a few things. Just a few, don't you dare say a word, not one," Rose warned. "Just some spaghetti. And Johnny shot a turkey for me last fall that was taking up too much room in my freezer."

"And pies?" Sam asked.

"How'd you know?"

"Lucky guess." Sam threw her arms around Rose and held on for dear life. There was a substantial amount to hold on to. Rose was large, not plump but big boned and rangy like her son. Her hair was a salt-and-pepper bristle that stood out from her rawboned face like a halo. Everyone who knew her thought she was beautiful.

"Just think, you and my Joey been married now for four whole years. And this house." Rose squeezed harder. "This house is something, Sammy. Something like out of some magazine. Teddy was just saying it ought to be written up somewhere, weren't you, Teddy?"

Samantha looked over Rose's shoulder at Johnny's wife, red-haired, long-legged Teddy, who had been a Giovanelli long enough to roll with the punches. "Something very similar," Teddy said.

"And all that food on the table. You're a regular cook, Sammy. A real Giovanelli woman. I've had to slap hands already. Two times already. We've gotta get somebody to guard the table till everybody else gets here, or there won't be nothing left. Nothing." Rose frowned, as if she had just announced the end of civilization.

"I'll guard, Mama," Teddy said.

"You, you'll eat yourself silly and not gain an ounce for evidence."

"Watch me." Teddy stationed herself in the doorway, but she didn't say a word to the herd of children who snitched a slice of cheese apiece as they raced through the room.

More family streamed in, followed by friends and neighbors. Reluctantly Sam separated herself from Rose. Joe was one of seven children, the second oldest boy of three. Francis was two years older and Johnny two years younger. Behind the boys, as if they had waited to make a more impressive entrance, one girl had arrived each year, each as stunning as the next. Now the Giovanelli tribe had grown to such proportions that Sam had to keep a written list so that no one was forgotten on holidays. All Rose's children had married young and presented the world with more just like them.

All except Joe and Sam.

The din increased as the day wore on, but Sam relished the noise. Surrounded by family, by neighbors and close friends, she could almost forget that all was not well in her marriage. She saw Joe at the edge of a group of adults, Joe spiking a volleyball over a net strung between a magnolia and a pine, Joe chatting with Polly and other teachers from both Foxcove Elementary and the high school.

But the places where she didn't see him were the most significant. She never saw him with his sisters' babies in the crook of each arm as he crooned lullabies in the front porch rocker. She didn't see him passionately arguing politics with Francis, or holding a weeping Teresa, whose husband, Jeff, had just shipped out on a naval destroyer. He hovered at the edge of real involvement. Most important, she never saw him anywhere close enough to touch.

Not until Rose declared it was time.

A corner of the living room was heaped high with housewarming gifts. One of them was a ship's bell, a gift from Teresa and Jeff to hang on the front porch. Rose took it outside and tested it herself, and when everyone had gathered around, she called Samantha and Joe to stand beside her.

"I guess I'm the family matriarch," she said. "Joe's papa should be here to say these things, but he's watching from up above, I know. So here goes. Joe and Sam have been married four years today. And in those years they took a terrible old store with rats and mice and broken glass and hay and dirt and—"

"Enough, Mama," Joe said.

Everybody laughed.

"And everything there shouldn't have been," she continued. "Everything! The stories Sammy could tell. Anyway, they made this out of it. Now I know that anything is possible." She turned to Sam and beamed. "And while I can, I want to say something about their marriage."

Sam didn't move, but she stiffened with dread and her smile felt as if someone had painted it on her face. Then she felt Joe take her hand. She wove her fingers through his to keep him beside her.

"First time Joe brought Sam home, I didn't know what he was getting into," Rose said. "She didn't weigh ten pounds soaking wet. And she didn't know how to hug. And she didn't know how to yell at anybody, especially my Joey. Now she hugs and yells, and I can swear she eats a little, sometimes. This marriage doesn't work out, I'll marry her off to somebody else in the family. She's as good a Giovanelli as anybody born with the name, and I'm proud to call her my daughter.''

Rose opened her arms, and Sam went into them to the applause and hoots of everyone gathered there. Someone turned up the stereo, and their carefully cultivated lawn became a dance floor. Francis came up to swing his mother into a slow dance right on the porch, and Sam turned to Joe.

"Will you dance with me?"

He held out his arms, and she stepped into them as courageously as she had the first night they'd met.

He waltzed her down the steps to catcalls and hoots, then he pulled her closer. "You look terrific in that dress."

She flushed with pleasure. "Short enough for you?"

He ran his hand down her side. "Nearly."

Her entire body reacted to his touch. She was like a starving woman who had just been thrown a crust of bread. "Are you having fun?"

"It's a great party. All your hard work shows."

"You were right about the food. There was enough for an army, and now it's almost all gone."

"When I was a kid we were never sure where our next meal was coming from, but we were always sure when it came we'd enjoy every bite."

Sam moved a little closer. "The party should be breaking up soon. Most of your family's got a long way to drive, and some people are moving on to the Warwicks' at seven."

"Were we invited?"

"Sure. But we're not going."

"We're not?"

"I'm not. This is all the partying I can manage for one day. Unless somebody suggests a private party for two."

"We can take a bottle of wine out to the lake."

"Pond."

It was an old argument. "Lake."

"Either one'll do if I get you all to myself." She thought he tensed, but she couldn't be sure. "Joe, I've missed you. If I was out of line yesterday, that's the reason."

"I'm sorry I've been away so much. It's been a busy year."

"It's been a tough year." She searched his face. "For both of us. But it's going to be tougher if we don't come through this together."

"We're together."

She couldn't argue; this wasn't the right place. And besides, she wanted him to be right. She wanted to believe that they were together, that the events of the past six months hadn't destroyed their marriage, that they could come through their hard times stronger, closer, happier.

"I *always* want to be together," she said.

Another couple appeared a few feet away. Sam realized Johnny was closing in with Teddy in his arms. He was a shorter, heavier version of Joe, and although he looked a decade older, she saw with a sinking heart that his best younger-brother leer was firmly in place.

"You two look at each other in bed like you're looking at each other now, you'll make Mama a grandma again." Johnny winked. "Got to pass the Giovanelli genes along, Joey."

Sam forced a smile. "Teddy, make your husband behave."

"Listen, you married one just like him. You tell me if Joey does anything you say," Teddy said.

"Hey, a man's too well behaved, he can't make babies," Johnny said. "Mama's not getting any younger. She told me to tell you, she wants a grandbaby for Christmas."

Sam answered before Joe could. "Well, you'll have to tell Mama she asked too late. We already bought her a nice new set of towels. Now go away so I can make eyes at my husband.''

''Just so it leads to something.'' Johnny swung Teddy away, and Sam and Joe were alone again.

She didn't know what to say.

''Johnny ever presses his legs together, he won't be able to think,'' Joe said.

She felt Joe's rage and shame in every inch of flesh that touched hers. She tried to pull him closer. ''It's not Johnny's fault. Every one of you kids was raised to think you were God's gift to the next generation.''

''The music stopped.''

It had, and people were beginning to drift away. Desperately she tried to think of something to cheer him, something that would make him stay by her side. She thought of the fort, Joe's pride and joy, and the battle royal that was undoubtedly being staged right now by their nieces and nephews. ''Do you want to walk down to the pond and see if any of the kids are still there?'' she asked.

He looked at her as if she had asked him to strip naked in front of their guests. She realized with horror that perhaps she had done just that. She put her hand on his arm. ''I'm sorry. I didn't realize...''

He shrugged off her hand. ''I'm going to say goodbye to Chuck and Sally.''

He didn't run, but he was gone before she could reply. She watched him stride away, a lithe, male animal with the broken heart of a little boy. She listened to the shouts and laughter of the people she loved most in the world, and she wondered how she could feel so alone.

Joe had always loved parties. He had never longed for silence as a child. He was comforted by laughter, by loud music and voices raised in argument. Now he could hardly wait for the rest of his family and guests to go home.

Except that then he would be left alone with Sam.

He said goodbye to Teresa and her brood and turned to the next car. Johnny had drunk too much, something he only did at occasions like this one when he knew Teddy would drive him home. As Joe watched, Johnny hung his head out the passenger window and crooked his finger. His eyes were too bright and his grin too cocksure, but he was still Johnny, Joe's little brother, the Johnny he had fought for and fought with all the years of his childhood.

Joe approached warily. Erin, Shannon and Patrick fought in the back seat of Johnny's green sedan. With a surname like Giovanelli Johnny and Teddy had chosen Irish names for their kids. It was a family scandal.

"You had too much to drink. Go home," Joe said.

"'Member what I said." Johnny's smile widened.

Joe started to turn away, but Johnny had never learned when to stop. "You get busy on that baby, Joey boy. You don't know how to do it, I can give you a tip or two." He gave a broad wink.

Joe twisted Johnny's shirt collar in his hand before he realized what he was doing. He saw Johnny's smile die and awareness make a slow return to his eyes. He twisted harder. "What Sam and I do is our business," he said softly. "You remember that, and you practice keeping your mouth shut. Understand?"

Joe heard a gasp behind him and knew who it had come from. He dropped his hand, and Johnny fell back in the seat. It had all happened so quickly that the kids were still fighting and pushing, oblivious to the front-seat version of the same thing.

"Johnny, I'm sorry," Sam said, stepping around Joe. "It must be the heat. Who would believe it's not even summer yet?" She was smiling a perfect finishing-school smile. "Now you have a safe trip home, and thanks so much for coming. It wouldn't be a party without you." She stepped away and Teddy, every bit as refined and tactful, raised her hand in a wave. In a moment the sedan shot out of sight.

"Joe—"

"Don't say it. Don't say a damn thing." He stalked away, covering the ground to the house in a long stride that got him there in record time.

There was no one inside. His mother had been the first to leave, and the rest of the family had drifted away afterward, with Teresa and Johnny the last to go. A few neighbors and friends still strolled the grounds, but Joe knew that Sam would say his farewells.

In the bathroom he stripped and stood under a cool shower. The house wasn't air-conditioned. There was still work to do on the wiring—one of his summer projects—and the heat made him regret that he hadn't completely updated it before he sanded floors and built cabinets. Sam insisted that she didn't mind, but *he* minded. He was a powder keg waiting for the right match to set him off. Today it had been his brother; tomorrow it might be something as simple as a thermostat one degree above what he considered acceptable.

He hung his head and let the water sluice over his hair. The sight of his own body disgusted him, and he closed his eyes. But even with his eyes closed he knew he was the picture of youth and masculinity. He ran five miles every morning and worked out in the afternoons in the weight room at the high school gym. His muscles were well-defined, his legs and chest covered with silky, dark hair. In graduate school he had posed nude for a senior-level art class to help with finances, and he had seen in charcoal renderings exactly how he appeared to women.

And none of it mattered.

Out of the shower and dressed once again he took his time going downstairs. The house was absolutely quiet, and the only noise from outside was the trilling of a mockingbird. He called Sam's name and received no reply. For a moment he wondered if she had left, too, if she had finally gotten tired of his absences and his anger and his silence. Then he realized where she had gone.

The path to the lake crunched under his feet. Under the trees just at the forest edge he stood and watched her picking dandelions. Her new dress was the color of spring grass, a clear meadow green with sprigs of flowers dancing over it, and her golden hair floated behind her in the light breeze.

"Sam?"

She straightened and turned. "You look cooler."

"You ought to give it a try."

"I was considering a swim, so I waded. But the water's still ice-cold. None of the children were able to get in, either."

"We have a houseful of flowers. What are you doing with those?"

Sam looked down at the dandelions. When she looked up, he had moved closer. "Actually, I was thinking about Corey."

"What for?"

She sat on the grass and patted the space beside her. He joined her, even though it felt like a trap.

"I was watching your brothers and sisters with their kids today. The way a child is raised matters so much. Nobody here today was a perfect parent. Francis yells too much, and Magdalena is spoiling Sarah rotten because she has asthma. But they're good parents. They care, and their kids know it. The kids come first with all of them."

"What does this have to do with Corey?" He felt her shift beside him and knew she was looking at him, but he kept his eyes straight ahead. He knew what he would see if he turned: the most beautiful woman he had ever known.

"What happens to kids when they don't have that kind of devotion, Joe? What happens when nobody loves them,

and nobody puts them first? How do they feel about themselves when they grow up? We've got prisons full of people
like that, prisons and other kinds of institutions. When are
we going to learn?''

"You can't change the whole world. You're a professional. You know what happens. Some parents grew up in
homes like you're describing, and they don't know how to
give love. They expect it from their kids, and when they
find out what being a parent is really like, they abuse or
ignore their kids altogether.''

"I know, but it's one thing when I'm talking about kids
I've never seen and another when I'm talking about a child
I care about.''

"You shouldn't.''

"Shouldn't what?''

He leaned back so he could see her face. He wanted to
pick a fight with her. He realized it, but he felt completely
powerless to stop himself. He wanted distance from her
pain, more distance than he had been able to put between
them in six months.

"You shouldn't care. For God's sake, you're a professional. You're going to have kids like Corey in every class
you teach. If you go around and let your heart bleed over
every one of them, you won't be any good to anybody.
There won't be anything left of you.''

She was silent for so long that he thought she was considering his advice. Then her gaze found his. "And what
would that matter? There's nobody else who needs anything I have to give.''

He had wanted a reaction; he had wanted distance. But
when she got up and started toward the house clutching her
ragged bouquet of dandelions, he cursed his own selfishness
and insensitivity. He adored her; he had since the moment
she had sat at the best table at a restaurant called La Scala
and stared longingly at him with her dreamy, silky-lashed

eyes. He had known that night that they would have a life together, a life full of ups and downs and sinfully acute pleasure.

He remembered the afternoon that life had really started. He had no desire to wallow in the memory, but it seemed he was powerless to stop himself from anything self-destructive today. As Tinkerbelle's kittens romped in the long grass, he sank back with his head pillowed in his hands and watched the sun descend.

4

Samantha Whitehurst, blue-blooded, hot-blooded and possibly his. Joe had thought of nothing but Sam all morning as he fried eggs and flipped pancakes. He had seen her image in the shining chrome of the coffee-shop toaster, in incandescent soap bubbles and shimmering steam clouds. After only a few short weeks he knew her so well that he could see Sam in anything.

She still looked away sometimes when she talked to him, as if she was afraid he might think she was too silly or not quite bright enough for a Bryn Mawr coed. He loved it when she turned her head and cast her sapphire gaze to the ground. He loved her profile, the graceful curve of her chin, the subtle lift of her eyebrows, the way her pale skin stretched over bones sculpted to perfection by a hundred years of scrupulous Anglo-Saxon breeding.

Unfortunately there was nothing about Sam he didn't love. Not the touch of shyness, the sophisticated reserve, the way she fought against the passion that threatened to overwhelm them both. In the two months since he'd met her Joe had found nothing about Samantha Whitehurst that didn't make his blood sing and the most masculine part of him swell with longing.

Today he carried flowers to their meeting place. She deserved pale, perfect hothouse roses. He had settled for brilliant red and yellow zinnias, orange marigolds, deep purple heliotrope so fragrant and feminine that it almost embarrassed him to hold it in his hands. On his way to work that morning he had picked the flowers in three different yards, choosing only those blossoms that had nodded at him between fence posts. He'd taken a second, but no more, to rationalize his theft. The flowers had been doomed to be crushed by the next pedestrian.

Samantha was twenty-one, but the meeting place they had arranged was not her home. Her parents knew that she was seeing him, and in their few face-to-face encounters with Joe since La Scala, they had been coldly polite. It was he, not Sam, who had asked that she meet him somewhere away from the ice shower that was Kathryn and Fischer's warmest welcome.

He would have braved anything for her, stood up to any dignitary or defended her against the worst dragons of Chevy Chase. But he couldn't stand to see what Sam's parents did to her self-esteem. When she was with him, she was funny, bright and passionate, with only the occasional endearing moment of shyness or uncertainty. When she was with her parents, each moment was a fight for dignity. It was a battle she would never win until the outcome no longer mattered to her. In the meantime he didn't want to watch.

He crossed the street against the light, darting with city aplomb between honking cars. The afternoon was already scorching, with humidity like descending dew. The temperature was no hotter than his thoughts or the blood coursing through his veins. He had only to think of Sam these days and he was no different than a stag in rut.

He spied her hiding behind a tree at the east end of the pocket park where they had agreed to have lunch. He wished he could afford to take her to one of the city's best restaurants, to lavish champagne and the finest cuisine on her, fill her hands with diamonds and roses and her ears with the strains of a string quartet.

Unfortunately sandwiches, cola and the trash-strewn grass of a downtown park were more his speed. The restaurant that had hired him after his dismissal from La Scala was not in Georgetown, and not the trendiest hot spot. He was lucky if his tips covered his rent. Last week he'd begun to work the morning shift as a short-order cook at a downtown coffee shop so he could save some money.

He approached the tree as if he didn't know she was there. He whistled off key—the only way he knew how—then sidestepped and trapped her neatly between his body and the tree.

The part of him touching her responded immediately. He edged away and tried to joke. "Mine at last, me proud beauty. Scream if you must, but it will do you little good." He fondled a nonexistent mustache.

"You've never heard me scream."

He couldn't help himself. He moved a little closer again. "But I have heard you moan."

She blushed, something she did with regularity and intensity. He loved to watch the color wash over her cheeks and creep up her neck. Usually she averted her eyes, too, but today her gaze was fastened on his. "Not as much as you'd like me to, I bet."

"That goes without saying." He kissed her then because he couldn't wait any longer. Her lips warmed to his immediately. He felt her body warming, too, warming and clinging and moving in an age-old rhythm to the beat of his. He thought he was dying.

When he finally pulled back, her lips were an unnatural red and her eyes were clouded with desire. "I thought we were just having lunch."

"I do everything with passion."

"I can't speak to that. There are some things I haven't seen you do."

He smiled, a lazy, self-assured grin that covered up the way his heart had just dropped to his kneecaps. "Name the time and place."

"Now. At your room."

He stared at her, digging deep for the humor in her offer. "Before lunch?"

"I've been eating for twenty-one years. There are other things I've never done."

He touched the knuckles of one hand to her cheek. Her skin was as smooth and soft as the petals of the bouquet he hadn't yet given her. He traced the curve of her lips with his thumb as he watched the expression in her eyes. He wondered if she could feel his hand tremble. He wondered if she knew how much he wanted to pull her to the grass right here in front of office workers, homeless men and a trio of small children playing in a flower bed.

"I don't think so," he said at last.

"Why not?"

He straightened and moved away so he could hold the flowers out to her. They were a barrier of sorts. He needed armor. "I'm a good Catholic boy. I drink, but not much. I don't smoke and I don't do drugs. I don't want any hopeless addictions. And the first time you climb into my bed, that's what you become."

She stared at him and didn't raise a hand. "Hopeless?"

Desire smoked up his voice. Even to his own ears he sounded brusque and unfeeling. "Look at us, Sam. My old man sold salami and pepperoni in a Brooklyn meat market. Yours manipulates the world financial markets. You think you want me now, but one morning you're going to wake up and realize it's Italian bread and black coffee every morning for breakfast because that's all I can afford. And it's not going to get much better. I'm a teacher, someday maybe I'll be an administrator. I've never wanted anything different, and I never will. I'd give you anything I could, but that's not saying much. It's not saying enough.''

She slapped the palms of her hands against his shoulders and pushed him. It happened so quickly he stumbled backward. By the time he recovered she was yards away.

He knew he should let her go, but he caught up with her and grasped her shoulder. "You know I'm right!"

She whirled. "What about that first night? You said we were going to spend the next twenty-one years together."

"I was as drunk as you were, only it was your damned perfect face and body and that little-girl smile that had me going!"

"And now you're tired of me?"

He closed his eyes. "No. I'm besotted." He didn't know where the word had come from, but it was perfect. He dropped his hand and opened his eyes. "Damn it, I love you. And if I make love to you, it'll kill me when you see how impossible this is. What else do you want me to say? I love you. I can't sleep with you because I love you!"

He watched her expression melt by slow degrees. Then she was laughing. She threw herself into his arms, and he, fool that he was, held her tightly against him, stabbing her back with the wiry stems of zinnias.

"You can't sleep with me because you love me? That's perfect. That's priceless, Joe. I love you, too! I love you! And I want to sleep with you forever! I don't care about Italian bread and coffee. And I love you because you teach. I'd hate you if you were a stockbroker or a banker or an investment counselor. We can teach together. We can live together. We can sleep together." She pushed away so she could see his face. "Let's sleep together, Joe."

Resolve began to disappear. He told himself she was offering herself freely. He told himself that she knew what she was getting into, that he had clearly warned her. He told himself that he would survive if she changed her mind.

He wouldn't survive.

"Not unless you marry me," he said.

She stared at him. "Marry?"

He wasn't sure where the words had come from, but he knew they were right. "That's it, Sam. Marriage or nothing. You want me in your bed, you marry me first."

"What century is this?"

He grabbed her shoulders. The flowers fluttered to the ground. "You marry me, or else. That's it."

"You're going to withhold sex unless this is blessed by a priest?"

"I'll settle for a justice of the peace. I can compromise. I can't wait until you convert."

"Until...I convert?"

"I want us to be a team. I want our kids to see us at Mass together on Sundays. I want you holding my hand when they make their first communion."

"Kids?"

"Kids are part of the package. I want a lot. Little girls with blond hair, boys with black. A laughing, brawling, pack of sassy, mouthy kids. No lonely little princesses in castle towers. Dirty little kids with scraped knees and runny noses."

"I don't know. There's genetics to think about. We're bound to have at least one kid with brown hair."

He stared at her. Her eyes were laughing. The rest of her face had collapsed into shock.

"I can't be what I'm not." He had to lay it all on the line for her. He knew that this was his only chance because he would never find the courage to do this again. "I won't be rich, and I can't be Protestant. I can't settle for a lifestyle that's foreign to me. I know I'm asking you for everything and giving you nothing. And I don't expect you to say yes. I'm just telling you everything so it'll be easier to say no.''

''Nothing's easy to say with you going on and on. Take a deep breath and shut up!''

He had run dry, anyway. There was nothing left except all the good things—and those would sound like pleas. He could tell her how much he would cherish her, help her, support her. Tell her about a lifetime of stolen bouquets and stolen moments, Italian bread and coffee brought to her in bed, nights spent rocking their babies so that she could get some sleep, days spent thinking of ways to tell her how much he loved her.

She drew a finger down his cheek. ''I don't care what church we go to, as long as we go together. I don't care how many children we have, as long as they're yours. I don't care how much money you make, as long as I have some say in how we spend it. But I do care that you don't trust me to love you enough. I care that you don't see that I want exactly and only what you can give me. You're not my adolescent rebellion. You're not some three-bourbon fantasy, Joe. You're the man I love, the man I'd like to love for the rest of my life if you'll just stop laying down ultimatums.''

He wasn't sure he had heard her right. But in a moment he knew his ears hadn't betrayed him, because she spoke again.

''Now,'' she said softly, ''shall we go to your apartment?''

His apartment was one room above a paternal uncle's grocery store on a noisy corner of northwest D.C. that was half an hour's bus ride away. He spent an hour's tips on a cab that took ten agonizing minutes to get there, minutes spent in back-seat purgatory.

They took the steps two at a time. The smells of cabbage

from the garbage bin drifted upstairs with the fumes of traffic, but his room had never seemed so welcoming.

"It should be more special," he said in the doorway, giving her one more chance to back away.

"It couldn't be more special, could it?"

"Did you mean it when you said there were some things you'd never done?"

"I've been waiting for you."

He told himself it didn't matter, and he knew that it did. Virginity was a standard he hadn't been able to meet, and he didn't expect more of Sam than he had expected of himself. But her answer had told him so much about the woman, her fears, her commitments. Most of all it told him about her decision today.

He clasped her to him and buried his face in her hair. He'd had just enough women to know what the fair sex thought of his sexual prowess, but apparently he'd had too few to get him past this moment. He felt like a virgin, too, a clumsy, bumbling oaf who knew only the most basic features of sex and none of the embellishments. He doubted he would have the skill or control to make this easy for her, much less pleasurable.

"You should have married me first," he said, his voice already harsh with desire.

"Why?"

"Because then it would be harder to scare you away."

She was braver than he. She laughed a little and her hands slid along his spine, fanning out like butterfly wings. "You can't scare me, Joe. I've seen movies. I've read books. Even my big, bad Italian stud won't be any surprise."

Judging by the way his body was reacting, he was afraid she was going to be surprised, anyway. He tugged her blouse from under the waistband of her slacks and kneaded her bare skin. She shuddered against him, and shuddered again when he unhooked her bra.

He had caressed her before, but never with unbridled longing. Always he had kept a part of himself in check with her. Now there was nothing kept in check. He explored her as she stood against him, savored the silky smoothness of her skin, the pillow softness of lush breasts that had seemed so refined and model perfect when covered by clothes.

She helped him unbutton her blouse, blushing proudly when it was on the floor beside them. He was so overcome with desire that the signals in his brain were hopelessly crossed. He couldn't taste and touch and see her all at the same time, and one need thwarted another until he thought he might go crazy with longing. He slid his hands under her waistband and eased her pants over her hips. Desire poured—hotter, heavier—through him, pounding in his ears, roaring through his bloodstream until each sense blended into the others.

He wasn't sure how they got to the bed. He thought maybe Sam had led them there, because he wasn't at all sure that he was capable of independent movement. She unbuttoned his shirt—he knew that much because the aching purity of her hands against his chest was crystal clear. She unzipped his jeans and smoothed his pants over an arousal that should have frightened her witless.

She gasped when he pulled her naked body tightly against his own, then just as he was gathering control, she pressed herself against him.

They fell to his bed together. He had just enough sense not to take her immediately. He filled his senses with her scent, his lips with her flesh, his hands with her breasts and the seductive, sensuous curve of her hips. He parted her legs with one knee and she eased them wide apart in invitation.

Finally he sank into her like a man going home.

He felt her tense, then relax as he held himself still. He could do that much for her. She was small boned and fragile; he was not. He eased himself slowly deeper, reciting the alphabet, stanzas of poetry from high school, lists he had memorized in catechism class. At last he rose on his forearms to look at her face, and the fragile control he had gained was almost lost.

She was crying.

"Sam." He wanted to cry, too. Worse, so much worse, he wanted desperately to finish what they had started. He wanted to sink into her again and again, and it was only the sight of her tears and a thread of decency that kept him still.

"Oh, Joe, I love you so much."

The thread broke. He gathered her in his arms as he never had another woman. He held her against him so tightly that there was little room for movement. He thrashed against her and felt the answering call of her body. And when his control was exhausted he raised himself higher and filled her with the love he had saved only for her.

It wasn't a masterly performance. When it had ended he wasn't sure that his audience was appreciative. He took her with him when he rolled to his back, afraid that he had disappointed her terribly. He caressed her, traced the curve of her hip with his palm. Then, because he couldn't wait any longer for the review, he spoke.

"It's not always great the first time. I sort of lost it there. I'm sorry."

"That wasn't great."

He shuddered and shut his eyes. Then he realized that she had said the words as a question. "I mean, sometimes it's not," he said.

She giggled. It sparkled through him. "Are you asking me if I had an orgasm?"

"I was trying to be a shade less clinical."

"I'll be a shade less clinical. I saw stars. Is that good enough?"

"Four or five?"

"How many was I allowed to see?"

"A universe." He turned her so he could see her face. "Did you see a universe?"

"I saw infinity." Her cheeks were still wet. "Joe, please don't tell me it gets better."

"I think eventually I get a little more skilled and you get a little less tender."

"It was perfect." Her gaze ran the length of his body and back to his face. "*You're* perfect."

"I'm in love." He framed her face. Her hair fell over his fingers like spun silk. "I'll always love you, Samantha Whitehurst. And I'll do everything a man can do to make your life easy and joyful."

"Joyful?" The expression in her eyes sparked an answer inside him. "I understand joyful, I think. Better than I did a little while ago."

He pulled her close. He couldn't give her joyful again. Not in the next few minutes, anyway. But he could give her all his love and the promise of joy.

As he held her, every fear he'd ever had that their life might not be perfect fell away.

Samantha stepped out of the shower and into her robe. Joe still hadn't come back from the pond despite the fact that twilight trembled in the air. She doubted he would return until it was completely dark and the fireflies could light his way back home. Then he would find another excuse to avoid her, a project he had to work on, a friend to visit, some unfinished detail at the school that he had suddenly remembered.

She was tired of pretending right along with him. She

was tired of a lot of things, of sleepless nights when Joe lay awake and silent beside her, of lovemaking that was increasingly rare and always unsatisfying, of conversations they couldn't have and feelings they couldn't share.

Of living with a stranger.

As she had predicted it was dark by the time he returned. She had sliced Rose's leftover turkey for sandwiches and set out two plates with tiny portions of half a dozen salads. Without a word she handed him one when he came into the kitchen.

"Would you like something to drink?" he asked.

"Lemonade would be nice."

He poured them both a glass and brought it to the kitchen table. It was large enough to seat a substantial family. Once they had sat beside each other. Now he chose a chair across from her. "It's cooling off."

"About time."

They ate in silence. Sam finished first and stood to clear her place.

"You didn't eat much," he said.

"I guess I had too much earlier. I'm not really hungry."

"Would you like to go out tonight? There's a couple of good movies on."

She was surprised at the offer. For a moment she felt like a dog who had just been patted on the head. Joe had noticed her, noticed the fact that she wanted to spend the evening with him, noticed it was their wedding anniversary. She started to say yes, but she found herself saying something else.

"Is that the best you can do?"

His expression didn't change, and he didn't answer.

"I asked you a question." She fought to control her tone, but her anger was obvious.

"No, you made a statement." He stood and shoved his plate across the table at her. Then he turned to leave.

She knew she couldn't let him go without finishing this. "All right, I did. It's our wedding anniversary. I want to spend it with you. I want to talk, make love, pretend we have a marriage that still works. I don't want to sit beside you in a movie theater. I can do that by myself."

"Maybe we don't!"

"Don't what?" She shoved the plate back at him. It slid off the edge and shattered against the floor.

"Don't have a marriage that works! Maybe I have a wife who nags until I'm sick of it! Maybe I don't want to spend the night listening to more of the same thing!"

"You don't want to spend the night listening to me because you're so caught up in your own self-pity you can't listen to anybody but yourself!"

For a moment she was frightened she had gone too far. His face contorted. She had never seen him so angry. Then as she watched he slowly mastered it. But his eyes were as cold as his words when he spoke. "You don't have to stay, Sam. You want to leave, leave."

He left, and she sank back into her chair. She put her head in her hands and shut her eyes, but nothing could wipe away the image of Joe's face.

The contrast with other anniversaries was so radical that visions of them danced in front of her eyes. Joe with the deed to the store and the world's biggest sheepish grin. Joe with theater tickets for a weekend in New York and a bottle of the best champagne Foxcove had to offer. Joe at a mountain cabin in front of a roaring fire.

The last memory was the most painful, but it was the one she couldn't push aside now. In a way it was that night that had led them to this one.

They had been married a year, one passionate, desperately poor, learning-to-accommodate year. They had married immediately after the afternoon in the room above the grocery store. Neither of them had had the presence of mind to think about birth control, and Joe had used potential pregnancy as an excuse to rush the wedding.

But they hadn't really needed excuses. When her period had started two days after their five private minutes with the justice of the peace, neither of them had felt cheated. They had married because they couldn't keep their hands off each other, because they both knew that there would never be anyone else they loved as much and because they could no longer bear even the shortest separation.

They had spent the remainder of the summer patching up their relationship with Sam's parents and forging relationships with Joe's family in North Carolina. At first Sam had been overwhelmed by the Giovanellis. They had no mercy and no restraint. They poured over her like marinara sauce on spaghetti, poking and prodding and making her theirs in the process. But before long she had fallen in love with them. She saw Joe in all his brothers and sisters, and that was all she needed.

In the fall Sam transferred for her final credits to a small college near the site of Joe's temporary teaching job in a North Carolina mill town. Since her parents refused to spend even one further dime on her education, she worked in the county library to pay her own tuition. But despite poverty, classes and homework, housework and the arguments of the newly married, she and Joe were blissfully happy. In May, after an internship at a local elementary school, Sam graduated with honors and a certificate to teach in the state of North Carolina.

On the afternoon of their first wedding anniversary, Joe packed everything they owned into suitcases as Sam watched, perplexed. Then he loaded her along with the cases into their car. Three hours later the secondhand Mazda climbed its first mountain. An hour after that, in the midst of a spectacular sunset, he stopped in front of an old log cabin.

"It's beautiful!" Sam threw herself into Joe's arms as soon as she could make her way around the side of the car. "But how can we afford it?"

"It's free for the summer in exchange for doing some fixing up."

"But your summer job! You told me you were going to find another job waiting tables so we could save some money."

"I lied."

She couldn't believe it. As far as she could see there were only trees, mountain laurel and wild azaleas. There were no other houses in sight. "But what about a job for me? I'm no handyman, Joe. I can't fix a thing."

"You get the summer off."

"What?"

"We both do. I'll enjoy puttering around here fixing plumbing and putting shingles on the roof. But most of the days will be free." He cut off her protests. "Look, Sam, we deserve this. We've both worked too hard this year. We'll have next to no expenses here, and with my job all sewed up for next year—"

"What?" She pushed him away so she could see his face better. His last contract had been for only one year, a substitute for a junior high school social studies teacher who had been on sabbatical. The job had been his third one-year stint. Permanent jobs were hard to come by because of a statewide recession. Joe had assured her repeatedly that he would find another job, but to her knowledge the search had been fruitless. "The guy you replaced isn't coming back, after all?"

"No, he's coming back. We're moving. To a place called Foxcove. It's about two hours from the coast and an hour from most of my family. I'm the new assistant principal at the high school there."

She stared at him. "Assistant principal?"

"Francis does some contracting for the school board. When he heard the job had come up he thought of me. They were looking for somebody outside their own system who could be tough and still relate to the kids, and since I've had a variety of experiences and I'm twelve hours into my Ph.D. I had all the right academic credentials."

"But you've only had three years' experience in the classroom."

"I charmed their socks off."

She threw herself into his arms. "You did all this without telling me?" She beat on his chest.

"I flew to Foxcove while you were visiting your parents in the spring. I didn't want to disappoint you. It was such a long shot."

She could only think that they had a real home now. They no longer had to live from job to job, wishing and hoping that Joe would find something permanent. Not only did he have a real job, the pay would surely be high enough to live on.

"What about me?" She leaned back and searched his face. "What about a job for me?" They had agreed from the beginning that Joe would find a job first, then she would start her search in the same geographical area.

"There's all kinds of potential there. But I have another idea."

"What?"

"Let's go in, and I'll tell you."

They carried a load of suitcases inside. The cabin was two-room-tiny, with a loft for sleeping and a fieldstone fireplace that spread halfway across one wall of substantial chestnut logs.

Joe started toward the loft. "The owner said he'd leave

some food to hold us over. I'll unpack if you'll rustle up something for dinner."

Her curiosity piqued, Sam searched the kitchen alcove cabinets and refrigerator. As she worked she watched Joe moving back and forth from outside, first with luggage, then with logs. By the time she finished, a fire roared in the fireplace to take the chill off the air, and Joe lay on the rag rug in front of it, propped against an old sofa.

She joined him carrying a platter of cheese and smoked oysters, crackers and fruit. He took it and set it on the stone hearth. He patted the floor between his legs, and she sank against him. "This is heaven. How did you find it?"

"I just answered an ad. God helps those..."

"You're a remarkable man."

"Tell me about it."

She fed him oysters and cheese heaped on a cracker while she considered. "You're energetic and committed." She laughed when he sucked on her fingertip. "And sexy as hell."

"You can forget the rest."

"I still can't believe you found such a terrific job." She stopped and frowned, turning a little so she could see his face. "What's the catch."

"Oh, ye of little faith."

"Joe?"

His smile died. "It's a small town, and not terribly progressive. It's a pretty area, rural and unpolluted, but we'll have to drive a good distance for any kind of culture."

"Mayberry?"

"A good facsimile."

"I'll love it."

She thought she saw relief. "Really?"

"But why didn't you consult me?"

"It's my job to support you, and this was the best way."

She had heard different renditions of this speech in the

year of their marriage. Sometimes Joe was an old-fashioned man masquerading in a modern man's body. He washed dishes and clothes and made a mean ravioli, and she knew when they had children he would share the responsibility. But underneath his genuine belief that they were equals was a niggling corollary that he had to be just a little more so.

"It is not your job to support me," she said gently. "It's your job to love me."

"I adore you." He took her into his arms. "And if you hate Foxcove I'll quit the job immediately. You know I will."

She did know it, just as she knew that she wouldn't hate Foxcove. She would be there with him, and that was all that mattered. "What was that idea you had about my plans for the next year?"

He turned her in his arms until she was lying on top of him looking into his eyes. "It's too late to find a teaching job for this fall. Why don't you have a baby instead?"

Her eyes widened. "Joe…"

"We've been married a year. I'm twenty-six. I can support a family now. We'll have insurance, and we can find a house cheap in Foxcove. If you get pregnant right away— and why shouldn't you?—you'll be due sometime in late winter. The baby would be nearly six months old when you started teaching…if you did."

"If?"

"You might want to stay home and have another."

"Joe…"

"Would that be so awful? I know you want to teach, and I want you to. But we need to start our family, too."

More and more often her thoughts had drifted in the same direction, although she hadn't discussed that with him. Some urge as old as time had taken hold of her in the past year.

"A baby…"

"Our baby." He framed her face with his hands. "I love you. We've got everything anyone could ask for except that. Our child, Sam. A symbol of our love."

She thought of Joe's child growing inside her. A part of Joe to nurture and cherish. A little boy with Joe's dark eyes, or a little girl with his devastating smile.

"You know that diaphragm of yours?"

She smiled dreamily and said nothing.

"I didn't pack it," he finished.

"You can't make these decisions by yourself."

"Hey, I know that. We can drive back for it. Or we can forget about making love this summer."

"Now there's an idea." She stretched up to kiss him. "Will you stay with me while I'm in labor?"

"No one could tear me away."

"And in the delivery room?"

"I'll be right there rooting for you."

"Do you want a boy or a girl?"

"Right now I just want you."

She put her arms around his neck and brought his lips to hers. She imagined that the glow in his eyes was fierce enough, passionately male enough, to impregnate her.

"I'm yours, Joe. I'll have a million babies if you promise you'll always look at me this way."

"One will do for now." She felt his hand on her breast. And when she was undressed and his lips had replaced his hand, she imagined Joe's child suckling there.

Midnight had come and gone before Joe returned home. Sam heard Killer's muffled roar, then only the chirping of crickets. She lay stiff and silent in the bed, wondering if he would come upstairs or choose to sleep on the couch.

Minutes later the bedroom door creaked open, and closed with a muffled click. She heard Joe undressing, heard him go into the bathroom, then heard him return. The bed sagged beside her. She lay very still and very alone, but when she had almost given up hope she felt the length of his legs against hers and his arm draped possessively over her breasts.

She said nothing, and neither did he. She moved a little closer; he pulled her a little closer. Finally, cocooned in his warmth, she shut her eyes and went to sleep.

5

Corey Haskins stopped only twice on the long hike down Old Scoggins. The first time she jumped to one side and watched as a pack of cars raced down the road. Dust settled over her as they disappeared, fine red dust that tickled her nose and made it hard to breathe.

The second time she stopped to rest under a tree shading the wide ditch that ran beside the road. She found a cool spot for the milk carton that she had cradled in her arms on the long trudge from town, then she lay on the grass and shut her eyes.

She knew that the bird nestling inside the carton didn't look so good. 'Course, he hadn't looked too good when she'd put him in the carton, either. Even though she'd put grass and stuff on the bottom.

And a worm, in case he got hungry.

Mr. Red—that's what she called him now—might need water. When she got back up maybe she could get him some from the ditch.

She was thirsty herself. She guessed she hadn't had anything to drink all morning. There'd been cereal for breakfast, but there hadn't been milk to go with it. And her mama had yelled at her and made her go outside before she could stick her head under the faucet for a drink. They didn't have more than a glass or two, and Mama kept those high because a while ago Corey had dropped one.

She wished there was a fountain here like the one at school. Once Miss Sam had lifted her up so that she could get a drink from the grown-ups' fountain because the little kids' fountain wasn't working. She remembered the way that had felt, Miss Sam's arms around her and all. She'd felt like a little baby, but it had felt good, too. Miss Sam always smelled nice, and her hands were soft.

She would never hit anybody with those hands.

Corey hoped she could find Miss Sam's house. She knew it was on this road somewhere. She dug stuff out of trash cans when nobody was looking. She'd found a letter to Miss Sam once in the classroom trash can, and it had said Old Scoggins on it. She was just glad she could read. There were lots of things she could find out now that she could.

She hoped Miss Sam was home. Miss Sam might give her a drink. And she might be able to help Mr. Red.

Miss Sam could do just about anything.

Impossible was the word. Impossible that one seven-year-old girl could be so filthy, so sweaty and smelly, so completely lacking in childish appeal.

A barefooted Corey Haskins, with all the style and tact of a Brazilian street urchin, stood defiantly in front of Sam clutching half a plastic milk carton in her thin arms. "I walked all this way, Miss Sam. And it's a long way. You got anything birds like to eat?"

"Corey, how on earth did you find me?"

Corey glared at her. The noon sun might have sparkled in her white-blond hair if it had been clean, but as it was, the sun only pointed out suspicious specks in the chopped-up locks.

"Don't matter," she said sullenly.

"*Doesn't* matter, and of course it does. You must have walked five miles or more if you came straight from town. How did you find me?"

Corey shrugged.

Sam stepped closer. "And what did you bring me?"

Corey held out the milk carton, but not too far. Sam could see that she was ready to snatch it back if she didn't like Sam's reaction. "Just an old bird."

The bird in question was a male cardinal with an obviously broken wing. The last rites were in order. "Oh, poor thing," Sam murmured.

"I give him some water, but he didn't want it."

"That was the right thing to do," Sam assured her. "He's very lucky you found him, but I'm afraid it's too late to be much help. I think the best we can do is make him comfortable in the shade."

"He's gonna be fine. You can fix him, like you fixed my face that time."

Sam saw genuine distress in Corey's eyes. "How did his wing get like that, Corey?"

The little girl shrugged again, but the expression in her eyes grew bleaker. Something suspiciously like tears began to form.

Sam made an educated guess. "Did you maybe throw a stone at him and hit him by mistake?"

"I was just swinging a stick. That's all."

Sam squatted in front of her. "You can't hit a bird, Corey. Not if you try for a million years. He must have been sick to start with. It's not your fault, honey."

"I kilt him."

"Not on purpose. Besides, he would have died, anyway. And look what good care you've taken of him." Sam looked at the bird and saw that the discussion about his death was now academic. She held out her hands and Corey set the milk carton in them. "I know just the place for him. It's a good place to be buried."

Corey began to cry. Sam was immediately impressed with how foreign the whole process seemed to her. The tears made tracks down her dirty cheeks, and she didn't even seem to know to brush them away.

Sam set the carton beside her and gathered Corey in her arms. This, too, was obviously foreign. The little girl held herself stiffly, as if she didn't know what was expected of her. But she didn't try to move away.

Sam put her head against Corey's, despite the fact that it might mean a trip to the drugstore for medicated shampoo. "Poor sweetheart," she murmured. "Go ahead and cry."

"I ain't crying."

"Sure you are. It's okay."

"I *ain't* crying."

Samantha held her while Corey finished not crying. Then, when Corey's shoulders had stopped shaking, Sam brushed her hair back from her face. "You must be hot and hungry. Come on inside and I'll call your mother. She's got to be worried about you. Then I'll fix you something for lunch. How does that sound?"

"We gotta bury him first." Corey pointed at the bird. "Gotta."

"He'll be fine out here while we eat."

"I ain't going nowhere till we bury him."

"You're not going anywhere," Sam corrected.

"That's what I said."

"Okay. Wait while I get a shovel." Sam left Corey standing under the tree, tears still dripping down her cheeks. She wondered what Joe would say if he came home now and saw the ragged little girl one step from the impatiens he had planted in early May.

Now that it was mid-July the summer was shorter by

half, and the night of their anniversary was a month and a half behind them. They had patched up their fight the same way they communicated about everything now. She hadn't commented on it again, and neither had he. Anyone watching would think that nothing was wrong between them, but anyone watching would have been wrong.

Things were terribly wrong, and Joe's absence today was proof of it. He had left the house early, just as he did most mornings, but today he hadn't even bothered to tell her where he was going. He was probably at the school, but she didn't need to know because she wouldn't need to call him. They seemed to have nothing to say to each other.

She found the shovel right beside all of Joe's neatly organized garden tools. Organizing the tools had been just one of his summer projects. Most of them had been outdoor activities. The message in that was not lost on her. She assumed that if she found things to do outside he would suddenly decide to finish the wiring and install the air conditioners.

When she returned she saw that Corey hadn't moved. Joe's impatiens were perfectly safe. "Let's go down to the pond," Sam said. "I'll bring the carton."

"No. Mr. Red's *my* bird."

"Mr. Red?"

"Yeah. That's his name."

"And a fine one." Sam led the way, checking occasionally to be sure Corey was behind her. She stopped near the water's edge at a soft clump of earth where Joe had removed a tree stump. "I think this will be perfect."

"You own a lake?"

Sam wondered if Joe just might like Corey, after all. "A pond."

"You got kids?"

Sam saw that Corey's gaze was fastened on the log cabin. "No kids."

"How come you got a playhouse?"

"We've got lots of nieces and nephews."

"They live here?"

"No." Sam began to dig. One foot down she stopped. "What do you think, Corey? Is this deep enough?"

Corey peered into the hole. "Deeper."

Sam was already damp with perspiration from the walk and work, but gamely she dug on. Two feet down she stopped. "Now?"

"I guess." Corey knelt beside the hole and lowered the bird, carton and all, into it. "'Bye, Mr. Red."

Sam wondered if she should say something. Corey looked up expectantly. Sam bowed her head. "We commend the spirit of this bird into his heavenly father's hands." The image of a great red bird in the sky filled her mind, and for a moment she was afraid she was going to laugh.

Then she looked down at Corey and saw that the little girl's hands were folded and her eyes closed. Sam would bet that Corey had never been inside a church in her life, but somehow she had learned what was expected of her. It was another sign of the child's intelligence.

"Amen," Sam said.

"Amen." Corey opened her eyes. "Can I fill the hole?"

"Sure." Sam handed her the shovel, which was longer than Corey was. Gamely she struggled with the dirt, finally figuring that scraping it into the hole was the simplest way to accomplish her mission. When she had finished she patted the dirt with her bare foot.

"What if he's not really dead?"

Sam had visions of being required to dig the bird up again as proof. "He was very, very dead. I'm absolutely sure."

"I was hoping he could be my pet."

"I think you'll need to find something else." Sam held

out her hand. "Let's go back to the house. I really do have
to call your mother. She must be worried sick."

"Oh, she won't care."

Sam was terribly afraid that the little girl was right, but
she knew her duty. Inside the house she made Corey wash
her hands and face, then she settled her at the kitchen table
with a peanut butter sandwich and a giant glass of lemonade while she looked up Verna Haskins's phone number.
Corey, with an IQ near genius level, swore that she couldn't
remember it herself.

The phone rang half a dozen times before there was an
answer. By the time Sam hung up, she was shaking.

"Your mother was glad I called," she told Corey.

The real conversation echoed in her head as she smiled
and lied.

*Corey? She's 'round here someplace. What? She's at
your house? Hell, I didn't know she was gone. No, don't
bring her home. Make her walk. It'll wear her out, so's she
won't be so much trouble tonight.*

Corey didn't answer. She was chewing so fast Sam was
afraid she was going to choke. "Slow down, honey. If you
eat too fast you'll be sick."

Corey chewed faster, as if she was afraid that Sam was
going to snatch the sandwich out of her hand.

"What else would you like to have with it?" Sam asked,
trying another tack. "Potato chips? An apple? I think I've
got some cookies."

"All!"

Sam was shaking harder by the time Corey had finished
her lunch. She had never seen a child eat this way. Even
in school Corey hadn't eaten as if she were starving. But
in school she had gotten a free breakfast and lunch—after
the principal had threatened Verna if she didn't fill out the
necessary forms. What did she eat in the summers? The
answer was only too clear.

Corey scratched her head, and Sam closed her eyes. "Corey, you need a bath and a shampoo."

"Don't!"

"Yes, you do. And you know what? I've got something I think you might like to wear."

Corey looked suspicious, but Sam led her into the guest bedroom and opened a drawer. There was a pile of children's clothes inside, clothes left by various Giovanelli offspring who had stayed overnight in the first years they had moved to Foxcove.

"Look." Sam held up a blue T-shirt and striped shorts. "I think these'll fit. And the color will be pretty with your hair. You've got beautiful hair."

"I don't." Corey ran her hands through it until it stood on end. "Ma cut it all off when I got pine sap in it."

Sam remembered that day. As bad as the shorter cut was, it was an improvement. Corey had had a full yard of tangles before her mother had gone after her with scissors.

"Would you like me to wash it and trim it a little? I could even it out so it would look better. I don't think your mother would mind." She doubted that Verna would even notice.

Corey shrugged, but she looked interested, despite herself.

An hour later she hardly looked like the same child. She was clean from head to toe—and to Sam's delight she had found nothing on Corey's scalp except dirt. Now Corey's hair was almost as short as a boy's, but at least it was all one length, and as it grew out it wouldn't look ragged. She was much too thin, all eyes and legs like a newborn colt, but she looked presentable.

Samantha stood her in front of the bathroom mirror. "What do you think?"

"How come I'm not pretty?"

Sam didn't know what to say. Corey might very well be

pretty someday. But now, despite Sam's efforts, she still looked underfed and awkward. "You're pretty to me."

"Not to me."

"Your hair's a wonderful color, honey, and your eyes are such a dark brown your hair looks even lighter. It's a very nice combination."

"I wish I looked like you."

"If I had a little girl I'd be happy if she was as pretty as you are." She heard herself say the words, then she heard them echoing through the room when she looked up and saw that Joe was standing in the doorway.

"Joe." She didn't know what else to say.

Corey whirled. "Who the hell's that?"

"Corey!" Sam couldn't imagine a worse introduction.

Corey glared at Joe. Joe stared at Corey. His face was a blank mask.

"Joe, this is Corey Haskins. She was my student last year. Corey, this is Mr. Joe, my husband."

"Why is Corey here?" Joe asked. He continued to stare at the little girl.

"It's a long story. I was just about to take her home."

"That sounds like a good idea." He disappeared.

"How come he don't smile?" Corey asked.

"How come you didn't?" Sam got to her feet. She suddenly felt very tired.

"Don't have to."

"I wish you'd wanted to. You'd like Mr. Joe if you got to know him."

"Don't think so."

Joe was in the living room when they walked through. "Why don't you come with us, Joe?" Sam asked.

"Sorry, but I've got things to do."

She was sure he did. Anything he could find. "Well, I'll be back in a little while."

He nodded at Corey. "Goodbye, Corey."

She stared at him, narrowing her eyes. "Miss Sam's a good teacher. Are you a good teacher?"

"I'm a principal."

"Same thing. 'Cept you spank kids and stuff."

"I don't spank anybody." He lifted a brow. "At least, I haven't spanked anybody yet."

"Look like you would."

Sam put her hand on Corey's shoulder. "We're going right now." She glanced once at Joe as she left the room. He was staring at the wall.

She measured the miles to Corey's house. The little girl had walked nearly six miles to bring her Mr. Red. Six miles on a July afternoon along country roads with no sidewalks. By the time she reached the dismal old house that had been sectioned off for three separate families, Sam was steaming. But there was no one home at Corey's to vent her anger on. The door was locked and Verna wasn't there.

"It's okay," Corey assured her. "She don't need to be home. I can get in through the window."

Sam turned back to the car. "We'll wait."

After dark, after three walking tours of Foxcove's small downtown, a hamburger, fries and a giant milk shake, one trip to the grocery store and another to the park to swing, Sam passed by Corey's house for the fourth time and saw a light in the Haskins's portion. "I think your mother's home," she said.

"Looks like it."

Sam walked Corey up to the door. The woman who opened it was overweight, prematurely aged and only slightly better groomed than her daughter had been before her bath. Verna snatched Corey inside and began to scream at her. Sam stuck her foot in the door so that Verna couldn't close it.

"Now listen and listen good," she said quietly. "I'm reporting your behavior to the authorities. And when they come to check on Corey tomorrow, I'm going to tell them to look her over carefully to be sure you haven't beaten her tonight. Do I make myself clear?''

"Who the hell do you think you are?" Verna screeched.

"I'm the mother she should have had."

Sam took one last look at Corey, who didn't seem nearly as upset by her mother's behavior as Sam was, then she turned and walked down the front steps.

If I had a little girl.

Joe poured rye over ice and swallowed it without a pause. It was hours since Sam had left but he still heard her words as if she had just said them. *If I had a little girl.*

But, of course, she would never have a little girl. She would never have a child of either sex. He had cheated her out of the opportunity.

When the door closed he poured himself another drink. The room was nearly dark, but the liquor was easy to find.

"Joe?" Sam came in and turned on the lights. "Did you start dinner? I called to tell you I was going to be late, but you must have been out. Did you get my message?"

"No."

"I hope you weren't worried. Next time check the machine."

"Where in the hell have you been?"

"Corey's mother wasn't home, and I couldn't just leave her there, although that's obviously what they both thought I should have done. I waited until she got home."

"She's not your problem."

"What?" Sam's voice was soft. It was usually soft when she was ready to explode.

"I know you couldn't just leave her. I understand that. But she's not your problem. You've got to let go. You shouldn't have brought her here today."

"I didn't bring her. She came on her two little feet carrying a dying bird she wanted me to fix."

He swallowed another drink. Three burning gulps, and somehow, the pain was welcome.

"Next time should I just turn her away?" Sam asked. "Is that what you would do? Tell her to walk the seven miles back home, never mind that she's only a baby and she could get killed by some joyriding teenager?"

"No."

"Then what should I do?"

"You should call the child protective agency and report her mother. Then let them handle it."

"What a great idea. So great, by the way, that I've already done it. I called the abuse hot line and told them the whole story. They'll investigate and they'll find out that Verna's just inside the law. They'll check for a while, maybe even do a little counseling, then they'll close the case."

"Your faith in the system is admirable."

"I have no faith!" Sam threw her purse on the chair. "What kind of faith am I supposed to have? Verna doesn't deserve that child! She's never going to be a good mother to her, no kind of mother at all! And then there's people like you and me—" She stopped.

"Go on, Sam." He faced her. "What about people like you and me?"

She lifted her chin. "Then there's people like you and me who would be wonderful parents, but we can't have children."

"But that's not quite it, is it?" He tossed down the rest of his drink. "You can have children. You're certifiably equipped to conceive and bear them. I'm the one who's deficient."

"You're the one who's infertile," she said. "There's nothing deficient about you, Joe."

"Except that I have no good sperm. A small deficiency."
She started toward him, but he turned away.

"Joe, if it had been me, how would you have felt?"

He didn't want to answer her; he didn't know how the conversation had started in the first place.

"Joe?"

"Leave it alone, Sam."

"No. It's a legitimate question. What if I had been the one who couldn't conceive? Would you have loved me less? Would you have thought I was less of a woman?"

"It's not the same thing."

"It very nearly is."

He felt her hand on his shoulder. It was all he could do not to shake it off. "I don't want to talk about this. We've been over it. Life goes on."

"But it isn't going on. You're so tied up with our infertility, so angry and hurt that you've completely shut me out. I love you. I need you."

"You need children!" He faced her. "Damn it, don't you think I can see that? You were born to be a mother. And I can't give you kids! Don't you know how that eats me up?"

"You can give me kids."

"No!"

"Joe, we can adopt. We both love other people's kids. That's why we do what we do for a living. We can raise other people's kids, too, and make them ours. Do they really have to have our genes?"

"Yes!" He turned away again. "I don't want somebody else's children." *I want my own,* hung unspoken in the air between them.

"This isn't about adoption or having kids at all." Her hand tightened on his shoulder. He could feel the sharp bite of her nails. "It's about Joseph Giovanelli and the way he feels about himself. It's about your pride."

He faced her again, and her hand fell to her side. "I don't need your psychological assessment, damn it! If you're not happy with things as they are, then you're married to the wrong man. I can't give you kids any way at all. If you can't accept that, then we have nothing to say to each other."

"So how would that be different? When was the last time we had anything to say to each other?" She moved closer. "I can't keep fighting this demon that's come between us, Joe. Not by myself. Give me something to hang on to. I can live without kids, but I can't live like this. I need you, but I'm not going to go on saying it over and over. I've got pride, too."

He wanted to grab her and hold her forever, but he couldn't reach out. He couldn't reach out.

She stood there for a long moment, then she turned and walked away. He watched her go, and he knew that one day she would leave and close the door behind her.

He wondered why she hadn't closed the door the day the doctor had told them that they would never be parents.

6

Johnny and Teddy lived in Goldsboro, where Johnny was a sales representative for a North Carolina furniture manufacturer. At the age of thirty-three, just after her husband's untimely death, Rose had pulled up stakes in Brooklyn and moved her young family to Goldsboro, where she had a brother to find her work and help with the raising of her brood.

Over the years all the Giovanelli children had drifted— but not far—to settle permanently in the state they'd grown to think of as home. Johnny was the only one to stay right in Goldsboro. When Rose complained that Johnny had stayed to watch over her, Johnny grinned the famous Giovanelli grin and refused to reply.

On the morning after the fight with Sam, Joe pulled in to Johnny's driveway. His brother's house was a comfortable brick ranch that was set apart from its neighbors by exquisitely perfect landscaping. Teddy was slowly pursuing a degree in landscape architecture, and their yard was an ongoing laboratory.

Johnny was in the garage working on his car when Joe got out. He looked up from under the hood, then went back to work without saying a word.

"What's the problem?" Joe asked.

"If I knew that, I'd be fixing it, not looking for it."

"Want some help?"

"From you? Since when did you know anything about cars that I didn't?"

"Forever." Joe took off his wristwatch and pocketed it before he ducked in beside his brother.

Johnny didn't look at him. "What are you doing here, anyway?"

"I was just out for a drive."

"That's a pretty long drive. Where's Sam?"

"At home."

"Too bad. She and Teddy could have gabbed."

"She's not in a gabbing mood."

"Neither are you most of the time."

Joe ignored what was an obvious opening. "What's this old wreck doing that it shouldn't?"

"Running rough."

"When? Low speed? High speed?"

"High, mostly. When I've been on the road too long."

"Could be a lot of things."

"You think I don't know that?"

"Did you reset the choke?"

"Not yet."

"Check the plugs?"

"I just got here! Check them yourself."

Joe dove in to do just that. Johnny attacked the air cleaner cover and both men were silent for a while. Finally Joe straightened. "Look at this." He came out from under the hood and stood by the door holding two spark plugs in his hand. "See the spots on the insulators?" He held them out to Johnny. "They're overheating. Maybe you got a vacuum leak, or maybe they were just put in wrong. You do them yourself?"

"Yeah, I did them and did them right. But they're a

different brand than I used to use. Maybe I should try colder plugs again.''

''That could be it.''

''Help me check the choke plate.'' Johnny fumbled in his pocket for keys and threw them to Joe. ''Floor it.''

Joe got behind the wheel and pushed the gas pedal to the floor. Then he stuck his head out the window. ''See anything?''

''Looks fine. Start the engine.''

The engine roared to life and Joe got out to poke his head under the hood with his brother. ''Open just a crack, like it's supposed to be. Looks good so far.''

''I'll let it run awhile. Want to come in and have some coffee?''

Joe thought about the friendly, family atmosphere of Johnny's house. Once he would have liked nothing better. ''Not yet.''

''Then what do you want to do?''

''Close the damned garage door and stick my head under the hood.''

''Are you going to talk about this sometime?''

Joe didn't want to talk about his feelings ever, but he owed his brother an apology. He owed the whole world an apology. He was a walking apology, and he couldn't seem to get two words past the permanent barricade in his throat.

''Coffee on the patio, and I'll threaten the life of anybody who bothers us.'' Johnny disappeared before Joe could refuse.

The patio was another example of Teddy's genius. Planters of sculpted miniature pines were set at angles along the edge, with smaller planters of cascading annuals to soften the stark effect. The table backed against a stone barbecue that Johnny had built himself. Before their confrontation at the housewarming, they had planned to build one down by the lake at Joe's house.

"So, what is it?" Johnny asked. He set a tray of coffee and ham biscuits beside Joe. Joe saw Teddy's handiwork in the biscuits, the colorful pottery and linen napkins. He knew she would keep the children from bothering them as they talked. She was a lot like Sam.

He still didn't want to talk about his problems. "Did you check the choke again?"

"Yeah. It's open all the way. I'll try cooler plugs and see if that does it. No sense in checking everything else if that's the problem."

Joe sipped his coffee and stared at the backyard built around the needs of Johnny's children. There was a swing set, a tree house and a sandbox large enough for the entire Giovanelli younger generation when they visited.

Johnny spoke. "Are you and Sammy having troubles? I know I had too much to drink. I was out of line at the housewarming, but I didn't know I was stepping on toes. You've always been so happy together."

"We can't have kids, Johnny." Five words. Joe hadn't been sure he'd ever be able to say them. But he didn't feel better; he just felt exposed.

"What do you mean, you can't have them?" Johnny was incredulous.

Joe didn't laugh; he didn't even feel angry. Johnny's reaction was so much like his own that he understood it completely. He remembered the day the doctor had told him.

When Sam hadn't gotten pregnant during their summer in the mountains, neither Joe nor Sam had been particularly concerned. They made the move to Foxcove and settled in a small apartment while they looked for a house to rent or buy. Just a week before the school year started, one of the first-grade teachers at Foxcove Elementary fell ill and ten-

dered her resignation. Sam was the only qualified teacher
waiting anxiously in the wings, and she was given the job.

Since the school district had a generous maternity-leave
policy, Sam and Joe decided to continue trying to have a
baby. Even if she got pregnant immediately she could still
finish most of the year. A more likely scenario was that the
baby would be born in the summer. But even that scenario
didn't come to pass.

A year after they had begun trying, Sam made her first
trip to the office of a fertility specialist in Raleigh. The
doctor did some simple preliminary tests, then told her to
go home and return in six months if she still wasn't pregnant. Six months stretched to twelve before she made another appointment. Joe was opposed to Sam consulting a
specialist at all. He told her stories of other couples who
had taken time to conceive. Medical intervention seemed
like an invasion of privacy.

When Sam finally returned to the specialist, she returned
alone. Joe refused to participate, and Sam underwent the
next round of tests without his support. But finally, when
almost every avenue was exhausted and there seemed to be
no medical reason that Sam couldn't conceive, Joe reluctantly returned with her.

He hated the tests every bit as much as he'd expected.
But he hated the results most of all.

The morning they went in for the verdict had been cold
and dreary. Sam had repeated some tests, too, and she was
nervous. The drive to Raleigh was a long one. He snapped
at her for choosing a doctor so far away; she snapped at
him for not cooperating earlier.

But by the time they arrived at the office they were a
team again.

"It's going to be all right," Joe said, squeezing her arm.
"We're going to get through this okay. If we've got a problem, they'll be able to help us. At least we'll know."

She was pale, clearly apprehensive. Her mother had been able to conceive only one child before a tumor had forced a hysterectomy. Despite the doctor's reassurances, Sam was convinced that her problems were going to be similar.

The waiting room was lavender, with expensive watercolors on the walls. Joe had seen the bills Sam had submitted to their insurance company. He had a good idea who was paying for the watercolors.

A nurse dressed in a soft print that matched the walls ushered them into the doctor's office. The doctor stood to greet them. Then he turned to Joe.

"It's me with the problem, not Sam," Joe told Johnny. "I'm allergic to my own sperm. How do you like it? Couldn't have been dogs or dust, it had to be my sperm."

"What are you talking about?"

"A doctor in Raleigh did some tests. My sperm count is low to start with. The ones I manage to produce are attacked by antibodies before they can go anywhere. I've got as much chance of getting Sam pregnant as flying to Mars."

Johnny was silent. Then, "God, Joey, and what I said at the party…"

"You were just being your usual obnoxious self."

"But can't they do anything?"

"We tried a round of steroids. I reacted badly. It's not much of a help, anyway, even if the sperm count's high. A real long shot. Now there's nothing left to do."

"I don't know what to say."

"That makes two of us."

"How long have you known?"

"I found out late in the winter."

"And you didn't tell me?"

"No."

"What kind of brother keeps this to himself?"

"My kind." Staring straight ahead, Joe finished his coffee.

"You're ashamed of yourself, aren't you?"

Joe didn't answer.

"Like you had something to do with it. That's stupid. You know that, don't you?"

"And how would you feel?" Joe faced him. "What if it was you who couldn't get your wife pregnant? What if your backyard was full of nothing but Teddy's flowers and shrubs? What if you didn't have that tree house or sandbox or those kids watching television in there? How would you feel?"

Johnny's shoulders slumped. It was answer enough.

Joe set his cup down carefully, even though he wanted to send it crashing against the barbecue. "I wanted you to know. I don't want to blow up again at anybody in the family over this. And I don't want Mama to be sitting around waiting for us to reproduce. Because we aren't going to. Not ever."

"You want me to pass on the word?"

Joe felt the barrier in his throat again. He nodded.

"You've considered the alternatives? Other ways of making a family?"

"I've considered them, yeah."

"No go?"

"No go."

Johnny didn't argue, just as Joe had known he wouldn't. Johnny was brash and outspoken, but there was nobody living who would understand Joe's feelings better.

"You're no less of a man, Joey."

Joe didn't answer. He couldn't call his brother a liar to his face.

Corey stopped to rest under the same tree that had sheltered her on her first trip down Old Scoggins. She was getting used to the walk. It was quiet here, not like around her house. The people next door fought a lot, and Corey could hear them late at night, yelling and throwing things.

She didn't know why they had to throw things. She guessed it made them feel better. Her mama had thrown a pot at her once, but she couldn't throw too good, and she'd missed. Still, it had scared Corey, because she knew that if her mama's aim had been better, that pot would have hurt pretty bad. Most of the time Mama just left her alone, but sometimes she got so mad Corey had to sneak around and hide until Mama went off somewheres.

She was off somewheres today. The house had been empty when Corey woke up. It was quiet, nice for a while. She'd eaten some peanut butter out of the jar and drunk all she liked from the faucet. She had even stayed inside and watched cartoons on television all morning, but after a while she'd gotten bored.

And then she'd thought about Miss Sam.

Her mama had told her not to go to Miss Sam's house again. Her mama had yelled a lot about Miss Sam making trouble and stuff. Corey didn't believe it. Miss Sam fixed trouble.

But if Mama found out that she'd gone to see Miss Sam again, she would be real mad. She might throw things at Corey, or she might do worse. When she hit, she hit hard.

So Corey hadn't visited Miss Sam again. Not exactly, anyway. She had been to Miss Sam's house. She had hidden in the trees beside her driveway and watched cars come and go. Once she had seen Miss Sam in the yard, planting something. She had been wearing yellow, the same color as her hair. She had looked all fresh and cool, like a drink of water after a long walk.

Corey had wanted to call her name, but she had been afraid. Her mama wasn't the only reason. Part of it was Mr. Joe. He was the biggest man Corey had ever seen. And he had the meanest eyes. He looked like he was mad at everything. She knew he didn't like little girls, not the way Miss Sam did. He didn't even look like he liked Miss Sam very much.

So Corey hadn't called Miss Sam's name that day, and she wouldn't call it today, either, even if Miss Sam was outside. She didn't want Miss Sam to see her. She just wanted to see Miss Sam. She didn't know why exactly.

She just did.

Joe stayed at Johnny's for lunch, braved the assaults of his nieces and nephew and gave them beloved uncle piggyback rides. But by the time he was on his way home, he felt as if he had been to hell and back.

He still had to face Sam. They hadn't spoken after their argument. Their days had become an endless progression of frostbitten conversation marked only by eruptions of rage. He didn't know how to change the pattern, or even if he wanted to. When Sam was angry or distant he wasn't forced to relate to her—something he no longer knew how to do.

A storm had come and gone, but the sky was still light when he pulled on to Old Scoggins Road. Several miles closer to home he realized he was driving faster than he should. Killer had become an outlet for his frustration. He had given dozens of lectures to juniors and seniors at Sadler High about the dangers of doing exactly what he was doing now, using his car to express his feelings. When he saw he was going sixty he lifted his foot from the accelerator.

But not soon enough.

A child darted across the road ahead of him. If he had been going thirty-five, as he should have been, he would have had plenty of time to slow, swerve clear and remain on the road. As it was, he hit the brake and fishtailed on the slick tarmac into a wide ditch. The car came to an abrupt halt against the root of a giant oak. He was thrown forward, but his seat belt just kept him from smacking the steering wheel. Killer shuddered twice, then died.

He didn't move for a moment. He was confused, because everything had happened so quickly. Then he was furious.

The door screeched ominously when he opened it and stepped into the ditch. It took only a glance to see that Johnny's car had needed an aspirin compared to the high-tech surgery Killer would need to recover from this.

Three steps and he was out of the ditch. Ten yards across the road he had his hand on the back of Corey Haskins's neck.

"What in the blazes are you doing here?" He looked around. There were no houses in sight, nothing but pasture land and acres of tobacco.

She kicked at him, but he held her firmly. He was furious, but not so angry that he couldn't see she was scared to death. "I asked you a question," he said.

"Ain't none of your business!" She kicked at him again.

"Were you going to see Miss Sam?"

"What if I was?"

He could have been killed. Worse—much, much worse—*she* could have been. She was seven, a pitiful, scruffy, unloved child, and he wanted to shake her into submission.

"I'm going to let go of you," he said through clenched teeth, "but when I do, you'd better not go anywhere until we're done talking. Understand?"

"Don't have to do like you say!"

"It would be...in your best interests."

She seemed to consider, then she went limp, and he removed his hand. She moved away, but not very far. She lifted her hands to her hips and stuck out her chin. "So?"

"I just crashed my car because of you."

"It made a lot of noise."

"I'm glad you were entertained."

Her eyes narrowed. "It was better than TV."

Obviously sarcasm was not lost on her, although it would have been on most children her age. Joe realized she was probably every bit as intelligent as Sam claimed. "Were you going to see Miss Sam?"

"I go there sometimes."

He only knew of one time. He wondered if Sam had purposely failed to mention the others. "Often?"

"Maybe, but I don't bother her," she said proudly. "Just go to look."

"It's way too far for a little girl to walk. And it's dangerous. You could have been killed running across the road like that."

"Wasn't."

"Because I crashed my car!"

"You drive too fast!"

He couldn't argue with that, but he disliked her even more for reminding him. "Does your mother know where you are?"

"Don't matter." Her face grew more sullen. "She don't care if I go off."

From everything Sam had told him, Joe suspected Corey was right. "Come on, we're walking to my house so I can call a tow truck. Then I'll take you home in Miss Sam's car."

"Don't want to walk with you. Don't like you."

"You don't have to like me."

"Good, 'cause I don't!"

His hand itched, and he suspected the only cure was to apply it rapidly to the seat of Corey's filthy shorts. But he started to walk, and before long she fell in step beside him. He forced himself to walk more slowly to accommodate her short legs.

"How often do you come out here?" he asked at last. He figured they had at least half a mile to trudge together.

"Don't know."

"Once a week? Twice? Every day?"

"When my mama goes away."

"And how often is that?"

"Whenever she can."

He suspected he was being baited by a seven-year-old, and he didn't like it. "How many times? One? Ten? Twenty?"

"Six, maybe."

"And Miss Sam doesn't know?"

"Told you."

Reluctantly he had to give the child credit. She hadn't uttered as much as one complaint. Time slogged right along with their footsteps. The road had begun to curve into the final stretch when she spoke again. "How come you got a playhouse and no kids?"

"Because we do."

"Miss Sam likes kids, but I guess you don't."

"I like kids who know how to behave."

"Like Alice Lambert."

"Who's Alice Lambert?"

"She's got shiny black hair like yours, and she can do cursive."

"Cursive?"

"You don't know what cursive is?"

"I know." He wished they were already home. "What's handwriting got to do with anything?"

"We're not s'posed to do cursive yet, but Miss Sam likes it. She says Alice's smart. Alice gets stickers on everything."

"How about you? Do you get stickers?"

"Not on my writing."

He told himself that one little girl's struggle with her

handwriting was not his concern. The words that emerged were somewhat different. "I couldn't get the hang of writing until I was almost in fourth grade. I printed everything."

"Must have been pretty dumb."

"Dumb, but not dumb enough to insult somebody almost four feet taller than me."

"Why do you live out here? S'nothing to do."

Fortunately for Corey, Joe saw his mailbox in the distance. "Because we like privacy. That means that we don't want people coming out here who haven't been invited."

"Miss Sam likes me."

"That doesn't mean you can keep coming. When I take you home I'm going to tell your mother she has to keep a better eye on you. And I don't want you coming here again. Do you understand?"

She turned away. He couldn't see her face. "*I'm* not dumb."

"But you sure are rude."

"At least I don't go staring at little girls and scaring them to death!"

"You don't act as if you're scared to death."

"Miss Sam's nice. How come she married you?"

He turned into his driveway. He was walking faster by now, and she was dragging behind. "So I could scare away everybody who doesn't belong here."

Her answer, whatever it was, was swallowed by the ferocious barking of a large Border collie who came streaking through the field beside the house. Joe recognized the dog as it closed the distance between them. Laddie belonged to Turner Insley, the man who had sold Joe his land. But Corey didn't know that the dog's only earthly pleasure was to round up everything in sight. When Laddie, yapping excitedly, darted toward her, she began to shriek.

Joe heard Sam's shouts from the driveway behind him,

but he didn't even turn. He leaped toward Corey and swung her away from the dog and into his arms.

She smelled the way she looked—which was terrible—and she weighed nothing in his arms. He held her tightly and kicked at Laddie to warn him away.

When the dog slunk off to find a cow or a butterfly to herd, Joe tipped Corey back so he could see her face.

"That's one of the reasons why you shouldn't be so far away from home by yourself," he said.

"Not by myself. I'm with you."

As Sam came up to join them, he set Corey firmly on the ground. "She's all yours," he said.

"What on earth is going on?"

"Your little friend will tell you." He glanced at Corey. She stuck her chin out defiantly. "Don't you forget," he told her. "I meant what I said. I don't want to see you out this way again."

"Don't know why I'd want to come out, with you here and all."

She stood like a soldier, as straight and defiant as a Prussian general. She was filthy—he'd never seen a child so dirty—homely and obviously undernourished. And still something amazing sparkled in her eyes. Under the defiance Corey yearned for more, for something she could see just out of reach. Joe couldn't give it to her; he had nothing to give anybody. But still, he could see her need.

He turned away, but not before he'd memorized that look. He knew it would haunt him.

Of all men, didn't he know what it was like to want something that he could never, never have?

7

For three full weeks Killer was the favorite topic of discussion at the Foxcove body shop. Parts drifted in slowly; opinions ranged on how best to complete the transformation. If Killer had been built in Japan or Germany instead of Detroit, the car would have been an antique by the time Joe was able to reclaim it. As it was, he had to reacquaint himself with the gearshift and clutch on the trip home. He drove slowly on Old Scoggins. If a turtle had ventured into the road, it would have had plenty of time to cross.

The pines lining the driveway rustled in a warm evening breeze. Joe parked next to Sam's sensible sedan. He had been away most of the day. He was back at work full-time now, preparing for the school year that would begin in a few short weeks. He wasn't sure how Sam was spending her time. The house sparkled, and there was always a wonderful hot meal at night, prepared with fresh vegetables from the garden she had dug and planted herself. But he doubted that the house and garden kept her so busy that she forgot about all the things that were missing from her life.

He opened the front door, expecting the scent of dinner. The house was dark and smelled only of lemon potpourri and freshly cut roses. He called Sam's name, but there was no answer.

He told himself Sam's car was in the driveway. She hadn't left. She hadn't left *him*. He called louder and began a search.

Ten minutes later he found her down at the lake, feeding the ducks, who were so tame she had to shoo them back into the water every time she went back to the house. She was wearing a strapless sundress that was the warm gold of her hair, and in the glow of a perfect sunset her skin was palest ivory. He sucked in a deep breath at the sight of her. His body responded in the most primal of ways.

She turned and only then did she seem to realize he was there. "Oh, Joe. I didn't know you were home."

He tried to sound natural. "I've been looking for you."

"Have you?" She sounded as if she doubted it.

"I'm later than I thought I'd be. I'm sorry."

"I'm never sure when you'll be home. I thought I'd wait and start dinner when you got here."

"Let's go out." He walked toward her. An arm's length away he forced himself to stop. "It's Friday. There's a fish fry at the Plantation House. Or we could drive over toward the coast and look for something there. We haven't been out together in a long time."

"Sit and talk over drinks and dinner?" She smiled sadly. "I think I've forgotten how."

He pulled her into his arms before he could think better of it. "I'm a bastard, Sam." She was stiff, but she yielded a little at his words. His blood heated and rushed swiftly to every distant appendage of his body. His arms tightened around her.

"Not a bastard. A stranger." She gazed up at him. "What happened to the man I married?"

He didn't know. But at the moment he felt exactly like that man. Desire and contrition crowded out all his anger at the fates and at his traitorous masculinity. He thought of Sam, of all the things she had been denied. Of how much he had denied her because of his own absorption in himself.

"I love you," he whispered. "That's never, never changed."

"No? Show me."

Desire was a freight train roaring through his head and blocking all his other feelings. He hadn't made love to her in a long time, so long he couldn't remember when. He had wanted to; God knows he had thought of little else. But each time he had tried to approach her, he had remembered...

The freight train picked up speed, and memory evaporated. Sam smelled like honeysuckle, like hot summer nights and a woman aroused. He ran his hands over her bare shoulders, down her arms, along the fabric-clad curve of her breasts. His breath caught in his throat; his hand touched the tab of her zipper.

"What do you wear under a dress like this?" he asked.

"Very little." She threw her head back. Her eyes were drowsy and passion glazed. No matter what was wrong between them, this was right. She wanted him as much as he wanted her.

"Then that's what you're going to be wearing." He inched the zipper down. He found her hair with his other hand. It was fine and as soft as dandelion down. He lifted it off her shoulders and bent to run his lips along her throat. She shivered against his lips. As the dress fell away, she shivered again.

"Don't tell me you're cold," he said.

"I won't." She wound her arms around his neck. "I'll tell you anything you want to hear."

"That you need me?"

"Desperately."

"And want me?"

"More than I can say."

"And you're going to do unspeakable things with me right here in the open?"

"Unspeakable, devastatingly intimate things."

He touched one breast, a feather-light caress as teasing as the warm breeze. She sighed, and he took advantage of her parted lips, plunging between them to taste her secrets.

She stroked her nails over the back of his neck, kneaded and stroked and drove him wild with her fingers and lips. He was breathing hard when the kiss ended, and she was smiling a woman's secretive smile.

She undressed him, but he couldn't stand quietly as she did. He filled his hands with her breasts, his lips with her sweetly scented hair. His mind was filled with nothing except thoughts of her, of the way she moved her hips when he made love to her, of her soft cries and murmured words. Of the way he filled her completely.

He filled her completely when they were both naked and stretched out together on a fragrant bed of clover and pine needles. She wrapped herself around him and drew him into her before he could even kiss her again. He lay surrounded by her, by her warmth, her scent, her love, and for a moment he forgot that he was giving her nothing but passion.

Then, in the throes of their mutual release, he remembered.

He held her afterward. Held her because it was expected, and he no more wanted to hurt her than he wanted to remember that the seed he had spilled inside her was devoid of life.

She drew a finger down his chest. "Are you all right?"

He closed his eyes. "Sure. That was terrific."

She turned so that she was facing him, her body strung languorously along the side of his. "You're a wonderful lover. You'll be wonderful when you're eighty. Nothing will ever change that."

He smiled, because it was expected, too. "You're every fantasy I ever had."

"Had?"

"Have. Have." He stroked her hair, although he wanted nothing so much as to be alone for a while.

"Shall I shower and change for dinner?"

"Is the dress ruined?"

"I doubt it. It landed on the grass. Would you like me to wear it?"

"If it's wearable."

"Then I will." She moved away from him and stood, a wood nymph moving gracefully against the darkening sky. He watched her find her dress and underclothing and slip them on for the trip back up to the house. Then she was gone.

He lay with his hands under his head, a man who should have been blissfully happy. Somewhere far in the distance he heard the lonesome whistle of a freight train.

Wrapped in her robe, Sam dried her hair. It was growing late, and she was hungry, but she didn't want to hurry Joe. He didn't have to tell her that near the moment of his release he had realized that he couldn't make her pregnant. She had felt it in his sudden tension, seen it in the bleakness of his eyes. Until then he had been the sensual, confidently virile man she had married. His emotional withdrawal had stolen much of the pleasure of their encounter.

But he had made love to her. For minutes he had been the Joe she adored. Perhaps tonight was a new start. She could be patient if they were moving toward a better marriage together. If they could repeat tonight again and again, perhaps one night it would turn out completely right. He would hold her, look into her eyes and see that it didn't matter that he couldn't sire her children. He would finally realize that he was first in her life and always would be.

Her hair was nearly dry when he appeared in the doorway. "Go ahead and get in the shower," she said. "I'll just be another minute."

"I can wait."

"No, go ahead. I'm starving."

It was an opening for an appropriately sexy remark, but he passed over it. She watched in the mirror as he stripped off his clothes. In the years of their marriage he hadn't gained a pound, despite the fact that she fed him as well as his mother ever had. He would be a gorgeous older man, silver haired and olive skinned, a man who turned the silver heads of every passing older woman.

She listened to the water run as she dressed in the bedroom. Once upon a time Joe had sung in the shower, snatches of Mozart's *Magic Flute* and Mick Jagger's greatest hits. He had a terrible voice, gruff and tuneless. She yearned to hear it again.

She was nearly ready when he emerged. She watched him dress from the corner of her eye. He always threw on whatever shirt he came to first. She always made sure that the clothes in the front of the closet were coordinated.

She was just sliding on an earring post when the telephone rang. "I'll get it," she volunteered.

"Catch it downstairs. I unhooked this jack yesterday while I was working on the wiring."

She scurried down and grabbed the phone in the kitchen. The voice on the other end was unfamiliar.

"Mrs. Samantha Giovanelli?"

"That's right."

There was static on the line, possibly due to Joe's work on the wiring. Sam missed the next several sentences. The voice sounded far away. "...your niece."

"I'm sorry. Can you repeat that?"

"There's been an accident. Your niece has been injured."

Sam sank into the nearest chair. She swallowed. Joe had nieces on top of nieces. She loved them all. Fear closed her throat. She was terrified to ask who had been hurt.

"I'm calling from South Carolina."

"South Carolina?" She gripped the telephone. "I'm sorry. I'm having trouble hearing you. Did you say South Carolina?"

"Yes. Spartanburg."

No one in the family was vacationing out of the state. Sam was sure of it. The Giovanellis practically lived in each other's pockets. Rose would have told her if any of them had gone on vacation. But it was possible that one of Joe's brothers or sisters had sent a daughter to camp. Maybe they had given Sam and Joe's number for emergencies. "How badly is she hurt? And I'm sorry, but which niece is it?"

The line crackled again, and Sam missed another sentence. The line cleared. "But she's going to be fine. She has multiple bruises and a broken arm. She was thrown out of the car when it crashed."

"Oh, my God!"

"Now, don't worry. She's been checked over thoroughly and treated." There was a pause. "I'm afraid her mother wasn't so lucky, Mrs. Giovanelli. I'm sorry I have to be the one to tell you this, but Mrs. Haskins was killed instantly."

Sorrow washed over Sam. She didn't know how she was going to tell Joe. No man loved his family as much as he did. His sisters and brothers were his closest friends. She didn't know how he would get through this. Then, as the woman on the other end remained respectfully silent, she gripped the telephone harder.

Sam's voice was only a shade louder than a whisper. "Excuse me, did you say Mrs. Haskins?"

Sometime later she heard Joe's footsteps on the stairs.

"I decided I ought to get dressed up, since you were." He came into the kitchen in dark slacks and a gray raw silk jacket. "What do you think?"

"Joe..." She was still sitting down.

He frowned. "What's wrong?"

"Corey's been in an accident. In South Carolina."

"South Carolina?"

"Yes. A car accident." She saw concern on his face. Joe wouldn't wish anyone, not even the brattiest child, so much as a splinter. "She's pretty battered, but apparently she's going to be fine."

"Poor little kid." He sounded genuinely distressed.

"Her mother was killed instantly."

"No one should die like that..."

She finished his sentence. "Not even Verna Haskins."

"No. Not even Verna." He touched her cheek. She covered his hand and held it there. "I'm sorry, sweetheart. I know you care about Corey."

"It must be so hard on her."

"Yeah. Even the worst mother is still a mother." He squatted in front of her. "Do you still feel like going out?"

"Sure. I'm fine. It's so late, though. Let's go somewhere nearby."

"The Plantation House?"

"Perfect. I'll get a jacket."

As they drove into town he told her about his day at school. She listened with half an ear, responding with all the enthusiasm she could muster. It had been so long since he had talked to her about anything. They parked on the street that passed for Foxcove's major shopping area and window-shopped its length before they headed a block east to the restaurant.

The Plantation House had never been that; it was six years old, built of wafer board and Sheetrock. But the architect-proprietor had been smitten with self-importance.

Elaborate Corinthian columns graced an otherwise unassuming two-story building. The food was always good, traditionally Southern and high in calories. Inside, at a table in the center of the room, they ordered the fish fry.

"They hate to see you coming on Fridays," Sam said. "They lose money on an all-you-can-eat when you're here."

"But they gain it back with you."

"We've always been a balancing act."

They chatted casually—interrupted frequently by people who wanted to say hello—until it was time to tackle a plate of cole slaw and the first round of fish.

"Don't look now, but Bobby Ferguson's the busboy," Joe said. "Remember my stories about him the first year we moved here?"

Joe had stories about almost all the kids at the high school. And they had stories about him. He was the youngest principal in the history of Sadler County, chosen for the job after only a record two years as assistant principal, but it wasn't youth that had made him such a success with the students. Joe simply understood how to relate to teenagers. He possessed the magical combination of respect, suspicion and forgiveness.

Sam looked up from her plate. "You wanted to bring him home."

"Just for a week or two."

"I can't remember why."

"He had a problem with alcohol. I wanted to sober him up."

"And why didn't you?"

"His parents finally admitted he needed help. They sent him to a treatment program. This year he'll be going into his third year at Duke. Premed."

She heard something like pride in his voice. "You're a hands-on kind of guy, Joe."

"Sometimes that's the only way to get things done."

"I wouldn't have minded if Bobby had come to stay with us. I like helping kids turn around."

"That's why you're such a good teacher."

"Let's not forget how kind and full of love I am."

He looked up.

"And nurturing." She put her fork down. "Let's not forget how nurturing both of us are. How concerned about kids. How caring."

He put his fork down, too. Carefully. "We're not talking about Bobby anymore, are we?"

"Close."

"What have you done, Sam?"

She stared at him and prayed he would forgive her. "I've told the social worker in Spartanburg that we'll be there Wednesday morning to pick up Corey and bring her here to stay with us."

"I can't believe you!" Joe threw his sports coat on the hallway table and stalked toward the kitchen.

"Then you don't know me very well." Sam followed at a slower pace. She was in no hurry to continue the fight that had flamed since the moment they'd buckled up for the drive back home. Until that moment she had explained her position calmly and rationally, fully aware that even Joe, with his hair-trigger temper, wouldn't start a fight in front of half the town of Foxcove.

"Oh, I know you," he said. "Or I used to. But maybe I don't know the woman who would make a decision like this without consulting me!"

"And if I had consulted you, what would you have said?"

"No!"

"Somehow I knew that."

He slammed the refrigerator door in response. She

watched him toss half a gallon of iced tea on the counter, and she was glad the container was plastic.

"I know you feel sorry for Corey." He slammed cupboard doors until he found the glass he wanted. "I don't blame you for that. But volunteering to take her is another thing!"

"I'll go over this one more time, Joe," she said quietly. "Shut up and listen and see if it penetrates. Corey told them I was her aunt. That's why they called me."

"So among other things she's a liar."

"Don't you realize what that means? I'm the only person in the world that one little girl could think of who might, just might, be willing to take care of her. She lied about our relationship so they'd take her seriously. She has no one else. The social worker said Verna took Corey to Spartanburg to look for Corey's father. Apparently she wanted to dump her with him, even though Corey's never met him. And you know why? I think Verna was tired of having the child welfare people on her case. It was easier to dump Corey on someone else than to try to become a better mother."

"And how do they know all this? The part you're not guessing about, I mean?"

She ignored his sarcasm. "Corey told them. Verna told Corey she was sick of taking care of her and it was time for her father to take her."

"She could be lying. She lied about you being her aunt."

"You've heard a lot about Verna. Does it sound like a lie?"

He poured a glass of tea and drank it between glares.

"So what?" he asked at last. "She's free of Verna now. There are certified foster care homes in South Carolina. You've explained that we aren't related to her, and somewhere out there she has a father who may be searching for her."

"Not likely. Corey claims her mother said that her father probably wouldn't want her, either."

"If Corey's never met him, she wouldn't know."

"She's lived in Foxcove all her life. Can you really believe it would be better for her to wait in a strange state with strange foster parents until they find her father—if they do? Can you really believe that?"

"You know what I can't believe? I can't believe they're going to let you take her. Just like that. They've got laws."

"And we've got credentials up the wazoo. They'll investigate, sure, but we'll come out looking like God's gift to the system. I gave them the name of a psychologist who knows us, little Jeff Hartley's mother. They're going to call her, as well as Father Watkins. And the people at the agency here know how concerned we've been about Corey. They've been as helpful as the law would allow. They're not going to interfere if we're willing to keep her."

"*We* are not willing."

"You had better get willing, and quick." She heard the threat come out of her mouth, and she was astounded. But she couldn't take it back, because she had meant every single word.

He set his glass on the counter. "Just what does that mean?"

"It means that if you say no to me on this, I don't know if I'll ever be able to forgive you."

His dark eyes smoldered, but he didn't say a word.

"I've put up with hell for half of this past year, Joe. I've watched you withdraw until I've almost given up hope we can still have a marriage. I've watched you shut me out, little by little, and deny it the whole time. I've watched you cut off all the options that could have helped us deal with our infertility. You won't consider marriage counseling. You won't consider artificial insemination. You won't consider adoption. You. You. You."

She touched her chest. "Well, this time I want something to help me ease my pain. I want to take a child I already love and help her through a terrible time. I want to keep her here until the state of North Carolina can make arrangements for her, good arrangements, not something shoddy and temporary. I'm Corey's one link with the good things inside her. No one else is as qualified to help her as I am. If I can do this, if I can be allowed to do this, then maybe it won't matter so much that I'll never get to raise a child from start to finish."

She stopped. She had said too much; she had said too little. And no matter how much or how little she'd said, she wasn't sure he had heard any of it.

"You've boxed me in, Sam."

"If that's possible, I'm glad I have."

"She's a smart kid. She's going to know I don't want her. She's already decided she doesn't like me."

"The two of you are peas in a pod." Sam's knees shook. She leaned against the stove. "Give her a chance, Joe. Nobody's better with kids than you are. You don't have to love her. You just have to get along with her for a little while."

"I don't like ultimatums."

"Neither do I. But you've given me one right after another this year. I suppose my turn's been coming."

She could see he wanted to deny what she'd said, but he didn't. "One condition," he said at last.

"What?"

"You don't even think about keeping her."

Her gaze didn't waver. "She has a father."

"Who may not want her. Promise me if he doesn't, or if for some reason he's not acceptable to the state, you won't bring up adoption."

"I promise. Her stay will be temporary."

"Very temporary. It wouldn't be fair to Corey to give her false hope."

"I don't want this to come between us." She moved toward him. Slowly. Apprehensively. "We were just making a new start tonight."

"Were we?"

"We made love. And it felt new."

He didn't open his arms.

"This means the world to me, Joe."

"It must."

She stopped right in front of him. "I love you."

"You love me because I'm doing what you want."

"I love you because even though you're still wading around in your own pain, you're willing to help me with mine."

He opened his arms and enclosed her inside them. But even though they stood that way for a long time, when they climbed the stairs to bed, neither of them could think of another thing to say.

8

The hospital where Corey had been taken could have been plopped down unnoticed in any state of the union. The building was medium sized and nondescript, complete with the frog-pond cacophony of intercom, beepers and smiling personnel determined to give out as little information as possible.

Joe and Sam waited for the county social worker on imitation leather chairs in the lobby. After fifteen minutes Sam found a coffee machine and returned with a cup for each of them, only to find Joe immersed in conversation with a young brunette.

For a moment Sam wanted to throw herself between her husband and the dark-haired woman. Joe had been quiet on the long drive. Yes, he had agreed to take Corey, but only under protest. Perhaps even at this late date he had decided to renege.

Then she realized how little credit she was giving him. Joe never went back on his word.

She handed him one of the cups and extended her hand to the woman. "Miss Davis?"

The woman, cuter than she was pretty and young enough to be Corey's sister, stood to shake hands. "You must be

Samantha. I was just telling Joe that Corey's been a terror. You're not going to have an easy time of it.''

"Corey's always been a terror." Samantha didn't look at Joe. "We're prepared. Has she been told that she's coming home with us?''

"I told her last night. I'm sorry we had to wait so long, but I wanted to be sure all the paperwork was cleared up. I didn't want to disappoint her if we ran into any snags.''

"How did she take the news?''

Miss Davis hesitated. "I don't think she believed me. She thought we were just trying to get her to behave.''

"She's had a hard life. She doesn't have much reason to trust anything an adult says to her.''

"But she seems to trust you." Miss Davis turned to Joe. "I'm wondering, though. Have you had much contact with Corey?''

"Enough to be fully aware what we're getting into.''

"She, um, said that you don't like her very well.''

"She's not the kind of kid you necessarily like on sight.''

That seemed to satisfy Miss Davis. Sam appreciated Joe's tact. She owed him one. "Look, we know she's had a hard time, not just since the accident, but since she was born. But she responds to love. She's extremely bright, and she wants to please if she thinks it's possible.''

"Well, I can't tell you how glad I am that somebody wanted her. I think we might have had some real problems finding a foster home. Very few marriages can withstand the testing of a troubled child.''

Sam couldn't look at Joe. For the first time she had doubts about this decision. Their marriage was shaky. Was Corey going to be the final blow? "Can we see her now?''

"Your timing's good. She's just had her bath, and the doctor's discharged her. She should be ready to go home with you.''

But she wasn't ready. When they entered the room at the

far end of the pediatric wing, one nurse was holding Corey down as a second tried to comb her hair. Somewhere there was a karate studio willing to give a scholarship on the basis of Corey's perfectly aimed kicks.

"Corey!" Sam crossed the room and waved away the nurse with the comb. "What on earth do you think you're doing?"

Corey took one look at Sam and started to wail. Sam fell to the bed beside the little girl and put her arms around her. "It's okay, honey, you're going to go home with Joe and me."

"My mama's dead, Miss Sam. I ain't got nobody."

Sam held her tighter and rested her head against Corey's hair. Corey looked past Sam to Joe.

Sam couldn't see Corey's expression, but Joe could. Mixed with genuine misery was challenge. Her thoughts were visible to him. *I've got her now. See if you can top this, buster.* Joe told himself she was just a little girl. He told himself that she was a little girl whose life had been tough and sad.

He told himself that he and Sam were making a big mistake.

Sam put her hands on Corey's shoulders and gazed into her eyes. "I mean it, Corey. You're coming home with Mr. Joe and me until Miss Davis can find your father or somebody else in your family."

"I ain't got nobody. My daddy was s'posed to be living here, but my mama couldn't find him."

"Well, Miss Davis knows just how to look for him. She's going to do the best she can."

"I'm going to sleep at your house and stuff?"

"You certainly are."

"With him?" She hunched one shoulder at Joe.

"I'm not moving out for the occasion," Joe said dryly.

"We've fixed up a room down the hall from ours," Sam said.

"Do I have to go to school?"

"I don't know how long you'll be with us. But if you're still there when the school year starts you'll have to go to school, just like all the other children." Sam stood. "First you've got to let me comb your hair, though, or they aren't going to let you out of here."

"I got a bruise on my head. It hurts!"

"I'll be careful." Sam held out her hand to the nurse who gratefully presented her with the comb.

Joe watched as Sam lovingly combed the child's stubby locks. Corey sat absolutely still. Beside him Miss Davis murmured something.

"I'm sorry. What'd you say?" he asked.

She turned. He thought he saw commiseration in her eyes. "I wouldn't want to be the one who comes between those two," she said softly. "When I find Corey's father I'll let *you* be the one to tell your wife. And Corey."

Corey walked with a limp—an ankle was sprained and appropriately bandaged—but it didn't keep her from thoroughly exploring her new home.

"What's that?" she asked in Joe's study.

He stood in the doorway just waiting for her to destroy something. "Encyclopedias."

"What're they for?"

"To learn things."

"Anything you want?"

"Just about."

She pointed at the wall behind his desk. "What's that?"

"A mandolin."

"What's a mandolin?"

"It's an instrument, a little like a guitar. Do you know what a guitar is?"

"I'm not dumb."

"So you've told me before." He stepped into the room to keep a better eye on her as she wandered.

"Why's it up high like that?"

"I don't play it well, but I like to look at it. It belonged to my grandfather."

"Ain't nothing much. 'S all beat up."

"So was my grandfather."

To his amazement she giggled. It was a normal little-girl sound. "That's not very nice," she said.

"If my grandfather was still alive he would have been the first to say it. He was ninety when he died, and he could really play."

"Play it."

"I told you, I don't play very well."

"Let me play it."

"No." He crossed the room and reached for the mandolin, which hung beside a window. He leaned against the desk and strummed a few chords.

"'S that all you can do?"

"Afraid so."

"You ain't very good."

He put the mandolin back. "I think you've seen everything. From now on this room's off-limits. There's nothing to play with in here, but I have papers I don't want messed up. You'll need to stay out."

She frowned. "What kind of papers?"

"Boring ones. But Miss Sam's put drawing paper in your room, and if you need more we'll get you more. You won't need to take anything from in here."

"My room's awful big." She looked unsure of herself for a moment.

Sam had spent the weekend clearing out the sewing room upstairs for Corey. Once the room had been intended as a nursery, but those days were past. Since then Sam had taken it over for sewing and school work, but she hadn't seemed to mind turning it over to Corey. Against Joe's better judgment she had bought curtains and sheets covered with pastel kittens. She'd also bought a hundred dollars' worth of toys and supplies. He knew that tomorrow she intended to take Corey shopping for clothes. The hospital had provided the little girl with only the clothes she'd walked out in, and they were a size too large.

Joe felt a nudge of sympathy. He wondered what kind of sleeping arrangements she was used to. "Your room's not that big. And you can keep your door open at night."

"Don't need no door open. Ain't afraid."

"Good." He shooed her out of his study and toward the kitchen where Sam was just putting dinner on the table.

"I hope you like chicken," Sam said with a smile.

"Can we dig up Mr. Red tomorrow and see if he's all bones and stuff?"

Sam dropped the chicken on the table. "Whoops."

"Yeah, Sam, can we?" Joe asked.

She laughed. "Let's not talk about birds until after dinner."

"I want a drumstick." Corey reached across the table with her left hand. Her right was firmly held to her side in a sling.

"I'll get it for you," Joe said, moving the platter out of her reach. "You ask, and I'll serve you."

"I can get it by myself!"

"No, you can't. Because I won't let you." Joe ignored the plea in Sam's eyes. "This is the way we serve dinner here."

"Want a drumstick." She pulled her hand back, but her eyes were mutinous.

"May I have a drumstick, please?" he coached.

She narrowed her eyes and refused to speak. He ignored her and turned to Sam. "What would you like?"

"May I have the platter?" She narrowed her eyes. "Please?"

"Why, certainly. A pleasure to wait on such a well-mannered and spectacularly beautiful woman." He passed her the platter. "Would you please pass the mashed potatoes?"

"I...would...be...thrilled." She passed them.

"Corey, would you like some?" he asked.

She wove her uninjured hand into her sling and stared at him, her lip jutting a record two inches.

"More for me, I guess," he said. "That's good because I love Sam's mashed potatoes."

"I'll have some," Corey said. "Now!"

"May I have some, please?" he coached again.

"You already got some! The whole damn bowl!"

Sam sputtered. Joe couldn't risk even a glance at her. "You'll have to leave the table and eat by yourself if you talk like that while you're here, Corey. Use some manners and ask politely."

"I'm hungry! I ain't had hardly nothing to eat today."

He was not impressed. He had seen Corey eat the equivalent of half a cow at a fast-food restaurant that afternoon. He leaned forward. "May I have a drumstick, please?"

"Miss Sam, he's being mean to me!"

"Joe..."

He turned to Sam and lifted one eyebrow.

"Thank you for trying to teach Corey some manners," she said.

"You're very welcome." He turned back to Corey. "Chicken's getting cold, kid."

A lesser man might have been felled by the expression in her eyes. "May I have some chicken and some mashed potatoes and what all else that I got to say please about?"

"You certainly may." He helped her dish up her dinner.

Then he sat back to eat his own. The three of them chewed in a silent truce.

Corey opened her eyes. The room was dark, even though Miss Sam had left two night-lights burning. It smelled funny, too, like lemons and stuff. She liked the smell, but it sure didn't smell like home.

The bed was softer than any bed she'd ever slept in. She had wanted to keep her eyes open all night, so Miss Sam would stay. But she'd kept sinking down in the bed. Then she'd closed her eyes a little. Then next thing she knew, Miss Sam was gone.

Now Corey closed her eyes again, this time because she was frightened to leave them open. There were funny shadows in the room, like long bony fingers pointing right at her. Sometimes they moved. Miss Sam said they were just the shadows of tree branches, but Corey wasn't too sure. One of the shadows looked like the head of a monster, and she'd sure never seen no tree branch that looked like that.

Miss Sam had given her a teddy bear to keep in bed. It was brown, like a real grizzly bear. Miss Sam had given her a book last year about a grizzly bear, a book to take home and keep. She had said that Corey could have it because Corey read so well. Her mama had put the book somewheres and Corey had never found it again. But now her mama was gone. She couldn't take the bear the way she had taken the book.

Corey clutched the bear tighter. She had thought about her mama's death a lot. Mama had been so still when the men had gotten her out of the car. But she hadn't looked sad. Just kind of surprised.

Mama had been driving too fast; Corey remembered that. The car had sailed through the air and Corey's door had come open and she had fallen out before the car crashed. One of the policemen said she would have died, too, if she hadn't landed where it was swampy and all. She had heard him say it, and somebody had told him to be quiet 'cause she was listening.

She didn't miss her mama, and that probably meant she was bad. She was sorry Mama had died, but she didn't miss her. Mama had never been around much, and she hadn't wanted Corey, anyway.

She tried not to think about the things Mama had said that night, about how her father probably wouldn't want her, either, and how nobody would ever want her. Maybe her mama was wrong. Mr. Joe didn't want her. He practiced looking scary on her, just like tonight at the table. But Miss Sam was glad she was here.

Corey opened her eyes. The shadows were still there. She closed them again. The bed was soft. Softer than anything.

"She's asleep."

"So am I." Joe rolled over and stared at the moonlight pouring in through a bedroom window. It was well past midnight.

"No, you're not. You don't talk in your sleep."

He felt the bed sink. The provocative woman scent that always set his body on fire drifted over him. A long, smooth leg settled against the length of his. He felt the softness of breasts sinking against his chest. He put his arm around Sam before he could think better of it.

"It's a gorgeous night," she said. "The air's as soft as butter, and the flowers in the yard smell like the end of summer. I can smell the roses on the breeze."

"You'd know about the night. You've been up for most of it."

"I know, but Corey was scared. She's not used to a room by herself. She says she always slept on a couch in the living room in front of the television."

"While her mother entertained in the bedroom."

"What?"

"That's the rumor."

"Well, I never heard it."

"If it's true, it makes it unlikely that Corey's father is going to be genuinely pleased to have her dropped on his doorstep."

"We'll see what happens. I just hope it's something good. Can you see now what a special little girl she is?"

"What's called for here, the truth or a husbandly lie?"

"You must see how smart she is, and funny and..."

"I'm waiting."

"And endearing."

"I see three hundred teenagers every day during the school year. Three hundred kids with bad attitudes and learning problems and adult-hating smirks on their faces. I'd trade her for any one of them."

"Joe!"

He gathered her a little closer. "Actually, not for either of the Symonds girls. One of them comes on to every male teacher in the school and the other one makes a Saturday run over to Raleigh every weekend for a new supply of drugs."

"What are you trying to say? Corey places an easy third?"

"I wouldn't trade her for most of the wrestling team, either. One of these days they're going to gang up and get me in a headlock in the hallway. That'll be that."

"Do you know what she told me?"

"I can guess. She told you I was picking on her tonight."

"She said looking at you is scary because you're so big."

"I hope I stay big while she's here, then. A little fear can go a long way."

"You don't really want her to be afraid of you."

"I want her to know that one of us isn't going to be a pushover." He felt her stiffen. He continued to hold her until she relaxed.

"Okay," she said after a while. "I guess I deserved that."

"She's a manipulator, Sam. She'll come between us in a heartbeat if we let her."

"She's a sad little girl who's never been loved."

"And she knows it." He caressed her arm. "But that's not entirely bad. She's a survivor. She uses what little she has to try to make a place for herself in the world. If she didn't, she'd be even sadder."

"You just said something nice about her."

"No, I didn't."

"I heard you!"

He felt her hair against his lips. He inched his lips to her cheek and felt the warm, smooth curve of her flesh. "There's nothing nice to say."

"Joe, I love you for this."

"For what? Holding my own? Holding you?"

"For being the man I married."

That man lived somewhere else, somewhere in a fantasy land peopled by small children with cocky Giovanelli grins. He didn't respond, but she didn't seem to notice.

"I need your love and patience now." She kissed the curve of his throat. Her hair drifted over his cheek. "If I didn't have it, then I wouldn't have any love or patience to give Corey. You know that's the real test of a man, don't you? The way he supports his woman when she really needs him?"

He knew the real test of a man.

She continued. "The way he comforts her. The way he makes her feel like a woman. The way he shares his life with her. I wonder why fathers don't teach that to their sons? This world's full of children put here by men who think the only way they have to prove their masculinity is to shoot a few sperm in the right direction.''

She wasn't pulling any punches. She had danced around Joe's fertility problem for most of the year; now she was moving in for the kill. "I get your point, Sam." He didn't like the obvious tension in his voice. He didn't like the way she could see into his very soul.

"Not well enough. Let me show you what kind of man you really are.''

Her hands were cool against his skin. He wanted to push them away, but he couldn't seem to move. Impotence was not his problem. She had only to look at him to arouse him. It seemed like a terrible joke.

"You're the kind of man who knows how to make a woman feel like she's beautiful," she said. Her lips trailed kisses along his jaw.

"You *are* beautiful.''

"Not really. Pretty, maybe. I'll be an elegant old woman because my bones are good. But I lack the spark for beauty.''

"Ridiculous." He found himself turning toward her.

"No. And it doesn't matter. You've always made me feel beautiful. When you hold me and make love to me, I'm Christie Brinkley and Madonna combined.''

"Madonna?" He laughed, and the sound drifted seductively on the warm summer air.

"Sure. You make me feel sexy. Hey, I could pose in the nude, too, if it was you behind the camera. But the pictures would be too hot to print.''

"It had better be me behind that camera if you're posing nude.''

"And you're the kind of man who knows just what to do when the going gets rough." She stroked her hand over his chest. Lightly and thoroughly. Again, then again. "Remember when I told my parents we were getting married,

and my father said he'd cut me off if I married you? And
you said that was great because you wanted the pleasure
of supporting me all to yourself? Well, he's still mulling
that one over. It's the only time in his life that he couldn't
think of an appropriately quelling response.''

"Fischer's not so bad.''

"And you're the kind of man who forgives.'' She
stroked her hand over his hip, circling, circling the part of
him that was ready to sink into the very core of her.

"I would have walked out of their house in Chevy Chase
and never looked back,'' she said, "but it might have
ruined my life. You knew just how to handle my parents
so that they had an open door when they needed one. And
when they walked through that door you never said an unkind word to them. They're still trying to figure out why
they can't seem to dislike you. God knows, they've tried
hard enough.''

"You're trying to drive me crazy.'' His voice was thick,
charged with desire.

"*I'm* crazy. Crazy about you, Joe. You're the only man
I'll ever want. You're too much man for me sometimes. I
don't know what to do with you.''

"I think you've got it figured out.'' He took her lips,
tasted and silenced them. She was the flavor of the warm
night, the rose-scented breeze, the moisture-laden air. Her
flesh was as soft as the rich North Carolina earth. He pulled
her on top of him to feel her closer, to stretch her lithe
body along the length of his and relearn its familiar secrets.

"No! No!''

For a minute he couldn't imagine who was screaming.
Then Sam stiffened. "Corey!''

"No.'' He couldn't believe it. He had been ready for
anything except this.

Sam rolled to the bed beside him and swung her legs
over the side. "She sounds scared to death!''

"Her timing is impeccable."

"You don't think she's making this up, do you?"

He didn't. He wanted to, but he didn't. Joe knew terror and what it sounded like. He had suffered nightmares after the death of his father, and his mother had always been there, despite her own sadness, to comfort him.

"I've got to go to her." Sam had already thrown on her robe. The words stayed in the room longer than she did.

Joe stared at the ceiling, at the way the moonlight softened the swirls of plaster and cast shadows that looked like the heads of gargoyles. Then with a harsh sigh he got out of bed and found his robe, too.

"I was looking in my mama's grave." In the doorway Joe saw that Corey was sitting up in the lonely twin bed, her face wet with tears and the bear Sam had bought her clutched tightly in her arms. Sam was on the bed beside her, with her arm around Corey's shoulders. "I was looking, and I saw Mr. Red, 'cept he was all bones and stuff. And my mama was turning into bones, too."

Sam pulled her closer. "When people die they don't feel anything anymore. Same thing for birds or anything that dies. The Bible says we came from dust and turn to dust. That's the way it's supposed to be. But the real part of us, the part that makes us what we are, goes on to another, better place. And that's where your mother is."

Joe had real doubts about that, but he sure wasn't going to tell Corey. As the years passed she would come to terms with her memories of Verna, in her own way and in her own time. Now Sam was right to offer her comfort.

"She died real quick. Maybe it was a mistake. Maybe I was the one s'posed to die."

"No. Things happen the way they're supposed to. You're supposed to grow up to be a wonderful woman and live a good and happy life."

"Like you?"

"I don't know about that. I just know you're supposed to be happy. Your mother would want you to go on and be happy."

Corey looked doubtful. She looked up and saw Joe standing in the doorway. Her expression seemed to say that she thought Sam was probably wrong about Verna, but Corey wasn't going to tell her so.

Something inside Joe did a funny little lurch. Corey obviously didn't want Sam to feel any worse than she already did. She was protecting Sam. Corey would keep her secrets about her mother to herself, even if it might feel pretty good to share them.

"Why don't you pack up your pillow and blanket and come sleep in our room for tonight?" he said. He didn't know where the words had come from, but they continued. "We'll make you a bed on the floor next to ours."

She narrowed her eyes. "You'll step on me!"

"If I do, I'll try not to put all my weight on you."

Sam laughed. The look she sent him was laced with gratitude. "Would you like that, Corey? It might not be so lonely."

"If I can sleep on your side, Miss Sam."

Sam laughed again. "I'm sure Mr. Joe won't mind. Will you, Mr. Joe?"

He was going to mind terribly. He had other things he'd rather do in his bedroom than baby-sit tonight. But it seemed that one small child was already taking over his life...and his wife.

"I sure hope you don't snore," he said.

"I don't!"

"I'll be sure to tell you if you do." He started for the bedroom to set up Sam's exercise mat and a pile of sleeping bags as a base for Corey's new bed.

In the hallway he felt a hand on his shoulder. He turned his head.

"You're the kind of man who does what's necessary, even if it's not the least bit fun," Sam said. She stretched up to kiss him, a soft, lingering kiss that was filled with promise.

"I'm the kind of man who can't say no when he ought to."

"I hope that's the case, because tomorrow night I want to hear a resounding yes to every suggestion I make."

His heart beat faster as he went to fix Corey's bed.

9

Joe was gone the next morning by the time the county social worker arrived. Since he had early meetings he had promised to stop by her office in the afternoon to introduce himself and answer any questions she might have. Now Sam and Corey braved examination alone.

Dinah Ryan was a no-nonsense spinster, in sensible shoes and a conservative suit, who drove a spiffy red sports car that made Killer look sedate.

"So, Corey, how do you like it here?" She looked over the top of her bifocals.

"I like it fine."

"Settled in all right?"

Sam answered for her. "Would you like to see Corey's room?"

"You mean the room where Corey is staying?"

Sam heard the difference and was properly chastised. "Yes." She led the way with Corey right behind her.

"Very nice." Miss Ryan ran her hand over Corey's new comforter, then picked up the teddy bear. "A new friend, I see."

Corey grabbed the bear out of her hands. "Mine."

"I'm sorry, sugar, I should have asked your permission."

Sam relaxed a little. At least Miss Ryan understood children.

"This is a very comfortable room," Miss Ryan said. "Did you sleep all right last night?"

"I slept with Miss Sam."

Miss Ryan lifted an eyebrow. "Oh?"

Sam answered. "She was frightened. We made her a bed on the floor beside ours."

"A good idea. For a little while."

Sam relaxed a little more. "Would you like to see the rest of the house? We'd like to take you to the duck pond if you have time."

"It ain't no pond," Corey said. "It's a lake!"

Sam smiled and smoothed Corey's hair back from her forehead. "Tell that to Mr. Joe sometime."

They toured the house slowly. After a few minutes it was clear that Dinah Ryan was more interested in the antiques that Sam and Joe had refinished and the history of the building than whether the house was suitable for Corey.

Outside Corey, despite her limp, outdistanced them on the path down to the pond.

"I'd give my car and my mother's diamonds for more homes like this for our children." Dinah—formality had lapsed by the time they had reached the kitchen—spread her arms wide. "All this space. Everything's clean and tidy and open. You have room for half a dozen Coreys here."

"One Corey is plenty."

"I've followed her case for years. I can't tell you how many complaints we had about Verna Haskins. I shouldn't even tell you that much."

"Then why wasn't anything done?" Sam realized how belligerent she sounded. "I'm sorry. I'm sure you tried."

"And tried hard. It would have been easier if she beat

the child, but she didn't, or at least not often or brutally enough to qualify as abuse. But neglect is much more difficult to pin down. We can't take one set of standards and apply them to all families. Parents have different ways of raising their children. Sometimes the differences are cultural, sometimes it's just personality or ignorance. I can tell you that Verna was an abused child, herself. She didn't have much left inside her by the time she had Corey.''

"My husband and I can't have children." Sam didn't know where that little piece of information had come from. It had just seemed the right thing to say.

"And you look at people like Verna Haskins and wonder about fate?"

"Sometimes."

"I didn't have children, because I never met a man I wanted to marry. Over the years I watched the way other people ruined the lives of the kids they'd had, and I got so angry."

"But not anymore?"

"I figure I've had half a dozen children by now, if you add up all the kids I've worked with and loved and let go of."

"That's a nice way to think of it."

"There is always more than one way to skin a cat."

Or make a family. Sam heard an open invitation. Dinah approved of her. Heartily. And she would probably approve of Joe. If Sam and Joe were interested in becoming foster parents, or in adoption...

"Do you have many children who need homes?" Sam couldn't resist the question.

"Not babies. Most of the children we get are like Corey. Placing a newborn is almost unheard of these days. But we have children with physical or emotional problems who need families. Sometimes we have siblings. We work hard to place them, but sometimes we have to resort to looking outside the county. And we'd much prefer to keep our children here if we can.''

"What will happen to Corey if her father can't be found?"

"I'm not sure. What will?" Dinah inclined her gray head.

Sam couldn't answer. She knew what she was supposed to say, what she had promised Joe she would say, but somehow, the words just wouldn't come.

Sadlers was the closest thing to a department store in Foxcove. There were several strip malls out on the highway with nationally known chains. But Sadlers, with its two stories of odds and ends packed into nooks and crannies, was much more fun to shop in.

Sam determined Corey's size with one agonizing fitting. The little girl's hips and back were black-and-blue, and between her sprained ankle and broken arm, trying on clothes was a miserable experience. But once Sam had a pretty good idea what would fit, the fun began. Corey, wide-eyed and—for the moment, at least—enraptured, sat on a bench while Sam brought her things to look at.

Corey liked bright colors, and they looked surprisingly good against her tanned skin. She liked pants and jeans, but there was also a wistfully feminine little girl deep inside her who responded with enthusiasm to a red plaid dress and a skirt and blouse of fuchsia-and-gold print.

Sam discovered that she couldn't say no to anything Corey really wanted. She remembered shopping for clothes with her own mother. Kathryn had disapproved of most of her choices, and only rarely had Sam come home with anything that excited her.

Between that memory and the realization that Corey had never shopped for clothes at all, Sam knew she lost all perspective. Corey had grown up in hand-me-downs, and the expression on her face when she was allowed to choose what she wanted blotted out the sensible voice inside Sam that told her she was setting Corey up for a fall.

There was almost no chance that Corey's father would indulge her this way. And if she went to live in permanent foster care, it was doubtful that the state of North Carolina would spend money so lavishly.

But Sam couldn't resist.

Sam had an armful of bundles by the time they left Sadlers. In addition to everything else they had bought shoes and socks for school and play, a backpack for school—and notebooks and a pencil box to go in it—a sweater, in case it turned cold early, a hat to go with the sweater and half a dozen T-shirts and cotton shorts to last for the rest of the summer. Then there had been underwear, a new brush and comb, female fripperies for the youthful set.... The bill had been enormous.

Sam dumped the bags in the trunk of her car and slammed it just in time to see Polly and her youngest daughter, Mary Nell, who was just two years older than Corey, waving from across the street.

Sam crossed with Corey's hand in hers and greeted Polly and Mary Nell on the opposite sidewalk.

"Well, hello, Miss Corey," Polly said cheerfully. "My, don't you look fine in that cast. Looks to me like it needs some decoration. Don't you think, Sammy?"

"I think Miss Polly wants you to ask her to sign it," Sam explained to Corey.

"Me, too!" Mary Nell said. "I could draw a picture on it."

Corey seemed to like that idea. The four of them descended on the drugstore, which, despite bright, wide aisles and a thoroughly modern pharmacy, had left its old-fashioned soda fountain intact during remodeling.

They settled at a table and ordered root-beer floats.

"Come on, let's go look at the toys while they're getting it." Mary Nell, a wiry bundle of energy, was up and out of the booth before Corey could respond. Corey hesitated and looked at Sam.

"Go on, honey. I'll be waiting right here."

Polly watched Corey follow Mary Nell's path. "I can't believe you've got her."

"You'd believe it if you saw what I just spent."

"Overdoin' it a bit?"

"A bit."

"What's Joe think about all this?"

Polly knew all about the problems between Joe and Sam. She was the only person to whom Sam had been able to pour out her heart after the final visit to the fertility specialist.

"He's tolerating her," Sam said. "He's been wonderful, actually, considering that I forced her down his throat."

"It's not so bad to force a good thing down a man's throat now and then."

"You think this is a good thing?"

"Could be."

"He was fantastic last night. Corey was scared, and he made a bed on the floor beside ours so that she wouldn't be afraid."

"Sounds like our Joe."

"Then this morning he left with hardly a word to either one of us." Sam thought about the silent man who had shaved, dressed and grabbed a cup of coffee on his way out the door. Last night she'd thought they were making wonderful progress. This morning had been like old times—or new times. The tension between them had been going on for so long she wasn't sure what to call it now.

"You've never really understood what he's feelin', have you?"

Sam waited until the floats had been placed in front of

them before she answered. The girls still hadn't returned. "I understand. I'm just tired of it. I have feelings, too."

"Sure you do. Difference is, you're supposed to. He's not."

"That's not fair."

"No? Don't you think you married Joe 'cause he's strong and sure of himself? He likes to take care of you and everybody else. Nothing stops him, least nothing did till now."

"I married him because I love him."

"But what was it you loved?"

All the things Polly had just named. The answer was so clear that Polly might as well have said that, too. Sam looked down at her float. "Darn you."

"Oh, you can do better'n that, Sammy. I deserve at least a damn or two."

"But I don't expect him to be strong all the time," Sam said. "I really don't."

"Then give him some more time. Joe's used to bein' strong. Now he doesn't see himself that way anymore. And if you start naggin' at him to be stronger, it's going to make him feel weaker. Do you see what I'm gettin' at?"

"You ought to go into counseling and put Dr. Ray out of business."

"Now wouldn't that be a kick in the head?"

The drugstore's toy shelves were full of wonderful things. "Look at that." Corey pointed to a jigsaw puzzle with a picture of a teddy bear much like the one that Sam had given her. "And that!" She pointed to another.

"You ever been out to the toy store on the highway? They got lots of stuff there. Better puzzles than these. I've got a bunch, but I don't play with them much."

Corey liked puzzles a lot. It was like magic to take all those little, no-count pieces and put them together to make something big and pretty. At school, every time she put that last piece in she felt better about lots of things. She wasn't sure why.

"You can have them," Mary Nell offered. "Mine, I mean."

"Really?"

"Sure. I've done them all already. You'll have fun."

Corey couldn't imagine anyone just giving away toys like that. Mary Nell, with her long brown ponytail and rosy cheeks, looked so much like the little girls who had tormented her in school that Corey fully expected her to say she'd been lying. But Mary Nell moved down to the books. "Do you read yet?"

"Sure!"

Mary Nell looked doubtful. Corey chose a book, one with a picture of a horse on its shiny cover, and started to read out loud. "When the little colt E-E-bony was born, he couldn't stand on his wobbly legs."

"Eb—ony." Mary Nell pronounced it correctly for Corey. "But that's very good. I couldn't read that good in first grade."

"I'm in second grade now."

Mary Nell sighed. "Yeah. School starts pretty soon. I don't want to go back."

Corey reluctantly put the book back on the shelf. She wanted to find out what happened to Ebony. "I like school."

"Really?"

"Miss Sam's nice to me."

"My mom says your mom died and now you're staying with Miss Sam. That's sad." Mary Nell brightened. "I know, let's get some markers to decorate your cast." She took off down the aisle before Corey could answer. Corey started after her at a fast limp.

By the time she reached the school supplies Mary Nell

had chosen a big, fat box of markers. "We can pay for 'em on the way out. I need some for school, anyway." She took out a bright red marker and tested it on Corey's cast by drawing a big heart. "Look, they work good."

Corey took out a yellow one. She couldn't draw too well with her left hand—it wasn't good for much at all—but she managed to uncap the marker and start a yellow flower next to Mary Nell's heart.

"What are you girls doing?"

The two girls had been so absorbed in their artwork that they hadn't heard anyone approach. Now Corey looked up and saw a tall woman frowning down at them. Before either girl could answer, the woman took them by their arms. "Are you here with anybody?"

"My mom's at the fountain," Mary Nell managed to say as the woman began to drag them in that direction. "We were going to buy the markers. We were just trying 'em out."

"You certainly *are* going to buy them!"

Corey saw the look on Sam's face as she and Mary Nell were dragged toward the wrong table. Then she saw the look on the woman's face as Mary Nell pointed toward Miss Polly. "That's my mom," she said. "And that's Miss Sam. She's taking care of Corey now."

The woman dropped their arms. Mary Nell sprinted across the short distance and fell into the booth next to her mother. Corey didn't know what to do. Miss Sam stood and beckoned. Corey had never been so glad to be wanted in her life. She threw herself into Miss Sam's arms and buried her head against her.

"They were using markers on her cast." The woman said the last word as if it were somehow distasteful and pointed to Corey. "They didn't pay for them."

"We were going to pay for 'em on the way out," Mary

Nell told her mother. "I needed some for school. Remember?"

"I certainly do remember." Polly looked the woman up and down. "Next time, why don't you check with me before you scare my daughter half to death?" she asked in her best first-grade-teacher voice.

"I'm sorry. I really am. I just saw her—" she pointed to Corey again "—and I thought there was some trouble."

"Well, the next time, why don't you check with *me*," Sam said, "before you scare my...little friend here? She's staying with me now, and I'll expect her to be treated like any other little girl in town."

"Well, she's stolen things before," the woman said.

"Just a candy bar." Corey still had her head against Sam's side. "Once. Just one time." She wanted to add that she'd been pretty hungry that day waiting for her mother to come back home, but she didn't think it would make any difference.

Sam reached into her purse and fumbled for a dollar bill. Her hand was trembling. She held it out to the woman. "Consider it paid for."

"I don't want your money, Mrs. Giovanelli. I just didn't know the—"

"Take it," Sam said through clenched teeth. "And then we can both forget this ever happened. But I expect you to give Corey a fresh start."

The woman looked helplessly at Polly. Polly nodded. The woman stepped forward and took the bill. "This really isn't necessary."

"I think it is. Corey's part of my family now, and the Giovanellis take care of their own."

Corey didn't understand exactly what Miss Sam was saying, but she knew that from that moment on she wasn't going to have to be afraid of anybody in town again. She felt the way she always did when she fit that last jigsaw-puzzle piece into place. She didn't know why. She just did.

Joe watched Corey limp into the kitchen in one of the new outfits that Sam had bought for her. One of the many new outfits.

"It looks wonderful," Sam said enthusiastically. "You look wonderful."

"Don't," Corey said.

"You look very pretty," Joe said. "Did you get your hair cut, too?"

Corey looked away, obviously embarrassed at the attention.

"I took her in to my stylist to have her bangs trimmed and the rest of it shaped up just a little. She wants to let it grow long."

Like Sam's. Joe knew that as surely as if Corey had told him herself. If the child hadn't already worshiped Sam before today, now she would probably be willing to lie down on a holy altar as a human sacrifice to the goddess Samantha Giovanelli.

"How did you fit in all those appointments?" Joe had heard about trips to the pediatrician—Corey was basically healthy, although definitely undernourished; the dentist—Corey would definitely need more trips there; and now, the hairdresser. Not to mention a buying spree that would go down in Foxcove economic history.

"Well, we worked hard," Sam answered. "That's why we're having pizza from town. Besides, it's one of Corey's favorites."

"What don't you eat?" Joe asked Corey.

The little girl seemed perplexed, and he felt immediately ashamed of himself for putting her on the spot. "How do you feel about spinach?"

"Don't know."

He wondered if she had ever eaten vegetables at home.

Sam seemed to read his mind. "Corey's going to help me in the vegetable garden tomorrow. Then we're going to cook whatever we pick for dinner."

Corey wasn't as big as the row of withering cornstalks in the back of the garden or the hoe that Sam would probably give her to wield. She would be nothing but a threat to all vegetable life and a huge distraction. But Sam seemed hardly able to wait for the experience.

Joe could feel something simmering inside him. It had simmered since the morning and heated up since he'd come back home to find Sam and Corey trooping inside with half a ton of shopping bags. He didn't begrudge the money. His feelings had nothing to do with money.

"Corey, run on upstairs and wash your face and hands," Sam said. "Then why don't you unpack the puzzles Mary Nell gave you and start one on your desk? I'll call you when the pizza's ready."

Corey looked rebellious at the first suggestion, but the second seemed to intrigue her. She left the kitchen, and Joe could hear her clattering up the stairs in her new shoes.

"That was another stop I didn't tell you about," Sam said. "Mary Nell insisted we follow Polly home so she could give Corey about two dozen puzzles and a bagful of books, besides. You should have seen Corey's face."

"Thunderstruck, I'd imagine," Joe said.

"At least that. Anyway, this will keep her busy for a while so you and I can chat in peace. How was your day?"

"Calm by comparison."

"Oh, come on, things at the high school are never calm. Even when the kids aren't there yet."

He described his day in as few words as possible. She didn't seem to notice his brevity.

"Well, it sounds as if the year's getting off to a good start," she said.

He watched as she bent over to slide the pizza, cardboard box and all, into the oven. When she straightened her cheeks were flushed with heat. "I feel like I accomplished about a bezillion things today. And I'm still brimming with energy." She smiled, a seductive Samantha smile. "I hope you are, too, because I seem to remember we have plans for later."

He saw the sparkle in her eyes, the flush that wasn't fading in the cooler air, and he knew why she felt so alive. Not because of him and a promised night of lovemaking, but because today she had lived out her fantasies of motherhood, fantasies that his sterility had made impossible.

"Playing fairy godmother must be energizing," he said.

"Is that what I was doing?" she asked, still smiling.

"Yes. To Corey's Cinderella."

The smile faded slowly. "You're angry, aren't you?"

"No. I'm not angry. I just see the handwriting on the wall."

"What do you mean?"

"Do you know what it's going to be like for that child when she has to leave? Anybody ever give you a Christmas package and then snatch it away at the last minute?"

She looked away. "I thought about that. I really did."

"Not hard enough."

She drummed her fingers on the stove. "What was I supposed to do, Joe? Was I supposed to treat her like a secondhand piece of merchandise so she won't get used to feeling special? Should I have done all her shopping at the Goodwill store? Bought her only a couple of things and washed them every night?"

"You overdid it, big time."

"All right, I did. Like I said, I knew it. But I couldn't seem to stop myself. I remember what it was like to be that age. I can't tell you what I would have given to have someone focus on me and what I wanted."

"You? You had everything! What did you ever want that you couldn't have?" The words were out of his mouth before he could take them back. And it took only a second to realize how wrong and how cruel they were.

"I was given everything my parents thought I should have and not one thing more. And nobody ever looked me in the eye or paid attention to who I really was. Not until you came along."

He felt lower than an earthworm. He stood and took her in his arms. "I'm sorry."

She pulled away. "You know what I think? I think you're right. In the short term caring so much for Corey might make it harder for her when she has to leave. But I'm willing to take the chance that in the long run she'll remember that somebody did care, somebody paid attention, and it'll make her a happier, more secure person."

"No. You're setting her up."

Sam kept her voice low. "You're setting *me* up. You didn't want Corey here and you still don't. And now it's eating you up because it means so much to me. Today was wonderful, and now you're trying to make it a lot less so. You've forgotten how to look me in the eye and see what I really need. You've forgotten how to pay attention to anybody but yourself!"

"I'm not talking about you or me. I'm talking about that little girl and what's best for her." But even as he proclaimed his innocence, Joe knew she was right.

"Do you even care?" she asked. "Can you remember how to care about a kid, Joe? Or did you stop caring the day you found out that you were never going to father one of your own?"

Corey washed her hands and face, even though she didn't see why she should. Miss Sam had funny ideas about how clean a little girl should be. Sometimes she was afraid her skin was going to peel right off the way Miss Sam scrubbed. Washing the hand in the cast was hard, and using one hand to wash her face was harder. But she managed.

In her room she peered around warily. There were no shadows now. It was still early, and the room looked pretty nice. There were kittens on the curtains just like the ones on the bed. They looked alive, and almost as pretty as Tinkerbelle's kittens. Miss Sam had let Corey hold Tink's kittens in the summer, when she had brought Mr. Red here for her to fix. Corey was sorry the kittens were all grown up now and gone.

She hugged her bear, then stuck it down between her cast and her body. The cast was a lot prettier now. Mary Nell could draw real good. She thought maybe Mary Nell was going to be her friend.

She put the puzzles on the shelf that Miss Sam had said to use for her toys. Having toys of her own felt kind of strange. She'd had a few from time to time, but never so many and all at once. Besides the puzzles and books there was the bear, and all kinds of things to draw and color on and with. And there was a doll that sat in the corner and stared at her. Miss Sam said it was mostly a looking doll because it was very old, but she said that tomorrow she and Corey would shop for a playing doll.

Corey wondered if they really would.

She saved the best puzzle to dump out on the desk. It was a big one, with lots of bitty little pieces. The picture on the front of the box was a farm, with cows and horses and a little girl—blond like her and Miss Sam—feeding a rooster and a whole flock of hens. She was just about to start it when she heard voices downstairs.

They weren't loud voices, but they weren't talking voices, either. Frowning, she went to the door and poked her head into the hallway.

She couldn't hear what Mr. Joe was saying, but he

sounded angry. When Miss Sam answered, she sounded angry, too, almost as angry as she had sounded at the drug-store.

Corey remembered the way Miss Sam had talked to the lady at the store. She hadn't even asked Corey why she had stolen the candy bar that time. She had stuck up for Corey then, and Corey thought maybe she was sticking up for her again with Mr. Joe.

The thought pleased her. She liked Miss Sam a lot, but Mr. Joe was another thing. He didn't like her. She could tell. She guessed he would do just about anything to make her leave. But maybe if he and Miss Sam were mad at each other, he would leave instead.

That thought gave her real pleasure. If Mr. Joe left, then Miss Sam might just keep Corey there. She would need company, wouldn't she? And Corey could help out and stuff. She could do lots of things.

The voices stopped. When Miss Sam finally called her to dinner, Mr. Joe wasn't there anymore. Miss Sam said that he'd had to go out for a while. Sitting next to Miss Sam at the table, Corey hoped that he wouldn't ever find his way back home.

10

Sam kissed her mother's cool cheek and inhaled a faint drift of the specially blended scent that was as much a part of Kathryn Whitehurst as her perfectly groomed blond hair. Kathryn was dressed in clothes only she would consider perfect for a Labor Day family barbecue: white linen slacks with a knife-edged crease that pointed the way to powder blue sandals, a short-sleeved blue silk sweater and understated platinum jewelry. Never mind that a drop of barbecue sauce would ruin the slacks, a walk to the pond would ruin the sandals. This was Kathryn at her most casual. Sam was learning to be tolerant.

"I wish you could have come to see us, Samantha," Kathryn said after she had pulled away. "This was too much of a trip after all the traveling we did this summer."

"I know, but it would have been Thanksgiving before Joe and I could have gotten out of town. School starts tomorrow. I'm glad you decided to come."

"Your father decided." Her tone implied that she had been against it, but Sam suspected that Kathryn found some sort of pleasure in getting together with Joe's family, even if it was just perverse fascination that her only child had married into such a rowdy crew.

"Well, I fixed your favorite picnic food, just to make it worth the trip," Sam said.

"It was worth the trip just to see you," Kathryn said, unbending just a trifle. "And to catch a glimpse of this child we've heard so much about."

"You'll probably only catch a glimpse. Corey's off playing somewhere with the nieces and nephews." Sam turned to greet her father, who had been on the other side of the car talking to Joe. Joe was always unfailingly polite to both of her parents. He found them every bit as fascinating as they found the Giovanellis.

She said all the appropriate things to her father and listened politely to his responses, but her eyes flicked over and over again to Joe. His polo shirt was a blinding white against his tanned skin, and his shorts were just tight enough to hint at delicious secrets.

Unfortunately everything about Joe was secret these days. In the weeks since Corey had come to live with them he had thrown himself into his work with a fervor that, even for Joe, was obsessive. Sometimes she found herself longing for the days before Corey had come, days when there had been the occasional, if rare, shared moment. Since the day she and Corey had come home from their marathon shopping trip, Joe had been a total stranger.

Sometimes she wasn't even sure she was still a married woman.

Joe caught her gaze and held it as her father made one more comment about the house. Something simmered behind Joe's dark stare. She didn't know what; she would probably be the last to know. She wanted to take him by the arm, lead him into a sheltering bough of pine trees and demand that he talk to her. But she knew where that would lead. Nowhere. And she wasn't Kathryn and Fischer Whitehurst's daughter for nothing. She knew the duties of a hostess.

She settled her parents on the front porch with drinks and Rose. Rose adored Kathryn because she listened raptly to Rose's stories about her grandchildren. Sam suspected that her mother was in the market for a couple of grandchildren of her own, even though she had never mentioned the subject to Sam. Sam hadn't yet told her that there would be no children with Whitehurst-Giovanelli blood running through their veins.

Back in the empty kitchen she stood at the counter for a moment, resting before the next onslaught of guests. All Joe's family had been invited, along with Polly and her husband and Mary Nell, who to Sam's surprise seemed to genuinely enjoy spending time with Corey. Johnny and Teddy were already down at the pond with their children, who were having the last swim of the season. Francis and his brood were there, too, along with one of Joe's sisters and her family. The others would probably arrive later because they had farther to come.

She felt warm hands on her shoulders before she even knew that Joe was there. "Do you need any help in here?" he asked.

She experienced the rumble of his deep voice in parts of her body that had nothing to do with her hearing. She leaned against him, and his arms came around her. For a moment she was frightened to breathe, frightened that anything would scare him away.

"I could make another gallon of lemonade, boil water for tea, make more hamburger patties," he offered.

"Just do what you're doing."

He nuzzled an ear. "I'll add a thing or two."

"Oh, by all means."

"Mama's showing your mother my baby pictures."

"She's sure my mother loves you like a son."

"She can't imagine anyone who doesn't adore me."

"Neither can I." Sam turned in his arms and threaded hers around his neck. "I adore you."

He didn't smile, but his gaze remained fixed on hers. "I don't know why. But I'm damned grateful."

"Joe—"

He put his finger on her lips. "Shh... This isn't the time or place for confessions. But I'm sorry. I've made the past few weeks harder for you than they needed to be."

She kissed his finger; then she kissed him. He tasted like hickory smoke and sunshine, the end of warm summer days. "It's an adjustment having Corey around. I know it's hard sometimes."

"She's not your garden variety seven-year-old."

"That she's not."

"You're wonderful with her."

She glowed from the compliment. "Really? Do you think I'm doing all right?"

"I think you're spoiling her rotten, but along the way you're teaching her patience and manners. Even self-discipline."

"I'm still spoiling her?"

"The last part of the critique was the most important."

"Maybe I just need your level head to guide me."

He didn't answer, and she didn't push. "Let me finish up in here and I'll meet you down at the pond. You can take the cooler with the meat in it," she said.

"You don't need any help?"

"Everything's all done. All we need now are extra arms to carry things down to the picnic tables."

"I'll send likely candidates your way." He kissed her once more before he left the kitchen. The day took on a decidedly rosier glow.

She was packing a jug of lemonade and containers of salad into a box for someone to carry down to the pond when Corey ran inside through the kitchen.

"Corey!" Sam called her back.

"What?"

"What on earth have you been doing?" Sam had helped Corey choose her clothes that morning. Not one of the Giovanellis would care if Corey spent the day in rags, but Sam's mother would.

Sam wanted her parents to like Corey. She wanted them to see her for what she really was, a wonderful little girl with a facade that just needed an alteration or two. Her manners were improving, and so was her grammar. She laughed occasionally now, and the nightmares were disappearing. But none of those improvements were visible at first glance, and the visible improvements, the fading bruises, the weight she had already gained, were hopelessly obscured now by a layer of dirt.

"Corey?" Sam asked when the little girl didn't answer.

"I was digging for treasure!"

"Treasure?"

"Yeah. Patrick said there was treasure in the woods. Me and him and Mary Nell were digging for it."

"Find anything?"

"A whole lot more dirt!"

"Looks that way."

Corey took off.

"Corey!" Sam went after her. "Where are you going?"

"I'm gonna swim."

"You're going to wade," Sam said.

Corey narrowed her eyes. It had been a terrible temptation all summer to have the pond so close. But with the cast on her arm, she hadn't been able to do more than sink her toes in the soft mud of the pond bottom. And that wasn't much fun.

"You're going to have to jump in the bathtub first before you put on your suit," Sam said.

"But I'm gonna be in the water! I'll get clean."

"You have to take a bath."

"Why?"

Why, indeed. Because Sam didn't want her mother and father to pass judgment on the grubby little urchin standing in front of her. First impressions were important. But she didn't want to admit that out loud.

"Because you'll get dirt all over your bathing suit. And only your legs will get clean in the pond," Sam said. "Now scoot. You don't have to stay in long."

Corey looked rebellious, but she didn't argue. A few minutes later Sam heard the sound of water running.

"I wish you'd let me get you some household help," Kathryn said from the doorway, when everything was packed and ready for the trip to the pond. "Just someone to come in a couple of times a week to clean and cook."

"I don't need help. I like doing it myself."

"Do you?" Kathryn seemed genuinely interested.

"I like taking care of my family."

"Family? You and Joe and that little girl?"

"Corey."

"I'm still surprised that you and Joe took in someone else's child."

Sam heard all the things her mother didn't say. "It's temporary, Mother. Just until they can find her father."

"They haven't found him yet?"

"No. Apparently he moves frequently." Sam didn't add how unhappy that piece of news—delivered the previous week by Dinah Ryan—had made her. Apparently Corey's father hadn't lived in Spartanburg for more than five years, and Verna Haskins hadn't even been aware that he had moved. They had traced him to two more towns, but the trail had since grown cold. If Corey's father was ever located and he wanted his daughter, Corey would live the life of a vagabond.

"Well, it's kind of you to take her...."

"She's a wonderful little girl." Sam heard the water stop. "She'll be down in a minute."

"Isn't this rather an odd way to start a family?" Kathryn asked.

"I told you. It's temporary."

"You always wanted to take in strays."

Sam faced her mother. "Corey is not a stray. She's a child. And if you'll give her a chance, you'll see just how wonderful she is. But if you look at her like some mangy hound dog who followed me home from school one day, then you'll be missing something pretty special."

"About that mangy hound dog..."

Sam realized that what she had meant as merely a figure of speech had really been more. Now she remembered that there had been such a dog. Once, when she wasn't much older than Corey. The dog had been whisked away at the Whitehurst front door on Kathryn's command, and Sam's heart had been broken.

"I'd forgotten," Sam said, turning away. "There was a stray once, wasn't there? And you disapproved."

"No, actually, I took him to the vet, or rather, I had someone on staff do it. Melwin, I think."

"Melwin never told me."

"We didn't want you to know. The dog was sick, too sick to help, as it turned out. He died after a week of treatment. We thought it would be better for you to think that we had just chased him away."

"What?" Sam sneaked a peek at her mother. "Mother, you have a soft heart."

"Absolutely not." But Kathryn looked pleased with herself.

They talked about the Whitehursts' trip to Europe and friends that Sam knew until their fund of small talk ran out. Corey chose that moment to arrive. She had put on her suit backward, and her hair stood in wet spikes all over her head. Sam could see that she had tried to wash herself, but with one arm that had to be held out of the water, she hadn't succeeded very well.

"Come here, honey," she said. Sam took a clean dish-cloth from a drawer. "You missed a spot or two."

"I want to go to the lake!"

"I'll bet. And you can go just as soon as you put your bathing suit on right and let me wash your face and neck."

"I don't want to!"

"I don't blame you. It's hot, and you want to get in the water. But you have to let me wash your face."

Corey's eyes were slits in her face, and her bottom lip hung nearly to her chin. Sam turned away to wet the wash-cloth. And when she turned back, Corey was gone.

Sam saw the look of consternation on her mother's face. She chalked one up for Corey.

"Guess who that was?" Sam said with a nonchalance she didn't feel. She had wanted Kathryn to approve of Corey. It had been important to her, although she wasn't sure why.

"Samantha, what have you gotten yourself into?"

Corey came streaking back through the kitchen. Joe walked through the door a few moments later. "Upstairs," he told her in his best high-school-principal voice. "Turn the bathing suit around, wash your face and comb your hair."

Sam stared at him.

"I gather she was escaping," he said.

"How did you know?"

"She knocked down a Giovanelli and a Carter on her flight out of the house. Not to mention that she kept looking over her shoulder."

Sam had never been more grateful to him. "Thanks. I was going to come after her."

"Looks like you're busy. I'll just station myself at the

bottom of the stairs and do a little inspection when she comes back down. Did I miss anything?''

"That'll do."

"So you've met Corey?'' Joe asked Kathryn.

"Not exactly." Kathryn shook her head. "Samantha was just trying to explain why you've taken her in. Something about a wonderful little girl."

"She's not a bad little monster," Joe said. "Give her a chance. You might grow to like her."

Joe went to stand at the bottom of the stairs as Sam stared at his retreating back.

The afternoon was cloudless, the sky as blue as Samantha's eyes. But even if the weather had cooperated fully for a perfect Labor Day party, one small girl had not.

Joe watched Corey skipping stones over the surface of the lake. She missed one of his nephews, Magdalena's son, by inches.

Sam missed the entire breathtaking event, but Joe saw that Kathryn and Fischer had not. They exchanged looks that said what they thought of this child from the nether regions. He imagined that Sam, on the very worst day of her childhood, had never behaved half so outrageously.

Joe strolled to the edge of the pond and squatted beside Corey. She tried to move away, so he put his arm around her. Firmly. "You're about to go inside for the rest of the day."

"Let go!"

"Be smart and don't struggle. I'm bigger than you."

"Can't make me do nothin'," she said bravely. But she stopped trying to get away from him.

"Now, here's the deal. I know it's hot, and you want to swim. And I know you feel strange because everybody knows everybody else and you're new—"

"Don't care."

"And I know Miss Sam's too busy to hang all over you today."

"You're mean!"

"You're not the first kid who's thought so. But if you can behave a little better, even just a little, like stop throwing stones at people and stop spitting in the water, things like that, then I'll take you swimming. All the way in."

She was as stiff as her cast, but Joe could feel her yearning to believe him. He knew kids, and despite all his efforts, he was beginning to know this one in particular.

"Miss Sam says I can't go in the water," she said.

He felt a moment of real admiration. Despite her desperate longing to get in the water with the other children, her loyalty to Sam was more important.

"I'll clear it with Miss Sam. We'll wrap your cast in plastic bags, and I'll carry you out, so you can hold it out of the water."

"You won't drown me, or nothing?"

"With all these people watching?"

That seemed to impress her. He released her and stood. "But remember what I said. I've got to see some better behavior from you, or the deal's off."

"How long?"

"How long what?"

"How long I gotta be good?"

"As long as it takes to show everybody you're not really a devil child."

Clearly she thought that was a long, long time. On that one thing at least, they agreed.

He went back to his table, where Rose was rhapsodizing about something that Corey had said to her. Rose was used to bratty little kids. She'd given birth to a full measure herself. Joe supposed that Johnny had told her that Joe wouldn't be making her a grandmother again. She'd never said a word to him about it, but she seemed to have fully accepted Corey as a surrogate, despite the fact that Corey's days in their home were numbered.

"Then she says, she says, 'Well, how come, if you're Mr. Joe's mama, you don't make him come and live with you?'"

Joe grinned, despite himself. He caught Sam's eye, and she was smiling, too. "She'd like nothing better," he said. "Then she'd have Miss Sam here all to herself."

"Don't you think the child needs more...help than the two of you can give her?" Kathryn asked. "I mean, she's..." Her voice trailed off, as if there was no word strong enough that a woman of breeding could use.

"She's what, Mother?" Sam asked, a decided edge to her voice. "Lively? Spirited? Normal, considering what she's just been through? I think Joe and I can handle that."

Joe was always captivated when Sam stood up to her parents. Through the years of their marriage Sam had always chosen her battles well, ignoring the small skirmishes to save strength for those that were needed to win the war. Until now the war had been her self-esteem and independence. It seemed a new war had just been declared.

"Don't dance around it, Samantha," Fischer said, always the businessman cutting straight to the point. "The child's got problems. I don't understand why you're putting yourself through such a difficult time when she's going to be leaving, anyway. You've got enough to handle, don't you? And surely you're planning to have children of your own to lavish some of this attention on."

"No, sir," Joe said. "We won't be having children of our own." He waited until Fischer looked at him. "We can't and won't be able to conceive."

There was shocked silence. Kathryn was the first to breach it. "But surely there are doctors who can help." She turned to her daughter. "They're doing so much now. Test tube babies, for one thing. A friend of mine is married to one of the best fertility specialists in Maryland. I can get you an appointment——''

"I'm the one with the problem," Joe said. "Not Sam. And there's nothing to be done."

"The problem is both of ours," Sam said. "No matter who got the wrong end of the diagnosis. Joe and I can't have children, and that's that."

"So now you're taking in other people's problems? I don't understand the point," Fischer said. "What do you have to gain? That child is obviously not from a good family, and from the looks of her there's not much you'll be able to accomplish. She's rude and hostile and probably not very bright. She's not even pretty."

Joe saw the horror on Sam's face. He saw Kathryn's eyes widen in dismay. He didn't even chance a glance at his mother, who was probably gasping for breath.

He didn't know he was standing until he felt the ground firmly under his feet. "That *child*," he said slowly and distinctly, "is a member of my family. She may not be a permanent member, but as long as she's living here, she's mine. I hope you'll reconsider your opinion, Fischer, but if you don't, Sam and I don't want to listen to it again."

Now Fischer looked as shocked as everyone else at the table. Sam stood, too. "I think it's time to bring out the desserts. Joe, will you help?"

She marched off. He joined her on the path back to the house, waiting as Francis's children passed before he spoke. "I'm sorry," he said.

"For what? For putting old Fischer in his place? It was masterful. I wish I could have done it as well."

He stopped her with a hand on her shoulder. Her eyes were glowing, but not with anger. "Just be sure you understand," he said.

"Understand what?"

"That I was reacting to your father's attitudes, Sam.

What would life have been like for you if you hadn't met his standards? What if you hadn't been intelligent enough? Or, God forbid, pretty?''

"I guess I'll never know."

He saw that she did know, that all her life she'd fought for approval from both her parents when they hadn't had it in their hearts to give. He pulled her close for a rib-crushing hug.

"You stood up for Corey," she said against his chest.

"I'm a sucker for lost causes. That's all."

"What's life going to be like for Corey if nobody ever approves of her?"

"Corey's going to make it. She's a survivor, a tough little bird."

"You're standing up for her again."

"Not a chance."

She kissed him. He felt warmth flowing through him that had nothing to do with North Carolina sunshine. Then he felt something—or someone—tugging at his shirt.

"I been good a long time," Corey said.

He moved away from Sam to gaze down at the intruder. She was dirty again, and her cheeks were flushed from the heat. Her eyes were narrowed into slits. Most of the time he couldn't see enough of her eyes to tell what color they were.

"Not long enough," he said.

He watched her droop, a black-eyed Susan wilting in the sun.

"But I'll take you swimming anyway," he added.

She didn't smile or say thank-you, but he knew her well enough now to see that she was grateful. After all, she didn't kick him or spit on his shoe.

It had felt funny to have Mr. Joe hold her in the water. His hands didn't feel like Miss Sam's, all soft and smooth.

They were giant, wide hands that could crush her if he wanted. But he didn't. He held her just tight enough so she wouldn't sink.

At first she was scared. She didn't know how to swim, and if Mr. Joe dropped her where it was deep, she figured she'd drown real quick. But after a while she knew he wasn't going to drop her. Miss Sam liked her and all. It would be pretty hard to explain to Miss Sam that Corey was lying on the bottom of the lake somewheres.

It was a lake, too, not a pond like Miss Sam always said. Mr. Joe told her how it used to be nothing but a spring at the bottom of a hill, and how his brother Francis had come in with bulldozers and giant machines to make a lake. She couldn't imagine such a thing. She wished she had lived here then, just to see it.

She had been sorry when it was time to get out. Mr. Joe brought her up to the grass and wrapped her in a towel. Then she felt just like all the other kids. They were wet, too, shivering while the sun dried them off. Mary Nell had asked her if she wanted to play hide-and-go-seek, and she'd said sure. Mr. Joe had told her not to get too dirty again, or he'd have to throw her in the lake and leave her this time.

But he'd smiled when he said it. Then he'd gone off to help Miss Sam. She wondered if they were kissing again. If Mr. Joe and Miss Sam did a lot of kissing, it meant that Miss Sam wasn't going to need her to stay around and all, 'cause Mr. Joe wasn't going to leave.

By the time the sun went down, most of the other kids were gone. Only Erin, Patrick and Shannon were still around. Miss Sam's parents and Grandma Rose were gone, too. She'd wanted to like Miss Sam's parents, but she hadn't. Miss Sam's father didn't know how to smile, and her mother kind of looked like she smelled something bad all the time. Grandma Rose was different, though. She laughed a lot, and sitting on her lap just seemed like the right thing to do.

"Hey, Corey, want to go down to the fort?"

Next to Mary Nell, Corey liked Patrick the best of all the kids who had been at the party. He was seven, too, and he had red hair that stuck out all over his head, just like hers did sometimes. He was bigger than her, but he didn't act like it mattered.

She wanted to go. The grown-ups were just sitting inside the house now, talking and drinking coffee. The kids weren't supposed to leave the yard. With the lake and all, Miss Sam got worried if they went off where nobody could see them.

But Patrick didn't want to go in the lake. He wanted to play in the fort—she let him call it that, instead of play-house. Forts were fun, too.

She looked around. Erin and Shannon were up on the porch, playing with Tinkerbelle. They weren't old enough to go anywhere in the dark. But she and Patrick could find their way along the path. Maybe they could just go for a little while.

Somebody came to the window and looked out. It was Miss Teddy. Corey stood where she could be seen, then as soon as Miss Teddy left she motioned to Patrick. In a minute they were running toward the fort.

She stopped just before the entrance. "What do you want to do?"

"Let's go inside and see if there's any ghosts."

"Ghosts?" She didn't like that idea.

"Yeah, Indian ghosts. Used to be Indians around here. My daddy said so."

Corey let Patrick go inside first. The fort was real dark now without sunshine coming through the windows. It didn't look friendly. "Don't like it here," she said.

"Ghost gonna get you."

"Ain't no ghosts in here."

"Just can't see 'em."

She didn't want to believe him, but there was a sound outside now, like somebody moaning. Sometimes when her mama had left her alone at night she'd been afraid of ghosts, so she'd turned on all the lights. But there weren't any lights in the fort.

"I'm going back."

"Scaredy-cat," Patrick said.

He was right, and that made her doubly furious. "Am not!"

"Want to see if there's really ghosts?"

She stopped in the doorway. "How?"

"Light a fire."

"How're we gonna do that?"

"I'll show you." Patrick led the way outside to the stone ring that Mr. Joe and Mr. Johnny had built close to the water. There were coals glowing inside it, left from the wood Mr. Joe had used to cook with. And the metal grates were stored away now, so the coals were easy to reach. "We can take some of those inside the fort and build a fire. Then we can see everything."

Corey was doubtful. She didn't even know how they were going to get the coals. But before she could tell him, Patrick went down to the water's edge and came back with a metal pail that some of the kids had used to make castles with. Icky mud castles.

"We can put 'em in here." Patrick scooped the coals into the bucket with a stick. "Get some wood."

Corey was excited now. It would be their own camp fire. Like they lived in the fort all the time, or something. Beside the stone ring she found branches and a small log that hadn't been burned. Then she followed Patrick inside the fort. The wood was dry and the coals were still hot. There was wind blowing through the door and windows of the fort. Pretty soon the camp fire was burning.

"See," she said. "No ghosts. Told you."

Patrick looked disappointed. The light from the fire was so bright she could tell he wasn't happy. "I'm going to get more wood. There's ghosts here. I know it."

The night air was cool and the fire was warm. She was glad to be sitting beside it. When Patrick returned he threw a stick nearly as big as he was on the fire. The flames leaped higher.

"Still ain't no ghosts," Corey said. She watched the flames climb nearly to the roof. Patrick knew how to make a real good fire.

"I guess there's not," Patrick said.

"Miss Sam's gonna be wondering where we are."

"Yeah." Patrick stood, and Corey stood with him. "Gotta put this out first before we go back." The floor was covered with pine needles. He kicked pile after pile into the fire. The fire burned brighter and higher. He frowned. In the firelight Corey could see he was worried.

"We could throw some water on it," Corey said, remembering the pail.

They ran out the door together to go down to the lake. At the water's edge Corey swung the pail down deep, then turned. Smoke was pouring out of the fort now, through the windows and door. As she stared, the roof burst into flames. From the direction of the house she heard Miss Sam calling her name.

"At least neither of them were hurt," Sam said. "And it didn't spread to the woods. We were lucky they didn't start a forest fire."

"Why'd they do it?" Joe looked over the smoldering heap of ashes that had been the fort he'd built for the children he would never have.

"Corey says they were looking for ghosts."

There had been ghosts in the fort, but none Corey could see. Joe jammed his hands into his pockets.

"Patrick insists it was his idea," Sam said. "He was very gallant."

"Well, he's going to be very sore tomorrow. Johnny's raising his kids like we were raised. Swat, forgive, forget."

"Joe, I'm sorry. You worked so hard, and the fort was wonderful. All the kids are going to miss it when they come over."

"She has to be punished."

Sam moved away. He could feel the space. "Why? She knows she did something wrong. And she was scared to death when the fire started. Isn't that enough?"

"She knew she was supposed to stay close to the house. She knew she wasn't supposed to go down to the water without an adult. That's been the rule since the first day she came to live with us."

"I think she's been punished enough. Please. Let's just let it go."

"Earlier you said you needed my level head where Corey's concerned. Well, here it is. If she thinks she can get away with anything she does, she'll just keep doing more and more." Joe folded his arms. "You feel so sorry for her, Sam, you're not thinking clearly."

"And you dislike having her here so much, you aren't, either."

He was hurt. Then he was angry. "You're letting her come between us."

"No. Corey isn't coming between us. You are."

"You want her to stay with us, but you don't want me to have any say in what she does or what we do about it? Are those the rules?"

"I know her better than you do."

"She destroyed something that meant a lot to me. I have

the right to be sure she understands that our rules have to be obeyed so she doesn't destroy anything else.''

"You'll scare her to death."

He faced her. "You don't even trust me to be fair?"

She didn't answer.

"What's happening to us?"

Again, she didn't or couldn't answer.

He left her standing beside the ashes of his dreams. Inside, the house was silent. He took the steps upstairs to Corey's room two at a time. He paused at her door, but decided not to knock. He pushed it open. Her head turned toward the door. In the glow of two night-lights he could see that her eyes were wide open.

"You and I are going to talk," he said.

"Are you gonna hit me?"

"No. I don't hit little girls."

Her eyes glistened suspiciously. He told himself not to be swayed. "You really blew it tonight, Corey. You went down by the water without permission. You started a fire in the fort. You burned it down. Do you realize how serious all of that is?"

"Mama said I was just born bad."

He moved a little closer. "Well, she was wrong. No one's born bad. Sometimes people just do bad things."

"Well, I do 'em a lot." She moved to the other side of the bed as he got closer, as if she didn't believe that he wasn't going to hit her.

He stopped when he realized what she was doing. "I said I wasn't going to hit you, and I mean it."

"You look mean at me all the time, like you wanna hit me."

"I don't want to hit you." He thought that one over and decided that wasn't quite the truth, but close enough. "But you do make me angry. I built that fort, and now it's gone. And you could have been hurt, or worse, just because you disobeyed us. We're responsible for you. You have to do what we say.''

"Miss Sam's not mad. She says I didn't mean it.''

"You meant to go down to the water, didn't you? And you meant to start a fire.''

She didn't answer.

"Besides, it's what we do, not what we mean, that's important.'' He felt impotent. It would be so much better to give Corey consequences, to let her work off her guilt. But Sam had decreed otherwise. Now all he could do was talk, and talk without action was nearly useless.

"I'd like you to help me tomorrow after school. I'm going to have to start cleaning up that mess down there.''

"I don't wanna help you. I wanna stay up at the house with Miss Sam.''

Joe turned and saw Sam standing in the doorway. He waited for her to support him, but she said nothing. He turned back to Corey. "Go to sleep now.''

Sam started toward her. Joe put his hand on her arm. "Haven't you already said good-night?''

Sam's eyes were wide and angry, but she didn't protest. She turned and preceded him out the door.

11

There were only two words written on the card. *I'm sorry.*

Joe put the tiny card back in its tiny envelope and examined the Boston fern that had come with it. The card hadn't been signed; it hadn't needed to be. The graceful, feminine penmanship had been acquired at a prestigious New Hampshire residential academy, along with the social savvy to send a gift along with an apology.

"I really am," said a familiar voice from the doorway.

He looked up. "This wasn't necessary."

"Maybe not, but it was fun. Besides, it's always bothered me that you have this terrific eastern exposure and nothing to take advantage of it. I came prepared to hang." Sam held up a hook and a drill. "Have hardware, will travel."

"How did you know I'd still be here?"

"I know what the first day of school is like. In fact, this is a little earlier than I intended to get here. Are all your meetings finished?"

"They'd better be, because I'm not staying another minute."

"Not even to drill a hole for the plant?"

"Not a minute past that."

She smiled, and he smiled, too. She looked good enough to eat in a candy-cane-striped dress that she'd bought especially for this day. Her hair was loose, held back from her face with a narrow pink ribbon, and her shoes had low heels, to bring her closer to the twenty-five first graders who would be a large part of her world for the next nine months.

"How'd it go?" she asked.

"Chaos, pure and simple. I had people in here all day complaining, an even mix of teachers and kids. I thought about stowing them all in a locked room together and keeping them there until June."

"Well, that would solve some of your problems."

"But it might give me others when the school board found out about it."

"True." Sam moved a little closer. "You look tired."

"So do you. How'd it go?"

"Good. Three kids cried for a solid hour, another three cried on and off all day. One mother called twice and came by once, just to see how her little darling was doing."

"Problems separating."

"Just her. Her son looked relieved when she left him this morning. He whistled all day."

"Is it going to be a good year?"

"Different from last, I think."

"How so?"

She smiled sheepishly. "An easy class. No Corey."

"Except at home."

"At least there I can tackle her one to one." She moved a little closer.

Joe liked the way she edged toward him, the way she put the hook and drill on his desk to free her hands. Anticipation built. "Speaking of whom, where is she?"

"At home with a baby-sitter."

"What?"

"I got one of the Insley girls to come down and sit with her. I thought we could have a quiet dinner alone."

He realized that Sam had made this sacrifice for him. He had no doubts that she had been looking forward to sharing stories of Corey's first day back at school—and probably had shared a fair number already. But instead of a family dinner, she had left Corey at home and sought him out. She was telling him that he was more important than her own needs, that patching up their fight was more important.

She put her hand on his arm, slid it slowly to his shoulder. "Unless you don't want to go out with me."

"I want to go out with you." He moved a little closer until she was in his arms. She smelled like honeysuckle, like the last roses of summer. She felt like paradise with all its lavish sensory delights and tempting, forbidden fruit.

"Actually, I want to take you home, straight up to our bed, and make love to you," he said. He heard her breath catch. He smiled against her hair. "You, too, huh?"

"Joe, it's so good to hear you say that."

He gathered her closer. "I've forgotten to say it for a long, long time now."

"Maybe we could rent a motel room."

"Foxcove's notoriously short on the kind that rent by the hour."

"Maybe we could improvise. Aren't there beds in the clinic?"

"I think we'll just spend the evening in anticipation." He lifted her face to his, taking his time to woo her gently with a long, slow kiss. Her lips were soft and vulnerable. He felt her doubts, her fears, and he cursed himself for his failings.

When he finally pulled away her eyes were sparkling suspiciously. "It's a new school year, Joe. A new start."

He stroked her hair. "Yeah. I think we should celebrate."

"Where?"

"Somewhere that has fried chicken on the menu."

She cocked her head in question.

"If I had to make a guess, I'd say chicken's Corey's favorite food, wouldn't you?" he asked.

"Corey?"

"It's her first day of school, too. We're going home to get her. Then we'll drive somewhere out of town, where nobody we know will have to watch her eat—"

Sam laughed, low and throaty and suspiciously tear choked.

"And we'll feed her so much she falls asleep in the car on the way home so we can say seductive—"

"Provocative—"

"Passionate—"

"Erotic—"

"Lustful things." He dropped his hands. They weren't quite steady.

"Things like what we plan to do to each other tonight?"

"A good start."

"You're the best, Joe. You always will be."

"I won't ask you what I'm best at." He put his arm around her and started toward the door.

"We forgot to hang the plant."

"Come back tomorrow and we'll do this scene all over again."

She tucked her arm around his waist. "It turned out well enough to repeat, didn't it?"

Corey bounced on Killer's narrow back seat as they drove down the highway.

"Tighten your seat belt," Joe said, glancing over his shoulder. "If it's loose enough so you can bounce, it's loose enough to be dangerous."

Sam noted that Corey sat back and stopped bouncing,

but that she did nothing about her belt. Sam reached around and pulled the strap tighter herself. "There. Now, that's how it's done."

"Can't breathe!"

"You're talking, aren't you?" Joe asked. "You must be breathing."

"You'd like it if I didn't!"

"Didn't what? Breathe or talk?"

"Miss Sam!"

"*I'd* like it if you'd stop yelling," Sam said. "And Mr. Joe's right. It's not too tight. You're fine, and now you're safe."

"My mama didn't make me wear no belt!"

Silence greeted that pronouncement. Sam looked at Joe and he shrugged. Neither of them had the heart to point out the obvious.

"My mama didn't make me do nothing," Corey said.

"Saint Verna," Joe said under his breath.

"Why don't you tell Mr. Joe about your new teacher?" Sam said, hoping to turn the tide of Corey's hostility.

"Yeah, is she an old witch like that teacher you had last year?" Joe teased. "With a wart on her nose and no teeth? Does she ride a broom to school?"

There was silence from the back seat.

"Guess not," Joe said.

"She's not pretty like Miss Sam!"

"Nobody's as pretty as Miss Sam," Joe agreed.

"And she yelled at me."

"Did she, now?" Joe could understand that. He'd done it himself a time or two.

"And she said I couldn't read good enough to be in the apple group. I'm a banana!"

"Well, I've always been a banana fan, myself."

"But I can read better'n she thinks. Just didn't want to."

"How come?" Joe asked.

"'Cause the book's dumb. I read it already."

Despite himself, Joe was becoming interested. Sam could see it happening before her eyes. "Did you? When?" he asked.

"This morning. When everybody was adding and subtracting."

"Well, why weren't you adding and subtracting?"

"Already done it. Went on to the next page and got in trouble, too. She yelled at me again."

"Corey, I've never heard Miss Simpson yell at anyone. You're exaggerating," Sam said.

"She don't like me."

"Is that possible?" Joe asked Sam. He looked at her for an answer. She gave the tiniest shrug. It was answer enough. He frowned.

"Did you go outside for recess today?" Sam asked, changing the subject to something that hopefully would be more positive. "I didn't see your class."

"We was there."

"Did you have fun?" Sam remembered last year, when Corey had often been forced to play alone because the other children hadn't wanted anything to do with her.

"A little. Mary Nell came over and played with me."

Sam said a prayer of gratitude to Mary Nell. She was well liked by everyone, children and teachers alike. Her friendship would do more to help Corey become accepted than anything an adult could do.

"And then Jennifer Hansen came over and said she liked my new dress."

Sam added Jennifer to her prayers.

They stopped just off the highway at a restaurant with cheery yellow walls and polished pine floors. The menu was varied, with barbecue the specialty. The smell of smoking pork and tangy sauce permeated the room.

Corey's eyes widened. Sam wondered if she had ever

been in a real restaurant before. They had eaten fast food together, but this might be an entirely new experience.

Joe seemed to sense Corey's awe. "We'd like a table near a window," he told the hostess, a girl who probably hadn't yet graduated from high school. "I think this might be a first for one of us, and she'll want to see everything."

"Aren't you a cutie?" the hostess said, bending over to gaze at Corey. "You've got your daddy's brown eyes and your mommy's blond hair. What a combination. Some people are just plain lucky."

Sam didn't know what to say. Corey stared at the young woman, clearly puzzled. Joe cleared his throat. "No Smoking section, please, if you have one."

"Sure thing."

At the table Sam and Joe sipped iced tea from Mason jars while Corey worked on a lemonade. Sam didn't look at Joe. The hostess's comment still rang in her ears. She could imagine what he was thinking.

"How'd she know what color my daddy's eyes are?" Corey asked, long after Sam thought the subject had died. "And my mama didn't have no blond hair."

"She meant us, Corey," Sam said. "Joe and me."

"I thought maybe she knew my daddy." Corey didn't seem unhappy that she had misunderstood. "I never seen him. My mama never told me nothing about him. I don't know what he looks like."

"Do you see anything on the menu that you'd like?" Sam asked. "They've got fried chicken, ribs, hamburgers."

"She thought you were my mama and Mr. Joe was my daddy." Corey looked sideways at Joe. "You do got eyes like mine."

He narrowed his eyes. "Mean eyes?"

She giggled. "Go on!"

"I'm not going anywhere. I'm staying to eat. I'm getting spareribs and corn on the cob and potato salad."

Corey didn't look at her child-sized menu. "Me, too."

"Me, too," Sam said, closing hers. "And lemon pudding cake for dessert."

"Me, too," Corey said.

"Me, too," Joe said.

They were all smiling. Sam watched the way Corey's eyes widened and crinkled at the corners when she was happy. Like...Joe's. She looked down at the checkered tablecloth, too full of emotion to risk smiling for even a second longer at the two people she loved best.

"She's dead to the world," Sam said, tiptoeing down the stairs to the living room. She closed the double wooden doors behind her, just in case, so that they would be guaranteed privacy. "She's exhausted and full of more food than she's probably used to eating in a week."

"I hope she's not too full. I had doubts about that second helping of lemon pudding cake."

"She seems okay, but I'll get up with her if there's trouble. I'm the one who said yes."

"A word that comes easily to your lips."

She smiled seductively. "Well, shall I work on no, Mr. Joe? Is this the time?"

"Not a chance." He'd made a fire in the old brick fireplace, even though the night had only the faintest chill. As he opened his arms to Sam he had a fleeting vision of last night's fire. But suddenly last night seemed years away.

She joined him on the rug and settled herself against him. "This is heavenly. But both of us should be working. I've got lesson plans to finish. And if I know you..."

"I probably won't have to do a thing this year. I've worked so hard for the past six months or more that I'm caught up through the next century."

Since the day he had learned he would never be a father. Sam understood, and she was touched that he had admitted it. "In that case, maybe I'll just use last year's lesson plans and forget about working."

"Oh, I have some work in mind for you."

"Something I have some talent for, I hope."

"Something you were born for."

She softened against him, as if desire were melting her bones. "I was born for you, Joe."

He nuzzled her neck, inhaling the sweet fragrance of her hair. "Sometimes I think you were. Sometimes I think that destiny brought us together. That you knew I'd be waiting for you at La Scala that night. If you think about all the things that might have been different…"

She didn't want to think about any of them. "I wouldn't trade a moment of our life together."

"I can think of a moment or two I'd like to trade."

"Why? Because some of them have been hard? But there might be harder ones in store. What matters is that we come through them together."

"Are we coming through them? Together?"

She knew he wasn't really ready to talk about their infertility. But he was asking for reassurance. Something he had never done before. She loved him more because of it.

"We have to come through them together. You're the center of my days and nights, Joe. I could go on without you and I would if I had to, but I'd be hollow inside. The part of me you fill would be empty."

"There would be a dozen men in line if I walked out of your life."

She turned in his arms and put her fingertips against his cheeks. "None of them would be you."

"But all of them could give you children."

She gazed into his eyes and saw the flicker of despair. She shook her head slowly. "None of them would be you."

"There must have been times in the past months when you wished I was anybody else."

"There've been times in the past months when I wished *I* was anybody else, anybody who knew what to say or do to make everything all right."

"None of this has been your fault."

"But I should have been able to help."

"You helped more than you know." He didn't elaborate. He stroked her back, and let his hands apologize and comfort.

She caressed his bottom lip with her thumb. She loved Joe's face, the high, wide cheekbones, the square chin, the winged black brows and brooding eyes that made him look dangerously sexy, even when he was laughing. She had fallen in love with the face, then with the body, the long legs and lean torso, the wide shoulders and muscular arms. Last, but so rapidly she wouldn't have thought it possible, she had fallen in love with the man.

"I'd like to help some more," she murmured. She leaned forward to kiss him, brushing her lips where her thumb had been. "Suddenly I can think of a way."

His eyes glowed. "But who would be helping whom?"

"I'm fairly secure it's mutual."

"Are you?" His arms tightened. "What makes you think so?"

Her hands drifted down his shirt, slowly, with tantalizing pressure. They settled temporarily at his waist, then he felt his belt sliding open. "Going straight for the evidence," he said. "Is that fair?"

"All's fair in love."

"What happened to the rest of the saying?"

"There is no war here," she whispered. "Only love, Joe. Only love."

Corey came awake suddenly. At first she didn't know where she was, then she remembered that she was living at Miss Sam's now. She squinted at the ceiling and watched the shadows play across it. She had made her peace with the shadows. Most of the time now they seemed more like friends who came every night to dance for her when Miss Sam thought she was sleeping.

She heard a noise in the hall outside her room. It was Miss Sam laughing softly. Corey recognized the sound. When Miss Sam laughed it sounded like music. Mr. Joe didn't laugh much, but when he did it was different, like drums in a parade. Now she heard the rumble of his laughter, and she knew that he was passing her room, too.

She squinted into the darkness, directly at the crack where her door opened into the hallway, and saw them as they passed. She thought Mr. Joe had his arm around Miss Sam. They sounded happy.

She didn't feel happy.

She didn't feel good.

She got up and went to the window. She couldn't see another house from her window. Just trees and sometimes, when the moon was just right, water sparkling in the lake. It was a lonely view, and it made her feel even lonelier now.

She wondered if her daddy ever felt lonely. She didn't guess he did. Her mama had told her he didn't have any feelings. Mama had said he left her before Corey was even born, and when the judge said he had to pay money for Corey anyway, he still didn't. Mama used to tell her that a lot. It was just about all she ever said about him. Except for the day that they'd driven to South Carolina to find him. Then Mama had said he was a snake, and Corey could just go live with him, since Corey wasn't worth much, either.

Her stomach hurt. It had hurt sometimes at Mama's, but not like this. Then she'd known that if she could find something to eat, she would feel better. Now she didn't think eating would help much. She didn't like to think about eating at all.

She found her bear sitting at the table Miss Sam had put in the corner. Miss Sam had bought her a doll, too, a doll with blond hair like hers and a silly smile. Corey didn't know what that doll had to smile about. She liked the bear best, but she liked the books almost as much. She chose one now and took it to the window where she could see the pages in the moonlight.

It was a story about a little deer who'd lost his mama. She wished she'd picked a different book to read. This one made her sad. She turned the pages to the part where the little deer, Bambi, was born. His mama looked real happy, even though she had to have a baby in the woods and all. She turned more pages to the part where his mama taught Bambi how to do things. Then there was the sad part where the hunter shot the mama.

Corey was sad that Mama had died, too, but not the way Miss Sam seemed to think. She was sad because she couldn't be sad enough. That was hard to explain. It was funny. She thought maybe Mr. Joe, as mean as he was, might just understand. But if Corey told Miss Sam, she'd just feel bad. Corey didn't want Miss Sam to feel bad. Not ever.

Her stomach hurt worse. She put the book away and took the bear back to bed. Even when she held him close, resting him on her stomach, she felt worse and worse. Everything was all mixed up inside her. Miss Sam laughing in the hall, and Mr. Joe laughing, too. Bambi's mama being so happy, then dying. Mama being so angry at Corey and her daddy, then dying. Miss Sam maybe not needing her 'cause Mr. Joe made her laugh now.

She shut her eyes, and the shadows danced anyway.

Joe heard the bathroom door creaking before he heard the moans. He came awake immediately. In a split second he knew exactly what was happening. He turned to Sam, but she slept on, a replete, satisfied woman.

He didn't have the heart to wake her. He sat up and felt for his pants, pulling them on and snapping them as he started for the bedroom door.

In the hallway he turned to the bathroom. An extraordinarily pale little girl knelt on the tile floor with her head over the toilet. He smoothed her hair back from her face and murmured comforting words as she lost the rest of her dinner. He was sorry for a number of reasons, one being that she needed more weight on her thin little frame, and the dinner would easily have added a pound.

"I don't feel so good," she said, between heaves.

"Shh…" He smoothed her hair some more.

"I can't help it!"

"Of course you can't." He patted her back. He remembered holding Magdalena's head once as a teenager, when she'd had too much to drink at a party, and he had tried to keep the noise from waking Mama. Magda had owed him one after that, and she had quietly ironed his shirts for the rest of the month.

"Don't tell Miss Sam!" Corey could hardly raise her head.

Joe suspected she was finished. He stood and searched for a clean washcloth, then held it under the faucet. "Why not?"

"She'll get all worried and stuff."

The child was a smart little bugger, obviously aware of all the dynamics around her. For the first time he wondered how much of his own hostility she was picking up. He felt ashamed. "It's all right if she worries a little," he said. "She worries because she likes you so much."

"I don't want to make her sad."

He thought there was probably more to that sentence. *Because I know what it feels like.* He approached the toilet and flushed it, noting how careful she'd been to hit her target exactly. "Do you think you're all done?"

She nodded.

"Then let's see if you can stand up now."

He helped her to her feet, then he sat on the edge of the bathtub and pulled her to stand between his legs so he could wash her face. He felt her trembling against him. Before he knew what he was doing, he lifted her to sit sideways on his lap. "Here, this is better."

She scowled at him, but he ignored her. She was still shaking hard. He brushed the cloth across her forehead, then over her cheeks. She was as white as the thin cotton nightgown Sam had bought her. "Does that feel good?"

She nodded. Reluctantly, he was sure.

"You know, this happens to everybody at one time or another. We shouldn't have let you have second helpings of dessert. You just had too much to eat."

"Can't eat too much."

"'Fraid you can. Especially if it's as good as dinner was tonight. I've done it myself."

"You?"

"Yeah. Someday you'll have to taste my mother's lasagna." He heard what he'd said, and his hand paused. He had no right or reason to talk about the future with this child.

"I like Grandma Rose. How come you got a nice mama and Miss Sam don't?"

"I was born lucky. It's too bad we don't always get to pick who our parents are going to be."

"I'da picked Miss Sam."

"I know." He set her on the floor. "Feel any better?"

"Sure." She lifted her chin. She was still as pale as her gown.

"Let's get you some water to rinse your mouth out

with." He filled a cup with cold water and handed it to her. She did as he'd suggested.

"Come on, I'll tuck you back in," he said.

"You?" She made it absolutely clear that this was an inconceivable way to end the night.

"See anybody else who could do it?"

She stared at him, all big brown eyes and shaggy blond hair. For a moment he glimpsed the woman she would become if she was ever given the chance. Feisty, intelligent, inquisitive, pretty—possibly even more. "You know, Brown Eyes, you're a pretty neat little kid."

"Am not."

"Sure you are. Don't let anybody tell you differently." He thought about all the people who probably would, starting with the deadbeat father whom the state of North Carolina was trying so desperately to find. Anger filled him. He had an urge to hug her close for a moment, to somehow infuse her with the strength she would need to plow through the rest of her life.

Then he looked in her defiant dark eyes and saw that the strength was already there. He held out his hand. "Come on. Let's sneak back down the hall so we don't wake Miss Sam."

She looked doubtful that placing her hand in his was a good idea. He waited. The corners of her mouth turned down, but finally she stuck out her hand.

In her bedroom he pulled the sheet up to her chin before he perched on the edge of her bed. "Need anything?"

Her eyes were already drifting shut. "Bambi's mama died."

He couldn't imagine what that had to do with anything. "Yeah, I guess she did."

"But his daddy found him. In the forest."

Joe seemed to remember something like that. Bambi was a cartoon he'd avoided since childhood, Bambi and every cartoon and movie where an animal died. Life was already too sad.

"My daddy's no good," Corey said.

Joe suspected she was right. "You don't know that, Brown Eyes."

"My mama said."

"Maybe your mama was wrong about him."

"I'd like to have a dad...dy." The last word drifted into silence.

He stood and looked down at her. In the glow of her night-lights her face was wistfully angelic. "I'd like to have a little girl," he whispered.

Sam cuddled against Joe as he slid back into his own bed. He put his arms around her and closed his eyes. But sleep didn't come for a long, long time.

12

Turkeys made from brown paper shopping bags hung from the classroom ceiling grid on green and gold ribbons, and costumed Indian chiefs hand in hand with Pilgrim men in wide-brimmed black hats smiled from crayon drawings that lined the walls. Sam tidied tabletops so that she could place the children's chairs on top of them for the night. The school janitor always appreciated the help.

"Corey, help me gather up these workbooks, would you?"

Corey started on the other side of the room, piling books against her chest. The cast had been gone for weeks now, and her arm had healed perfectly.

The missing cast wasn't the only difference in the little girl. She weighed more, noticeably so. The extra weight particularly showed in her cheeks and torso. Corey would never be plump; she seemed to burn off most of what she ate. But she looked decidedly healthier, no longer pale and undernourished. Her hair had grown a bit longer and Sam tied it back from her face with ribbons or barrettes every morning. The effect was charming.

This afternoon she was dressed in a deep violet shirt with matching pants and bright pink sneakers. She wore plastic rings on every finger, and she wanted to get her ears pierced, just like Mary Nell. Sam was going to let her do it as a Christmas present.

If Corey was still living with her at Christmas.

"I'm getting tired, Miss Sam," she said. "Can I go out and swing?"

"Promise you'll stay in the school yard? No chasing after kittens or blue jays?"

"Just did that once!"

"Once was enough. I thought I'd lost you for good." The words had a hollow ring. Sam *was* going to lose her for good. It was only a matter of time.

Corey slipped into her jacket. "I promise."

Sam watched Corey skip out the classroom door, then she went back to her work. Only somehow she never quite got to it. She stared out the window until a woman cleared her throat in the doorway.

"Penny for your thoughts? Heck, you're worth more than that. I'll give a dime apiece."

Sam turned to smile at Polly. "Sorry. Nothing I'm thinking is worth even a penny."

"I just saw Corey runnin' down the hall. Mary Nell's still here, too. She went after her."

"Good. She'll be sure Corey stays around. Sometimes she forgets she's got someone taking care of her now. She's used to being able to go off and do what she wants, when she wants."

"Yep. Her life's different, all right. So's yours."

"That it is." Sam started clearing tables again.

"You going to the bonfire tonight?"

"Wouldn't miss it for the world."

"Well, we're headin' over that way, too. Thought, if you didn't mind, we'd take Corey home with us for the afternoon so she and Mary Nell can play. Then we'll feed her dinner and bring her to meet you at the high school."

"Mary Nell really enjoys being with her, doesn't she?"

"That's one smart little girl. Even keeps Mary Nell on her toes."

"I wish Carol saw it that way." Sam had already talked to Polly about the antagonism between Corey and her second grade teacher, Carol Simpson. Until Corey had become Carol's student, Sam hadn't realized how rigid Carol's standards were. But it had become increasingly clear as the months of school progressed that Carol disliked Corey as much for her high IQ as for her primitive manners and occasional grammar lapses.

"Have you tried to talk to her?"

"I don't know what to say. I don't want to make things worse for Corey, and I don't want to create a rift with Carol. I keep hoping she'll see what a great little girl Corey is and loosen up a bit. This can't be the first gifted child she's taught. She must have learned some strategies for coping."

"Yep. Shuttin' her eyes."

"Polly!" Sam couldn't help herself. She laughed.

"What's so funny?" Joe asked from the doorway.

"Polly's being outrageous." Sam went to greet him. She put her arms around his neck and gave him a light kiss on the lips. "That shirt should be illegal."

The junior clothing and fashion design class had made the shirt for Joe as a classroom project. Wide vertical stripes of red and gold traversed the width. The high school motto, Scholarship Is Its Own Reward, was embroidered on the pocket.

"Turn around, Joe," Polly ordered. "Let me see the back."

He complied. An appliquéd bulldog, sequined saliva dripping from three inch fangs, covered the whole panel. Once upon a time the Sadler High mascot had been—quite naturally—a fox, since the school was located in Foxcove.

But the first time it became clear that the new girls' varsity basketball team would have to be called the Sadler Foxes, the mascot had been changed. Jokes about being full of bulldog were easier to take.

"You can just stand next to that bonfire tonight and ignite it with that shirt," Polly said.

"He has to stand there to give a speech, anyway," Sam said.

Joe faced them again. "More like a pep talk. Rah-rah stuff. Why we're going to win the homecoming game tomorrow, even if we haven't won a game this season."

"Are we goin' to win?" Polly asked.

"Are you kidding? Half the team's in bed with the flu, the other half wishes it was. I might have to get out there and play, myself."

"Now that's a game I'd watch with real interest. Real interest. You in those tight pants and all." Polly patted Joe on the cheeks as she squeezed past him. "Don't forget, I'm takin' Corey. See you tonight."

"She's taking Corey?" Joe's eyes sparkled.

Sam laughed. "You sound like a man in the market for an uninterrupted dinner."

"I wish." He put his arms around her, even though there were people passing in the hallway. "But there's a pep-squad hot-dog roast before the bonfire. Did you forget?"

"I guess I did."

"You're invited, you know."

"Maybe I'll come. I can fend off the cheerleaders for you."

"Oh, the pleasures of having a wife."

"Don't think I don't notice they're all crazy about you. I know what goes on in the hearts and minds of teenage girls."

"Really? What does?"

"Things no teenage boy would believe."

"What about elementary school teachers? What goes on in their hearts and minds?"

"Exactly the same things."

He laughed, a deep, seductive rumble that made her wish there was no hot-dog roast. "I've got to be back at school early, but there might be time to run home and...change," he said.

The invitation was clear. She smiled her answer. Their relationship had been filled with unfamiliar twists and turns for almost a year now, but she was beginning to have faith that the road would straighten out for them again. If Joe wasn't exactly the same man she had married, he also wasn't the man who had withdrawn completely at the diagnosis of his infertility. He was quieter and more self-contained than in the early years of their marriage, but with his personal pain had come a new maturity, a new patience with the faults of others.

She still yearned for their old intimacy, for sex unhampered by shadows of their failure, for evenings spent planning their future. There was no talk of the future now, as if it were still in jeopardy. And despite what appeared to be a truce on the subject of Corey, it was still clear that Joe had no intentions of permanently welcoming her into their home if her father couldn't be found.

But he was still the man she adored, the only man she ever wanted in her life. And now, faced with the blatantly sensual flicker in his eyes, her heart beat gratefully—and faster.

"Samantha? Joe? I'm glad I caught you both."

Sam recognized the voice before she saw the man standing behind Joe. She watched Joe close his eyes, as if saying a prayer for patience.

"Ray." She stepped back to give Joe space to compose himself. Dr. Ray Flynn, the sole purveyor of psychological services for all of Sadler County, was not Joe's favorite colleague. Nor hers. "What can we do for you?"

"I'd like to see you in my office, if you don't mind."

"I've got a busy schedule this afternoon, and so does Sam. Can it wait?" Joe asked, turning to face him.

"It could, I suppose. But the problem just keeps growing and growing...."

Sam knew immediately what, or rather whom, the problem must be.

Joe nodded. "All right, then. But let's be brief."

Sam admired Joe for asking the impossible. Ray had never been brief in his life. He was a man who could take a full minute to say excuse me, half an hour to tell about his drive to school, half a day to recap the other half. And in addition to being long-winded, he was narrow-minded and shortsighted.

They followed Ray into his office. Sam had known Ray would want to talk to them here, where he felt relatively safe and in charge. In the hallway, with Joe looking down at his balding dome, Ray would feel his authority was under challenge. Here he could sit behind his desk and tap a pencil in emphasis as he spoke.

"Have a seat. Have a seat."

Sam wondered if Ray was going to repeat everything because there were two people in front of him. It promised to be a long session.

"I won't beat around the bush," Ray said after long minutes of doing just that. Sam knew he believed that small talk would put them at ease. Instead Joe looked like a man on the edge of an explosion. "I've been talking to Carol Simpson about the child."

Sam felt her temperature rising. "What child?"

Ray frowned. "Why, Corey. Corey Haskins."

"There are a lot of children in the building," Sam said pleasantly. "It does help to identify them by name."

"She is living with you? Still living with you?"

"Yes." Sam bit her lip to stop herself from repeating it.

"And you plan to continue letting her live with you?" His distaste was clear. He might as well have asked if Sam and Joe planned to continue to dump their garbage in the school hallway every morning.

"We plan to keep her with us until her father is found," Sam said.

Ray sat back and made a tepee of his fingers. Sam thought Elmer Fudd would look much the same sitting that way—except noticeably cuter. "And when do you suppose that might be? Do you know? Can you guess?"

Sam started to speak, but Joe interrupted. "Neither Sam or I predicts the future very well. The authorities are still looking. What's your beef?"

Ray's eyes widened with distaste. "I'm just trying to help, Joe. That's what the school board hired me to do."

"Well, we'd like to help, too," Sam said. "But we can't until you tell us what the problem is."

"The child is the problem."

"Corey, you mean."

"Yes, of course. Who else would I be talking about?"

Sam gave up trying to make her point. "Exactly how is Corey a problem?"

"She was your student last year. Just last year."

"Yes." Sam waited.

"Samantha, you know how disruptive she can be in a classroom. How disobedient. Yet you insisted that we not send her to a class for the disturbed. That was a very grave mistake. Very grave."

Sam remembered exactly how furious she had been last year at Ray's insistence that Corey be placed in a special class. Now she was twice as furious. Too furious to speak.

"Let me get this straight," Joe said, leaning forward.

"You've done tests, and the results show that Corey's emotionally disturbed?"

For a moment Sam thought Joe was using Ray to prove his own misgivings about Corey. Then she saw that Joe's foot was tapping. It was a sign Ray should heed.

"Yes, of course I've done tests."

"Exactly what?"

"The standard tests for a situation like this one."

"Which are?"

"Well, I'd have to pull her records. I test a lot of children. I can't be expected to remember every test I've given."

"Yet you called us in to give vague opinions? Even though you don't have any data in front of you?"

"Carol Simpson has been talking to me. Every day. To me."

"I saw the workup that was done on Corey last year," Sam said. "There was nothing, nothing at all that indicated she was really disturbed. She was an incredibly intelligent child in an unfortunate home situation. Her behavior was a reflection of both, not of any problems that couldn't be dealt with in the classroom."

"Your bias is obvious."

"Our bias." Joe touched his chest. "Ours, as in both of us. If Miss Simpson is having problems with Corey, then she'll need to give some consideration to better ways of solving them. We can give her suggestions. Like allowing Corey to read ahead, to supplement her daily busy work with some creative projects, like not raising her voice at Corey when she makes a mistake."

Ray looked stunned. "I can't believe what I'm hearing. Here you sit, two teachers—and you a principal, Joe—and you're refusing to listen to another professional? She's not even your child. She's living with you. Just living there."

"And as long as she does, we'll keep her best interests uppermost in our minds," Joe said.

"You're making a mistake. A big mistake." Ray began to tap his pencil. "Not just in defending her now, in spite of the assessment of a respected teacher, but in keeping the child at your home at all. You have a special place in this community. This isn't a big city. Maybe you don't understand. This is a small town, and we look up to our teachers and administrators here. We look up to them. Having that child stay with you is only going to hurt your image in the community. Your standing. You have your standing in the community to consider." He was getting more and more flustered. He tapped louder and harder.

Joe stared at him, narrowing his eyes like a certain blond hellion. "I want to understand, Ray, I really do. Let's both be absolutely clear about what you're saying. First, there's a young resident of Foxcove, a child born and raised here, who has no standing in this community herself?"

Ray swallowed audibly and tapped.

Joe went on. "And you're recommending that we dump this child somewhere else, somewhere out of this community, or at the very least in a program out of everybody's sight? Not because she's really disturbed, but because her family was poor, and her behavior isn't always exemplary? Am I clear about what you're saying?"

"She is disruptive. She is an angry, disruptive child."

"I have about a hundred kids at the high school who fit that description. Shall we send them all off, Ray? Shall we find homes for them outside Sadler County?"

"You're being unreasonable."

Joe stood. "Then I'll be reasonable. Here's what we're going to do. You're going to call a meeting with Sam and me and Carol Simpson. You're going to sit there and smile, and Sam and I are going to tell Carol exactly what she can do to make her job easier and more enjoyable. Luckily for her, we live with Corey, so we know what works and what doesn't. Luckily for everyone in Sadler County, see? Because now, Corey's got someone in her corner, and that should smooth over any problems that might come up.''

''But—''

Joe waved away Ray's response. ''And when we're all done, you'll enter our suggestions into Corey's permanent record. That way it'll be clear to personnel in any school she's transferred to that this is an extremely bright child who responds well to additional stimulation. Your notes will help one little girl find her place in this world, and you will have done your job. Admirably.'' Joe leaned farther forward. ''Admirably, Ray.''

''Well, that's not a bad idea, I—''

''You'll have to excuse us now. I hate to rush off, but Sam and I've got a busy afternoon ahead. Glad you cared enough to bring us in.'' Joe motioned to Sam and she leaped to her feet.

'''Bye, Ray,'' she said as Joe tugged her from the room.

''Tornado alert. Whoops, too late, it's already passed,'' she said in the hallway.

''I wonder how many kids have been pigeonholed and sent away by old Elmer Fudd in there,'' Joe said when they were halfway to their cars. ''I'm going to start pulling records tomorrow.''

''Joe...''

''No, I mean it. We're under obligation to provide the least restrictive environment for all the kids of this county. Tomorrow I'm going to find out if that's what we're doing.''

He was a knight on a white horse, Corey's personal knight. No one, Carol Simpson or any other teacher Sam knew, would willingly take on Joe. Intimidating was a bland word for the expression on his face.

"You went to bat for Corey," she said in the parking lot.

"Of course I did. I live with the kid. I know what she's about, and she's not disturbed. She's coped better with poverty and rejection and sudden changes in her life than any kid could be expected to. They try to put her in a special class, they'll have me on their doorstep."

"I think you made that abundantly clear." She took his arm. "Now, relax. You've got to be all smiles tonight."

He looked at his watch. He turned, his eyes full of regrets. "Now I really don't have time to go home and still get back for the beginning of the hot-dog roast."

"You're dressed appropriately, but I'm not. I'm going home to change, then I'll come back and join you. Save me a hot dog?"

"If you're smart, you'll grab something to eat at home and pass on the dogs. I know what the pep squad spent. If there was ever any real meat in those things, it just wandered through on its way somewhere else."

She made a face. "Thanks for the warning."

"But I'll save you anything that looks good."

"You look good." She rose on tiptoe to kiss him. "I could have handled Ray alone if I'd had to. But it was a lot more fun watching you take him down a notch. Thanks for caring about Corey."

"I wouldn't do what I do for a living if I didn't care about kids."

"I know." She kissed him again, lingering over it this time. "But I think Corey's growing on you."

His eyes were opaque. "Don't get any ideas, Sam. Nothing's changed."

But it had. She didn't know exactly what or how, and she certainly had no insight into where it might lead. But something had changed. The man in Ray's office had been the Joe she'd married. She welcomed him back with a third kiss before she left him standing in the parking lot.

Corey had never heard so much noise. She had been to football games with Miss Sam and Mr. Joe, so she was used to the band. But tonight they were louder than they'd ever been before. Some of the instruments were bigger than she was, and they rumbled and blared until her ears felt as if they were going to fall off her head. There was a lot of yelling, too. People jumping up and down, cheerleaders clapping their hands and doing cartwheels. She had yelled a time or two herself, and nobody had told her not to.

"Come on, let's go under the bleachers." Mary Nell motioned for Corey to follow her.

Corey looked around, to see if it was all right.

"Come on, my mom knows," Mary Nell said. "All the kids do it."

Corey wondered if she should tell Miss Sam, then she decided against it. Miss Sam hadn't paid her much attention since the bonfire began. She had been up front with Mr. Joe, laughing and shouting and clapping. She looked at Mr. Joe like he was the president or something, like he was a king. Corey knew what that look meant. It meant that Miss Sam didn't need a little girl to keep her happy. She just needed Mr. Joe.

The night was cold, but Corey's jacket was warm, warmer than anything she'd ever owned. She threaded her way across the seats, hopping from one row to another after Mary Nell until they were on the ground. The bonfire still burned brightly at the edge of the football field, but the cheerleaders had stopped dancing around it a while ago. Now some of the football players, dressed like cheerleaders in red-and-gold skirts, were out on the field pretending to do cheers while the crowd roared and clapped. One football player-cheerleader threw his pom-poms into the air and they landed on another one's head. They started a pretend fight.

Corey covered her ears as the noise grew louder. She saw Mary Nell beckoning her, and she ran along behind her. The noise was loud under the bleachers, too, because Corey could hear the feet stomping above her.

"Why'd you want to come here?" Corey shouted.

"Looking for friends."

"Oh." Corey looked around. She didn't see anybody else dumb enough to come down here. "I don't see nobody."

"You want to look for candy bar wrappers?"

"Yeah!" Corey and Mary Nell had started saving wrappers. One company, maker of several different brands, was giving away prizes for fifty or more wrappers. Corey had to save two thousand to get a bike, but she already had ten.

The noise receded. Corey began to pick over the trash under the bleachers. She wished there was more. The floodlights on the field shone in narrow strips between bleacher seats, and she couldn't see very well.

"Look! I found one!" Mary Nell held it up.

"Ain't... Isn't the right kind."

"I know, but it's a clue. There'll be more."

Corey went back to looking. At the back of the bleachers, where they had come in, she saw three little girls approaching. She turned to tell Mary Nell, but she was up at the front now, poking through the litter there with her foot.

Corey recognized all three girls. They were in Miss Simpson's class, too, and one of them, Ann Grady, was the teacher's pet. None of them liked Corey.

Ann reached her first. "What are you doing here?"

"Playing." Corey stood her ground.

"Playing what?"

"Looking for candy bar wrappers. You can save 'em and get prizes."

"Ick. That's dirty, going through other people's trash."

"I wash my hands."

"Corey's going through the trash," Ann told the other girls. "She likes trash."

Corey turned away. There was no use in trying to explain anything to these girls. They were never going to be her friends. She wanted to find Mary Nell and go back up where Miss Polly and Mr. Harlan were sitting. Or she wanted to find Miss Sam. Then she remembered that Miss Sam hadn't hardly looked at her that night.

"Corey likes trash," one of the other girls said. "My mama says Corey *is* trash, and so was her mama."

Corey turned back to her. "That's a mean thing!"

"I know Miss Simpson doesn't think you belong in her class. Maybe you belong in the trash can!" Ann danced with glee at her own joke.

"Stop it!" Corey said.

"Don't have to!"

Corey pushed her. Not hard, just hard enough to make her point. "Leave me alone!"

"Ooo... Your hands are dirty, trash girl. Don't touch me."

Corey pushed her again. Mary Nell appeared magically at her side. "Stop, Corey. What's wrong?"

"She called me trash girl!"

"Why'd you go and do that?" Mary Nell asked Ann.

"She's your friend, you're a trash girl, too." Ann didn't look quite so brave now that the odds were evening out. She had two friends with her, but Mary Nell was bigger than anyone there.

"Take it back," Mary Nell said. "Right now!"

"Not going to."

Corey pushed Ann again. "Take it back!"

"Not going to!" But now Ann's eyes were frightened.

"Oh, leave her alone, Corey," Mary Nell said. "She

can't think of anything else to say 'cause she's got no brains and no manners. Come on, let's go.''

Corey wanted to push Ann again. It felt good to scare her a little after she'd gone and said bad things about Mary Nell and all. She had started to follow Mary Nell out from under the bleachers when she heard Ann speak again. Quietly this time.

"My mama says Miss Sam's trash for letting you live with her.''

Corey couldn't answer. Her voice wouldn't work, as if somebody had just reached in and shut it off. Her hands began to shake, then her knees. She had Ann on the ground under her before she even knew what she'd done.

"Corey!" Mary Nell tried to get her off Ann.

Ann began to scream, and the two other girls screamed with her. Mary Nell tugged at Corey again. "Stop, Corey." She managed to drag her off Ann. "You'll hurt her!"

"I wanna hurt her!"

Ann jumped to her feet, but instead of running, which is what Corey had expected, she ran at Corey with her head lowered and aimed right at Corey's chest. In a moment they were a tangle of arms and legs on the ground.

"Corey!" Mary Nell yelled once more.

"Take it back!" Corey said, punching Ann again and again. "Take back what you said!"

"Miss Sam's trash!" Ann yelled.

Mary Nell heard her that time. She joined in the fight, grabbing Ann's hair. One of the other little girls jumped on her. The other one took off running.

The rest passed in a blur. Corey thumped Ann's shoulders against the ground, but Ann got her hair and pulled it till Corey's head felt as if it was on fire. Beside her she could hear Mary Nell and the other little girl thrashing and banging on the ground.

Then strong hands pulled her off Ann and stood her on

her feet. "Just what are you doing?" an angry voice demanded.

Corey looked up and saw a strange man, his eyes blazing and his face contorted in anger.

"She called me—"

"I don't care what she called you!" He bent to lift Ann to her feet. A crowd began to gather. First just one or two people, a man who separated Mary Nell and the other girl and a woman Corey had seen somewhere before.

Corey clung to Mary Nell, frightened for the first time. More grown-ups were coming. Somebody dragged her and Mary Nell out from under the bleachers. Somebody else separated them.

Corey saw Miss Polly at the edge of the crowd, trying to make her way through. Then she saw Miss Sam.

"What's goin' on?" Miss Polly asked. Corey tried to reach her, but there were too many people in the way.

"That girl there started a fight with my Ann," the man who had pulled her off Ann said. "Ann says she just jumped on her and started hitting her. That's what she was doing when I found them."

Miss Polly looked in Corey's direction. Her eyes said that this was a very serious matter.

Some people drifted away; the band was still playing and the pep squad was still shouting cheers.

Miss Sam reached her, but she didn't take Corey in her arms. She just stood beside her, several feet away.

"She hit me. I didn't do anything." Ann was crying now, her shoulders shaking. "She hates me. I didn't do anything."

"You called me names!" Corey started toward her. "That's not true, you called me and..." She didn't want to finish. She didn't want anybody to know what Ann had said about Miss Sam.

"Mary Nell? Who started the fight?" Miss Polly asked.

Mary Nell looked miserable. She hung her head.

"Did Corey start the fight?"

"Ann called her names," Mary Nell mumbled, loyal to the end.

"That's not enough of a reason to hit somebody," Miss Sam said. Corey could tell Miss Sam was angry, even though Miss Sam wasn't looking at her. Worse, Miss Sam was disappointed. Corey felt as if there was a hole inside her and all the good things were just draining out.

"We'll take care of this," Miss Sam said, still not looking at Corey. "In the meantime Corey will apologize."

Corey saw Mr. Joe approaching. She wondered if every single person at the football field knew about the fight. Her head was beginning to hurt, and she had a scratch on her knee. She looked down and saw that her pants, the nicest Miss Sam had bought her, were torn.

"What's going on?" he asked.

"There was a fight," Miss Sam said.

The woman, who had her arm around Ann, spoke. "Yes, that child you're taking care of attacked my daughter."

Corey realized Ann's mother was the lady from the drugstore. Corey glanced at Mary Nell, and Mary Nell rolled her eyes. Corey felt a little warmer inside.

"Corey attacked your daughter?" Mr. Joe turned to her. He had the same mixture of expressions on his face as Miss Sam. "Is that true?"

"I've already taken care of it, Joe," Miss Sam said. "Corey's going to apologize, then we'll straighten this out at home."

"Mary Nell will apologize, too," Miss Polly said. "Right now."

Mary Nell, looking at the ground, mumbled something that could have been the pledge of allegiance. Corey didn't know. But everyone seemed to think it was good enough. Then all eyes were on her.

"Not going to." She scuffed her toe in the dirt.

"Corey." Mr. Joe's voice was firm.

"Didn't do nothing wrong," Corey said, not looking at him. "It was her."

"Did you hit her?" Mr. Joe asked.

Corey nodded.

"Then apologize."

Corey looked up. She saw the expression on Ann's face, and she knew if she said she was sorry now that she would never be able to face her again. Ann and her friends would never leave her alone. "Not sorry," she said. "And it'd be a lie if I said so."

She turned her gaze to Mr. Joe because she was way too scared to look at Miss Sam. Something had changed in his expression. She couldn't be sure, but she thought maybe he'd liked her answer just a little, teeny bit.

"At least she's honest," he told Ann's parents. "We'll take this matter up at home."

"Mr. Giovanelli, from now on keep that child away from our daughter," Ann's father said. "Or I'll hold you responsible."

"Teach your daughter not to call Corey names, and I can guarantee that Corey won't have anything to do with her."

The man made a sound low in his throat, like a cough. Then he and his wife walked away with Ann between them.

Miss Polly marched Mary Nell up the bleachers, and the other little girl and her mother disappeared. Corey was left alone with Mr. Joe and Miss Sam. By now, everyone else had gone.

"I've got to get back out front," Mr. Joe said, kissing Miss Sam's cheek. "Are you going to take her home?" he asked, as if Corey wasn't even there.

"Right away."

"It's all right, sweetheart." He touched Miss Sam's arm. "These things happen."

"In front of the whole town?"

"Yeah, why embarrass us in private when it's much more fun in public?"

Corey hung her head. She realized that she had made a terrible mistake. She should have lied. She still couldn't even look at Miss Sam. Miss Sam started to walk away, and she realized she was supposed to follow. She wanted Miss Sam to put her arm around her. She wanted somebody to understand.

But Miss Sam just kept walking, and finally Corey followed.

13

Joe watched Corey out of the corner of his eye. She picked at her dinner, as if food no longer interested her. Her appetite had dwindled since the night of the bonfire a week before. Sam thought that since Corey had gained some much-needed weight, her appetite was tapering off to a normal level. But Joe wasn't so sure that was it.

"Want some cranberry sauce to go on that?" he asked. "Or are you just getting tired of turkey?"

"I'm tired of it," Sam said when Corey shook her head and didn't speak. "We've had it four nights in a row since Thanksgiving. The rest of the leftovers go in the freezer."

"Tinkerbelle deserves a holiday treat," Joe said.

"Got you. The rest goes to Tink."

"It was nice of your mother to pack this up and send it home with us. I'll give her that."

"Wonderfully generous, even if she didn't have to cook it or pack it herself." Sam got up and began to carry dishes to the sink. "And the fact that roast turkey is to Mother like stewed roots and grass is to the rest of us doesn't detract a bit."

"Give her credit. When she found out we were coming she made sure we had the traditional dinner." He didn't add that Kathryn obviously had pulled out all the stops just for Corey's sake. Kathryn, for all her faults, had made an attempt to include Corey in all the festivities. Even Fischer had mended his ways and addressed occasional booming questions in the little girl's direction.

Only Corey had refused to enter into the spirit of the gathering.

"Next year we eat at Mama Rose's house with everybody else." Sam returned for more dishes. "If my parents want to spend the holiday with us, they can come, too."

"No leftovers that way. There's never anything left over after my family gets through."

"More reason to go there." Sam stacked Corey's plate on top of the others. "Corey, will you help me with the dishes?"

"I got homework."

"Not enough to get you out of doing the dishes. Come on, Mr. Joe put out the dinner, so we've got to clean up."

"Can I feed Tinkerbelle?"

"Sure."

Sam had answered just a little too fast. Joe knew that, even though she wasn't admitting it, she was worried about Corey, too. But then, he and Sam didn't talk about Corey. They could talk about almost anything else now, but not Corey.

He stood to help them clear off the table, but Sam waved him away. "You've got work, don't you?"

"Just some papers I've got to look over."

"Why don't you do that now?"

Then there'll be time tonight for other things. The words were as clear as if Sam had said them out loud. She was looking straight at him, her eyes a smoky blue. He sent her half a grin and began to look forward to having Corey asleep.

In his study he sat back in the soft leather chair that had

been last year's Christmas present and leafed through the papers he was supposed to review. He was tired, and the words blurred in front of his face. He set them on the desk and rose to lift his grandfather's mandolin off the wall. He strummed a chord, then another. He had never mastered trilling, the quavery, signature strum of the instrument. He remembered how the same mandolin had sounded under his grandfather's tender ministrations. Much, much better.

He played another chord and tried to pick out a tune before he set the mandolin beside his computer. He had sat at his grandfather's feet countless times while the old man played and sang for him. Grandpa Giuseppe had never been too busy for his grandchildren. He had loved them all, enjoyed every moment he spent with them. Joe sometimes thought that he had gotten his own love of kids from his grandfather.

Sometimes, like tonight, he wished he was back teaching in the classroom rather than sitting in the main office. He missed the interaction with impressionable students, the heady feeling that they were clay for him to gently mold. He hadn't done enough teaching to get burned out. Now his favorite days were those rare ones when he had to hold down a classroom while a substitute was on the way or a teacher had an emergency.

Sometimes it seemed as if he spent more time with ledgers, with forms and all the other endless documentation that was required of administrators, than with kids. But none of that had mattered as much since Corey had come to stay.

Joe wasn't sure where that last thought had come from. It was too momentous to ignore. The thought wasn't new; it had cropped up before. He examined it, waiting for the pain that should arrive, too.

There was no pain. Just a jolt of anger. What was he thinking? He was grateful to a snot-nosed little kid because she had brought childhood, all its anxieties and sorrows, into his home? And who was he kidding? He was thanking Corey, troublemaker *extraordinaire*, because nothing was the same as it used to be, and every time he looked at her he remembered that he would never father a child of his own?

Apparently he was.

"Mr. Joe?"

The troublemaker in question stood in his doorway, her eyes—what he could see of them—filled with hostility.

"What do you want, Corey?" His voice came out harsher than he had intended.

"Miss Sam says there's a leak under the sink."

He stood, rounding his desk to squeeze past her before she could say any more. Only when he was in the kitchen and heard the throb of strings and the unmistakable splintering of wood did he remember that he had forgotten to put his grandfather's mandolin back on the wall.

"She's scared to death, Joe." Sam came out of Corey's bedroom and closed the door behind her so that Corey couldn't hear them arguing.

"She should be."

Sam motioned him toward their bedroom. Her hand wasn't quite steady. He followed, but only reluctantly. Corey had gone straight to her room after breaking the mandolin. He had wanted to storm right after her, but so far Sam had prevented him. That wasn't going to be the case much longer.

In the bedroom she shut the door before she turned. "Corey says she was just looking at the mandolin and it slipped out of her hands."

"Then Corey's lying."

"I know how awful this is, but please, don't make it worse."

"Worse?" He ran his hand through his hair, a sure sign he was furious.

"Yes, it's bad enough this happened, but maybe we can salvage something from it."

"Not the mandolin, that's for damned sure."

"We don't know that. There are repair shops that specialize—"

"She smashed it against the desk, Sam. She didn't drop it. The back is splintered, not cracked."

Sam wanted to argue. She didn't want to believe that Corey had been so willfully destructive, so calculated in her hatred of Joe. But Joe was right—the instrument was shattered. Even if someone was willing to reconstruct it, very little could be salvaged. It would never be more than a facsimile of the same beloved mandolin.

"She was making a statement," Joe said.

"We don't know that—"

"*I* know it. She was making a statement loud and clear."

"Let's just leave her alone for the night, until we're thinking clearly."

"No!" Joe had paced as they argued. Now he faced her. "What are you talking about, Sam? Is that what your parents did to you? You made a mistake and they let you lie awake all night and worry about what they were going to do to you in the morning?"

"Of course that's not what I'm saying. I've already talked to her. She knows we're unhappy about what she did."

"Unhappy? You think this is unhappy? I'm furious."

"Then you should give yourself time to calm down before we talk to her."

"*We're* not going to talk to her. I'm going to talk to her. You're going to stay in here."

"What?"

He moved closer. "I said I'm going to talk to her. Alone. This is between Corey and me."

"No. You can't!"

"What?"

"I said you can't. You don't even like her, Joe. You don't think she belongs here. You've made that point over and over again. And now you've got proof that she shouldn't be living with us. You'll be too harsh with her. You don't love her like I do!"

"Just who do you think you married?" He advanced on her. His fury was congealing into something as heavy as stone. "A monster? A man who doesn't understand kids? I grew up with kids! Half a dozen of them. I helped raise Johnny and my sisters. I'm a high school principal. I deal with kids every day, and I've never beaten one yet, and I've never ruined anyone's life or even his self-esteem."

"I know that, but this is—"

"Different? How? Because she lives here? Because you love her? How does that make it different? Suddenly you don't trust me? Suddenly you think that I've turned into some vendetta-seeking maniac?"

"But it was your mandolin—"

"Yes, it was." He let his words settle between them for a moment. "It was my mandolin, and that makes this my situation to settle. And if you can't trust me to do it fairly and compassionately, then you're obviously married to the wrong man."

"I love her...."

"Yes. Apparently you love her so much that your head's not screwed on straight anymore. You've forgotten everything you ever knew about kids. You don't leave them hanging, Sam. And you don't pretend they haven't done anything wrong when they have. You talk to them, then you tell them the consequences. There are always consequences, whether we set them or not, and I'm not going to let one of them be a wider rift between Corey and me.''

"But—"

He ignored her. "She was testing me. She wants to know my limits. She wants to know if we'll keep her after this kind of behavior. She wants to know if this will come between you and me so she can squeeze into the gap and fill it herself.''

Sam stared at him. "Come between us?"

"You bet. And it's working.''

Sam felt suddenly sick. The truth was so apparent that she couldn't believe she hadn't seen it. Worse, much worse, she hadn't trusted Joe enough.

She fell to the bed. "Oh, Joe…''

"You wouldn't let me deal with her when she burned down the fort. This time I'm going to deal with her no matter what you say. If you can't live with it, then Corey's won and we've both lost.''

"I'm sorry.'' She looked up at him. "So, so sorry. Of course you'll be fair. My God, what's wrong with me?''

"About one year of doubts and fears.''

"I—''

He waved her comment away. "We'll finish this later.'' He reached the door in two strides and opened it. He paused, but she didn't say anything else. Satisfied, he went out into the hall and shut the door behind him.

He knocked on Corey's door, but there was no answer. He knocked again louder and called her name. There was still no answer. He was glad there was no lock.

He pushed open the door and stepped inside. The room was lit by the soft glow of night-lights. There was a mound under Corey's covers, a little-girl-sized mound.

He crossed the room without a word and sat on the edge of the bed. Then he tugged down the covers.

"Go 'way,'' she said.

"Yeah, I bet you'd love that."

"I told Miss Sam I was sorry."

"Do you really think that's good enough?"

"Don't know what you mean."

Joe saw that she was clutching the bear Sam had given her. She never carried it out of the room; she was much too old and tough to be caught with a fuzzy teddy bear. But he had never seen her in this room when she hadn't been holding on to her teddy for dear life.

He was touched—he didn't want to be and fought it hard. But she was scared to death, and the bear was the only thing she had to comfort her. He was a hard man to impress. He loved kids, but with a professional's distance. Sentiment had little place in his job; it blurred the distinction between what was good for a kid in the long run, and what was the easiest or most comfortable response.

Now the easy, comfortable response was to walk out of this room. But it wasn't emotional distance that made him sit tight. Something else kept him there, something he had no time to examine.

"Let me tell you about that mandolin," he said. "It belonged to my grandfather."

"You told me!"

"I know. But I didn't tell you enough. He was a wonderful old man. His name was Giuseppe. That's Joe in Italian. I was named for him."

"So?" Her eyes were shining with tears, and despite all her obvious resolve her bottom lip trembled.

"Grandpa Giuseppe could really play that mandolin. I wish you could have heard him. And he had a wonderful voice. He'd sing, always in Italian, because he'd been born in Italy and that's the language he knew best. I can't sing at all, but when I hold that mandolin and strum a few chords, I can always see him."

He was silent for a while, and she said nothing.

"The best way to make somebody angry is to hurt them," he said at last. "If I really wanted to make you angry I would find something you really love, like your teddy bear, and rip it to shreds."

"No!" She clutched the bear harder.

"Yeah. That's exactly what I'd do if I was trying to hurt you and make you angry. But that's not what I'm trying to do. I'm trying to explain that I understand why you broke the mandolin."

"I dropped it! On accident!"

"No. You smashed it against the desk to make me mad. And you did. I'm mad, and I'm hurt because now I may never be able to play it again. I'll remember my grandfather, but not in that special way. Do you understand?"

"No!"

"You know what? I think you're smarter than that. I think you understand perfectly."

Her bottom lip trembled harder, and she didn't answer.

He stood and walked to the window. "What do you think we should do about this?"

"'Bout what?"

"About what you did."

Again she didn't answer.

"We have to do something," he said. "I think you should have some say in what happens to you. We don't spank little girls in this house, but we have to do something."

"Don't care."

"I think you care a lot. I think you want a chance to make this better. I'm giving you that chance." He turned and faced her. "What would be fair, Corey? I think kids always understand what's fair."

She sat up, still clutching her bear.

"Can you think of some jobs you could do for a while to help me?" he prompted. "Since I'm the one you hurt?"

She shook her head.

He nodded. "Okay. Can you think of something you might be able to do that would make me feel better, like bringing me the paper at night?"

She shook her head again.

He felt frustration build. He hadn't expected this to be easy, but he'd learned from experience that all but the most intractable kids usually came around in a discussion like this one. And usually the punishment they assigned themselves was twice as harsh as he would have given them.

"There are still some leaves that need raking," he said. "And that's a job I always do." He tried not to picture Corey with a rake twice as tall as she was. "Let's see. My car also needs washing."

She shook her head, but she didn't look at him. She looked down at the bear in her arms, then she held it toward him. "Here."

For a moment he didn't understand. "What?"

"Take Bear."

He moved closer. "You want me to take your bear?"

"Rip him up." The tears were flowing down her cheeks now, and she didn't try to wipe them.

"Not a chance. I'd never do that."

"Take him."

He reached for the bear. "You really want me to have him?"

She released it, and the bear was in his possession.

For a moment he couldn't speak. Then he pulled the words from somewhere. "Okay, this is what we'll do. I'll take the mandolin into town and have it sent off for repairs. When it's all fixed, I'll give you back the bear. Is that fair?"

"You're not gonna rip him up?"

"I told you, I'd never, never do that. I don't want to hurt you."

"But I hurt you."

"Yeah, but you're a little girl and I'm a grown-up." He sat on the edge of the bed, but not within touching distance. They definitely still needed space between them. "I don't want to hurt you, and I'm sorry I have to take your bear. I just want you to understand and remember that we have rules, and you have to obey them. The rules keep everybody from getting hurt, you, me and Miss Sam."

"Miss Sam hates me now."

"Nobody here hates you."

"You hate me!"

"Nope. I don't." He couldn't trust himself to add another word. He wasn't sure what would come out of his mouth. He was a roiling, seething mass of emotions, none of which were easy to understand.

"Bear's scared of the dark."

"Is he?" Joe looked down at the bear. "Then I'll be sure to put him by the window, where he can see the moon."

"He gets cold."

"Tell you what." He stood. "I think you'll need to come into my room before bedtime at night and tuck blankets around him to make him comfortable. None of this is his fault, after all."

"I can visit him?"

"Any time you want. And if you think of something you'd rather do than lend me the bear, just tell me."

"No. Bear'll make you feel better."

She was dead wrong. He was going to feel much, much worse. He wanted to stuff the bear back into her thin little arms. He wanted to tuck her in tightly and tell her she was forgiven. He wanted to kiss her wet little cheek and tell her how proud he was of her. He did none of those things, because he knew what was really needed.

He had to take the damned bear.

"I don't hate you at all," he said. "And neither does Miss Sam. We think you're somebody pretty special."

"Not." She burrowed back under the covers.

He was at her side before he knew it. He tucked the covers around her. He could feel her shoulders shaking, but she didn't make a sound.

"Everybody makes mistakes," he whispered. "Someday I'll tell you about all the ones I've made."

She didn't answer. He touched her hair. Just one quick, forgiving swipe of his hand. "Sleep tight, Brown Eyes."

Back in his bedroom he found Sam sitting on the edge of the bed where he'd left her. He held up the bear. "An exchange," he said. "I'm going to ship off that damned mandolin tomorrow morning and ask for a rush job. I don't care if they repair it with sheet metal. I can't give this back to Corey until I have the mandolin again."

"Joe..." Sam began to cry.

He set the bear on the windowsill, but he'd be damned if he was going to cover it with a blanket. "It was Corey's idea," he said, staring out the window. "She was the one who thought of it. I made the mistake of trying to explain that destroying the mandolin was the same as if somebody ripped her bear to shreds." His voice sounded funny, even to him.

"She wanted to make you feel better."

"Yeah. That's what she said." He felt Sam's arms sneak around his waist. "I feel like hell."

"She's so confused and unhappy, Joe."

"You don't have to tell me." He turned and gathered her into his arms. He pulled her hard against him and buried his face in her hair.

Sam's cheeks were damp against his shirt. "She doesn't know how to make people love her."

"She's done a pretty darned good job of making you love her."

"But you're right. I love her too much. I can't see clearly enough. I want to take care of her and protect her so much I can't see what's really good for her."

"That's where I come in." He held her tighter and realized what he'd said. But it was true. He balanced Sam's intensity with his own levelheaded good sense. His years of experience in a big family, his years of training, of teaching and beyond, had given him valuable insights. As painful as tonight had been for everyone, he had done what was right.

"You have so much to give her," Sam said. "And I've stood in the way. But not anymore. I promise, not anymore."

She lifted her face to his. He knew he should remind her that no real harm had been done, that the situation was temporary, anyway. But that seemed irrelevant. There was a more important message in her words, and he heard it.

You have so much to give.

"No, *I've* stood in the way," he said. "I'm the one who's been out of touch with what I have to offer. I've been so tied up with my sperm count. I've only remembered what I can't give you, not what I can."

"It doesn't matter."

"Yeah, it does." He buried his hands in her hair. "Somehow I let making you pregnant become the cornerstone of my whole existence. I've been brooding like a spoiled child."

"Never that."

"Too much like that. I haven't been the husband you needed. I haven't been the man you married."

"Don't you think I know how hard this has been for you?"

"So what? It's been hard for you, too. I'm sorry, sorrier than I can tell you. I've failed you miserably."

"Never, never failed. But we've both been wrong not to

face this squarely. You wouldn't talk, and I tried to cope by taking Corey—"

He put a finger over her lips. "Don't start on that. Having Corey hasn't been a bad thing."

"Really?"

"Really." It was all he could say; he didn't know what else he could add right now. He still had miles of unexplored territory inside him.

"Thank you."

He kissed her, promised her with his hands and lips that they would make a new start.

Later, asleep with Sam cuddled close beside him, he realized that for the first time in many months he had made love to her without remembering that he would never make her pregnant.

Tonight it just hadn't mattered.

14

From the corner of her eye Sam watched Corey plodding away at her homework on the kitchen table. Her teacher, at Joe's prompting, had begun to assign more creative challenges for the little girl. The reports from school were encouraging. Corey was more manageable in class and less disruptive. At home, though, she was simply listless. Sam had tried to compensate by lavishing more attention on her, but Corey's response had been erratic. Sometimes she clung, but most of the time she withdrew.

Sam didn't need a child psychologist to explain the problem. Corey was suffering the fate of many foster children. She knew her life with Sam and Joe was temporary. As time dragged on and her father couldn't be found, her situation grew more unstable. Sam never talked to her about the future, because she didn't know what to say. Until Corey's father was located, the future was, at best, a question mark.

"Did you finish your math?" Sam asked when Corey closed the book.

"It's dumb."

Sam sensed a rebellion brewing. "You won't think so

someday when you have to balance a checkbook. Bring it here and let me see what you've done.''

Corey slowly slid her chair back from the table, but the telephone interrupted her snail's-pace progress to the stove where Sam was stirring homemade vegetable soup.

"Stay right there," Sam told her when Corey looked longingly at the stairs. "I'll be back." She squeezed past the little girl on the way to the phone. The voice on the other end of the line was familiar.

"Samantha?"

Sam had talked to Dinah Ryan so often in the past months that now they were collaborators, never adversaries. "Hi, Dinah. Any news?"

"Are you going to be home for a while?"

Sam's heart beat faster. Usually Dinah's answer was no, nothing important to report. "Sure. Joe's going to be late. Corey and I are making soup. Would you like to stay for dinner?"

"Not tonight."

Sam's heart beat a little faster still. She lowered herself into a chair. "Are you coming right over?"

"Just as soon as I can get away."

"Fine. I'll be waiting."

"Find something for Corey to do while we talk."

"I will." Sam hung up. She pasted a smile on her face. "That was Miss Ryan."

"Are you gonna look at my math?"

"You bet." Sam got up and told herself to be calm. She took Corey's paper and stared at it, but the numbers blurred in front of her eyes. "Looks good."

"I'm not finished."

"Thanks for telling me. I didn't notice."

"Why'd Miss Ryan call?"

"You know how she is. She likes to come over and see us whenever she can. She's on her way over now."

If Corey knew Sam was lying she didn't contradict her. Sam imagined she didn't want to hear the truth. "Mr. Joe called earlier. He's going to be home late, but he said he has something good to tell you."

"What?"

"If I told you, it wouldn't be a surprise."

Corey didn't even pout. She seemed miles away.

Sam knew Joe's news. The local music store had found a man in the Smokies who made dulcimers, banjos and mandolins. For a sizable bribe he had been willing to make the repair of Joe's mandolin his first priority. According to the music store, the man was a superb craftsman. Best of all, the mandolin was now on its way back to Foxcove. If it wasn't the same instrument, it was probably nearly as good.

Joe was most pleased that soon he could give Bear back to Corey. More than once he had complained about the way Bear stared at him in the darkness.

Corey went back to the table to finish her math and Sam poured too much salt into the soup. By the time she heard Dinah's car in the driveway she was about to explode.

"Did you clean your room when you got home?" Sam asked Corey as Dinah parked.

"No."

"Well, after you say hi to Miss Ryan I want you to pick up your toys like we talked about. Then you can finish your homework up there, while Miss Ryan and I chat."

"Don't have any more."

"Aren't you supposed to read a book and tell about it in class next week?"

Corey mumbled something. By then Sam was on her way to answer the front door. She passed through the living room, decorated with the biggest pine tree that Joe had been able to get through the front door. They hadn't talked about reasons, but this year the Christmas tree had gone up earlier than usual. There were still almost two weeks before the holiday, but the house was in full regalia.

She and Joe had both wanted Corey to have some part of Christmas with them, even if she was gone by Christmas Day.

Dinah's expression was always as no-nonsense as her clothes. But today there was something different and impossible to read on her face. She greeted Corey with affection and listened to her report about school. She took a tour of the tree and the fireplace mantel with its collection of antique, hand-carved toys nestled among spruce boughs and sprigs of holly. She exclaimed over the candles that Corey and Sam had made the previous weekend and the gingerbread house that was suspiciously less ornate than before Corey had decided to eat the licorice fence. But when Corey finally went upstairs to clean her room, Dinah grew solemn.

"Let's talk in the kitchen," Sam said. "I made a fresh pot of tea."

Dinah settled herself at the table as Sam poured. When her cup was in front of her she just stared at it.

"Go ahead," Sam said. "I'm braced."

"I don't know if the news is good or bad," Dinah said. "I won't know until you tell me."

"We found Corey's father, or at least the man that Verna Haskins always claimed was Corey's father."

"You mean he's not?" Because of confidentiality Dinah had never told Sam or Joe the name of the man they had been looking for, and Corey had never mentioned it. Sam had never wanted to know.

"I mean he says there's no proof. And he refuses to take a blood test, which by law we might be able to insist on but only after an expensive legal battle."

Sam stared at her tea, too. "That sounds as if he's afraid of the results."

"There seems to be no real question he's our man. But it's almost beside the point. He's completely unsuitable whether he's Corey's father or not. Apparently he's fathered a string of kids from here to Savannah, and no court's ever been able to get him to be responsible. He has no income. He lives off women, then he moves on when they boot him out. He's been in and out of jail for the past ten years and seems to have no intention of improving his situation."

Sam looked up. "That bastard."

"Probably too kind a word." Dinah played with her spoon. "The point here is that we're willing to let him off the hook. Going after this guy for support would be an exercise in futility. And he says if we don't prosecute him he'll sign a statement admitting he's Corey's father and relinquish all his rights to her."

Sam could hardly breathe. "And he calls himself a man."

"Some men measure their manhood in very peculiar ways."

Sam knew Dinah wanted to say more, but years of good North Carolina breeding prohibited it. "How do I tell Corey?"

"I think the real question is *what* do you tell Corey?"

Sam looked away.

"I won't beat around the bush. Corey's going to be eligible for adoption very soon, Samantha," Dinah said. "We're going to accept her father's offer and terminate all his rights as soon as possible. And our thrust at the agency is to place children in permanent families. We're not going to let Corey linger in foster care. If we can't place her here in Sadler County, we'll send her away, to another state if we must."

"Who would be eligible to take her?"

"You would," Dinah said. "But only if you and Joe

both want her. And if you decide you really do, there's absolutely nothing to stand in your way.''

There's absolutely nothing to stand in your way.

The words echoed in Sam's head as she, Joe and Corey ate salty vegetable soup and biscuits for dinner. They echoed in her head as Corey fed Tinkerbelle and she and Joe cleaned up the kitchen. They echoed as she helped Corey pick out clothes for the morning, as she read her a story and tucked her into bed.

There was absolutely nothing to stand in their way.

Nothing but Joe.

Sam lingered upstairs after she tucked Corey in. She knew that she had to go downstairs and face Joe with the news. She also knew what she couldn't add. She couldn't ask Joe to reconsider keeping Corey. She had promised she would put that possibility out of her mind. These months had been tolerable for him only because he had known that they would come to an end. She had no right to ask that they strike a new bargain. The old one still stood.

Corey would have to go away.

She dropped to the bed and put her face in her hands. She had always known this would be hard; she had always believed she would find the strength to deal with it. But she had no strength. She couldn't love Corey more if the little girl were her own child, if she had come from her body as a tiny baby.

Corey was the child of her heart. She understood how a mother giving up her newborn must feel. Sam would never know where Corey had gone, or to whom. She would never know if she was happy, or fully accepted. She would never have the pleasures of watching Corey graduate from high school and college, of watching her marry and raise her own children. Corey would be dead to her.

Tears streamed down her cheeks. She wondered how she

could tell Joe. They had made a bargain, and she had no right to burden him with guilt about his part in it. From the beginning she had known his feelings on adoption. She couldn't ask more than he could give. She couldn't destroy her marriage with resentments. She had to be calm when she told him, and she had to be reasonable. Most of all she had to let him know that she didn't blame him. Because if she didn't let him know, all the good things that had slowly come back into their marriage in the past months would disappear again.

She hadn't heard the door open, then softly close. She hadn't heard footsteps. The first she knew that Joe was in the room was when she felt the bed sag beside her and his arm slip around her shoulder.

"Are you going to tell me what's wrong?" he asked.

She didn't want to tell him now. She wanted to be strong. She searched wildly for any explanation except the real one, but nothing occurred to her.

"Did you talk to Dinah Ryan today, by any chance?" he asked.

She nodded.

"They found Corey's father?"

She burrowed her face against his chest. "Yes."

"And he's going to come and get her?"

She knew Joe would immediately think that, because he was an honorable man. He would assume, despite constant evidence to the contrary, that other men would be as honorable. She shook her head.

"No?"

"He doesn't want her." She fought her tears. This was exactly what could not happen. She had no right to put Joe through this.

"What happened, exactly?"

His voice sounded strained. Hers sounded worse. She heard herself saying exactly the wrong things. "Oh, he's a real man, Joe. A real stud. He's fathered a bunch of kids. He doesn't have any problem getting women pregnant. Of course, he skips out on them and leaves them to raise their babies alone. But he's done his job, right? He's shared his fabulous gene pool. That's enough. He knows he's got what it takes.''

''What are you trying to say?'' He moved away from her.

She sat up straight and tried to wipe her face with her fingertips. ''I'm telling it like it is. Apparently Corey's father has prided himself on populating the southeast U.S. He doesn't support the kids he fathers, and when push comes to shove he doesn't even acknowledge them. He's happy just to do his manly thing and send a part of himself into the future.''

''He won't admit he's Corey's father?''

''He's not her father!'' She stood. ''Oh, he'll say he is if the state promises not to require anything from him. And he'll gladly relinquish all rights to her. But he's not her father! Maybe he's the man who got her mother pregnant, but he's no more her father than Verna was her mother. Even less so, because Verna at least tried to be a parent. She was a miserable failure, but at least she gave it a shot.''

''Is that why you're crying?''

''Yes.''

''You're furious.''

''Yes. At him!'' She faced him. She was still trying to control her voice, her thoughts.

''And those comments about real men, about sending gene pools into the future, they had nothing to do with me?''

She swallowed. ''No.''

''You're a damned lousy liar.''

She saw anger in his eyes. She knew that she had said

too much already, and that there was still so much more to say.

"I'm upset. I'm not thinking very clearly," she said. "We can talk about this later."

"We'll talk about it now." He stood and took her by the shoulders. "Make your point. Say what you really want to say."

"No."

"Do it, Sam."

She knew they had come too far, but not quite far enough. Worse, she knew that it was too late to turn back. "He has what you want, doesn't he, Joe? Corey's father? He can impregnate any woman he takes to bed. And does that make him a man?"

He dropped his hands. "It makes him an animal!"

"Joe…"

"Don't you think I can see the difference?"

"I don't know."

He turned away from her. He was silent for a long time. It was a silence she knew she couldn't break.

"I always thought I'd grow up and make a houseful of babies." He didn't turn around. Instead he went to the window. He touched Corey's bear, stroking it lightly as he talked. "I thought I'd be the kind of father my old man was. I was only ten when he died, but I remember him as if he was here today. He was never too busy to throw a baseball or go to one of Teresa's tea parties. Every Sunday he stood us in the hallway, tallest to smallest, and checked us over to be sure we'd do him proud at Mass. We were Giovanellis, and that was something special."

"It still is."

"You know what? Maybe it isn't. Or maybe somewhere along the way I got screwed up about what that meant. We weren't the kind of family you hardly see anymore just because he and Mama had one baby after another. We weren't happy just because we could trace our family tree back to a village in northern Italy. We were happy, we were special because he cared and Mama cared, and they let us know. They gave us strength. They gave us the desire to make something out of our lives. My old man was a real man. And he would have been a real man even if he'd never been able to make a single baby. He was a real man because he was a good man. It's that simple.''

She wanted to cheer; she wanted to cry harder. "You're a real man," she managed. "You've never been anything else."

"No, that's where you're wrong. I haven't been a real man since the moment I found out I was the one with the fertility problem. You asked me once what I would have done if I'd discovered the problem was yours. You know what?" He faced her. "I would have accepted it, Sam. I would have been sad. I would have felt as if we'd lost something. Then I would have accepted it. And I would have gone out and studied all the options that were left to us."

"Adoption?"

"Especially that."

"But it wasn't my problem."

"No. And I couldn't face myself. I was unhappy I'd failed you, but I was more unhappy that somebody up there had failed me. Somebody snatched my manhood away the day I found out the problem was mine. You know who that somebody was?" He put his fist to his chest. "Me. Only me."

"Oh, Joe." She wiped her cheeks.

"And now I see the difference, and where the problem really lies. I'm the problem. Not because of a screwed-up sperm count, but because of a screwed-up attitude. And you know what? Maybe I can't do anything about one thing, but I can damned sure do something about the other."

"What are you saying?"

"What's the state going to do about Corey?"

"She's going to be put up for adoption."

"Are you willing?"

She started toward him. "We can't make a decision this way. We can't take her just because you want to make me happy."

"You?" He hit his chest again. "Since when are we talking about you?"

She stood absolutely still. "What are you saying?"

"I'm saying what you think I'm saying. We're the closest things to real parents that kid's ever had. I think we should get one step closer."

"Keep her?"

"Things happen for a reason. There's a world of kids out there who need what you and I can give, and one of them is living under our roof. She needs us. And we need children. Nothing could be simpler."

"Oh, God, it's not simple!"

He took two steps and gathered her close. "It's as simple as a call to Dinah."

"I told Dinah you'd never consider adoption! I told her today."

"Did you? I'll tell her differently tomorrow. She'll understand."

"I don't know what to say. I don't know what to think."

"I'll tell you what to think. I love you. And there's a wretched, bratty little hellion down the hall..."

She lifted her face to his. "What?"

"I guess I want her to be my daughter."

She looked in his eyes and saw it was true. "You really do?"

"Yeah. I want to be her father. Her real father. So, you see, it's simple, after all."

"Joe..."

She felt his lips on hers, his hands flowing over her body. She wrapped her arms around him and held him close. She was dizzy with love. Through all Joe's torment she had never stopped loving him, but she loved this man who had emerged from the torment more.

"You're sure?" she whispered.

"I've never been surer of anything."

His hands were warm on her skin, strong, sure hands that skimmed over her as if he were relearning the contours and textures of her body. He was a man restaking a claim, a man who had just discovered that treasure, not the treasure first sought but one as cherished, as valuable, had always waited just under the surface.

He inched her blouse over her head and removed the rest of her clothes with the same unhurried exploration. Her breath caught as he lifted her and carried her to the bed. She lay quietly when he moved away to undress. Silvery moonlight lapped at the contours of his body. He was every woman's most dangerously exciting dream, the male to her female, the god to her goddess.

When he stood before her proudly, undeniably aroused, she opened her arms to him. He came to her without flourish or hesitation. The bed sagged and he was beside her, the muscled length of one leg stretched over hers, the breadth of his hard chest pressing against the soft curves of hers.

He smiled the smile that had never failed to excite her, and she saw the confidence of old in his dark eyes. "We're going to conceive our first child tonight, Sam."

Tears rose in her eyes. Tears of gratitude. She was filled with more love than she had ever known, love for this man who had come through so much and emerged stronger and somehow better.

"And I don't think she'll be our last," he whispered.

"Ours," she said. "In every way."

"In every way that matters." He touched his lips to hers, as if to seal his words. She trembled with pleasure and embraced him. The kiss deepened and became another until she could feel only desire. His hands wandered, stroking the most sensitive places of her body. He had always been a considerate lover; now there was no give-and-take, only mutual need and answering passion, pleasure that scorched them both.

She gasped when he entered and filled her completely. She was united with him in a way that she had never been before. In that moment Joe was part of her, and she could feel his strength and resolve. He began to move, sealing the commitment they had made so long ago. She looked into his eyes and this time she saw only love. She knew then that this love they shared, the love they were expressing so perfectly, would guide them safely down the path of parenthood and into the future.

As they found joy in each other's arms, she knew that a child had truly been conceived that night. A child of their hearts and of their love for each other.

There had never been a sweeter moment in her life.

Corey saw shadows dancing on the ceiling. Not the ones she had grown accustomed to. These were ghostly fingers, the very first things she saw when she opened her eyes after the nightmare. For a moment she wasn't even sure she was still in her room at Miss Sam's. Then, with a spurt of courage, she looked around and saw that she was, but the room was darker than usual.

She managed to sit up, even though she was scared to death that the shadow fingers would grab her. She saw that only one of her night-lights was burning, and most of the light was blocked by a chair.

She wanted to stand, to move the chair so that the light would shine brighter, but she was too scared. Tears welled as she thought about the dream. She had been chasing her father, a tall man with black hair, just like Mr. Joe. She had just about reached him when he disappeared. And then, when she had looked around to find Miss Sam and Mr. Joe, she saw that they weren't there. They hadn't been in her dream at all. She was alone.

Tears flowed down her cheeks. Miss Sam didn't think Corey had heard her talking to Miss Ryan, but she had. She hadn't heard it all, but she had heard Miss Ryan say that her father didn't want her. Then Miss Sam had said that Mr. Joe would never adopt. She didn't understand exactly what all that meant, but she was more afraid than she had ever been.

She had known Mr. Joe didn't want her. She had wrecked his car, burned down his fort. Then, because she didn't want to wait any longer to find out if he was going to send her away, she had broken his mandolin. At least, she thought that's why she had done it. It was all a confusion inside her. Sometimes she did things she didn't understand.

She did know that she'd tried real hard to make Miss Sam love her best. When Miss Sam and Mr. Joe fought, she had even thought that maybe it had worked. But they hadn't fought in a long time now. Not since the night she had broken the mandolin. They kissed sometimes when they thought she wasn't looking. And Mr. Joe held Miss Sam's hand in a way that made Corey's own hand feel real empty.

Sometimes she didn't think Miss Sam loved her at all. Not anymore. And now she was sure she wouldn't be staying with Miss Sam. She just didn't know where she would be going.

She wondered if Miss Ryan was wrong. Maybe her father would want her if he just met her. Maybe he'd love her right away and keep her with him.

She remembered his name. Her mama had said it over and over, like it was something bad. And he had to live somewheres in South Carolina, because that's where her mama had died.

The shadows moved again, and terror washed over her. All at once she was too terrified to think about anything except getting out of the room. She managed to get to the door and open it. Miss Sam's door was closed, but Corey thought she heard noises. She crept along the hallway until she stood just outside their room.

She heard Mr. Joe laugh, and Miss Sam laugh, too. She could hear the low murmur of their voices, although she couldn't understand what they were saying. They sounded happy, like people always sounded when they were telling jokes or secrets. They knew Corey was leaving, but they were still happy.

She wanted to knock on the door, to let Miss Sam hug her, maybe even to sleep on the floor beside their bed. But she heard Miss Sam laugh again. It was the loneliest sound she had ever heard.

She crept back down the hallway. Inside her room the shadows didn't look as scary anymore. There were some things scarier than shadows. She slid between her covers and pulled them to her chin. Then she lay in the darkness and said her father's name over and over again.

15

"This backpack weighs a ton." Joe hefted Corey's school pack and pretended to wince.

"Gimme."

He relinquished it. "Hey, don't be such a grouch. Miss Sam tells me you've only got half a day of school, then you're going on a field trip to the candy-cane factory."

She looked away. As she'd gotten ready for school that morning she had hardly said a word.

Joe was surprised, but he didn't have time to explore her bad mood. He and Sam had decided to place their call to Dinah Ryan before they talked to Corey. They wanted to be sure that nothing was going to go wrong with their plans to adopt her before they told the little girl that she was going to be their daughter. He didn't know how she would react to the news—an edited version—about her father, but he thought that when she'd had time to adjust, she would be happy she was staying with them.

"Hey, Brown Eyes," he said. "It's going to be a good day. Let's have a smile."

"Don't you have to be off to school, Joe?" Sam asked as she came into the hallway.

"Yes, Mommy," he said, with a very private wink.

She blushed. "Then get going."

"Okay, but I'm planning to be home early tonight."

"I'll make something special for dinner."

"Do that. Fried chicken's good."

"Would you like that, Corey?" Sam asked.

Corey shrugged.

Joe shrugged, too, then he leaned over to kiss Sam. He ruffled Corey's hair, but she moved away before he could do any affectionate damage.

"We'll be waiting for you," Sam said meaningfully.

"I'm looking forward to coming home."

Joe disappeared out the door and Sam went upstairs to get her purse. When she came back down Corey wasn't in the hallway anymore. "Corey?"

"Coming."

She wondered what Corey had been doing in the kitchen, but she didn't give it much thought. The second graders had been instructed to bring a lunch to school, since there was going to be an afternoon field trip. The children were going to eat on the bus. She imagined that Corey was just adding an apple or banana to her bag.

"All ready?" she asked when Corey joined her.

Corey looked around, staring for a moment at the tree. "Guess so."

"Good, I'm afraid we're running late." Sam shepherded her to the car, and once at the school, she sent her off to her classroom.

The morning passed swiftly, despite the fact that Sam watched the clock continually. Joe had wanted to make the call to Dinah Ryan himself. She imagined their conversation a hundred times, until by noon, when she heard the clatter of second grade feet in the hallway, she could hardly wait to talk to him.

Through the windows of her classroom she glimpsed the second graders boarding their bus. She wished she was going with them. She would have loved to share the field trip with Corey, but she could content herself with hearing an account of it that evening.

It promised to be a very special evening.

As soon as her own students made their way into the lunchroom she slipped into the office to call Joe, but his news was disappointing. Dinah was in meetings all day. He had left a message requesting she return his call, but so far she hadn't.

The rest of the day dragged. By the time the bus with the second graders returned, Sam felt as if she had lived two lifetimes. When the final bell rang she assisted the last of her students into their bulky coats and mittens and sent them on their way. While she waited for Corey to join her she straightened up her classroom, placing items in drawers and turning chairs over on tables.

She began to get concerned when there was nothing left to do. By this time Corey had usually arrived. She wondered if the little girl had gotten into trouble and been kept after class. She slipped on her own coat and gloves and turned off the light. Then she walked down the hall to Carol Simpson's classroom.

The room was dark and Carol was gone.

She checked with the teacher in the room next door to Carol's. Carol had left earlier than usual because she was having company for dinner.

No one in the main office had seen Corey that afternoon. Sam began to systematically check all the classrooms. Polly was just turning off her light when Sam got to her room.

"I can't find Corey," Sam said. "She's not with Mary Nell, is she?"

"No, Mary Nell's at home with the flu. Remember?"

Sam had forgotten. "I don't understand. She always comes to my room after school and we go home together. She's not in her own classroom. Where could she be?"

"I'll help you look. Have you checked the west wing?"

Sam shook her head. Polly started in that direction as Sam finished the east wing and the playground. They met in the hallway where one wing joined the other. "No sign of her," Polly said. "Did she go on the field trip?"

"Sure. I mean, I think so. She had her lunch and her permission slip. Why wouldn't she have gone? You don't suppose they left her there, do you?"

"Anything's possible."

"I'm going to check with the office again."

"I think you oughta call Joe."

"I'll call from the office. Thanks for your help, but I know you want to go home, Polly. You need to check on Mary Nell."

"Harlan's there. I'll just give him a call. I'm not leavin' till that little girl's been found."

"I appreciate it, but—"

"You think I'm goin' home and tell Mary Nell we went and lost her best friend?"

Sam squeezed Polly's hand. She was beginning to feel the first flutters of panic.

The office had no list of who had gone on the field trip or who had returned. But they began to make calls. Sam phoned Joe as she waited. "I can't get through to Dinah," he said when he answered. "I've tried three times."

"Corey's missing."

She hung up after he assured her that he'd be right over.

"Samantha?" The school secretary, a motherly woman who was usually unflappable, motioned her to the counter. There was no reassuring smile on her face. "I talked to one of the field trip chaperons. She doesn't remember seeing Corey after they got off the bus at the factory. There were a lot of kids. It's not time to panic yet...."

The principal arrived, fresh from a meeting at the administration building. By the time Joe got there, the office was filled with people trying to put together the events of the day.

Sam went into Joe's arms in front of everyone. She didn't care about image. She needed him. He stroked her hair and murmured encouragement.

Carol Simpson walked in the door. She was a pale woman, thin and high-strung. Now she looked on the edge of a breakdown. "This is my fault." She began to cry. "I didn't take roll on the bus. It's unforgivable. I just didn't do it. All the mothers had children assigned to be with them. I thought that would be enough."

Sam felt Joe's tension, but to his credit he didn't criticize Carol. "Did you see Corey?"

Carol shook her head. "I don't remember seeing her at all. I'm sorry. That doesn't mean she wasn't there."

"And you didn't notice that she wasn't at her seat when you got back to the classroom?"

"It was chaos. The kids were wound tight. I knew better than to try to get them to sit quietly. So in the short time we had left I let them do any activities they wanted. Some of them went to the reading corner, some to housekeeping—"

"Did you see Corey anywhere? Think."

"I just don't remember."

"Did you help her with her coat?" Sam asked. "Any time today?"

Carol appeared to be grasping at memory straws. "No. I just don't remember! I have twenty-six children in that class."

"Twenty-five," Joe said. "Because it looks as if you've lost one, Carol. Ours."

Corey knew better than to walk by the side of the road. There were lots of cars going real fast. Some of them slid funny when they rounded the bend she had just passed. The woods were wet, slick with rain like the road, but there was a path she could follow if she was real careful.

She had been walking a long time. She didn't know how long, but she knew it was a lot more than an hour. It was starting to get dark. She had forgotten how it got dark so early now that it was almost Christmas. There hadn't been much sun when she'd left the bus at the factory because it was such a cloudy day, but now there was hardly any.

Getting away from her teacher had been easy. She had gotten off the bus at the factory and told the mother she was supposed to walk with that she was going to walk with another mother. Then, when no one was looking, she had hidden behind a car in the parking lot and waited until everyone had gone inside. From there it had been easy to get back out to the road that the bus had come on.

On the trip she had paid attention to which way to go. She knew which way the bus had turned, so she had gone the other way. If one way led to Foxcove, the other had to go to South Carolina. That part had been easy.

Now she knew it was time to start looking for a place to spend the night. Her legs were tired and sore, and she was cold, even though she had brought an extra sweatshirt to wear over her school clothes and under her jacket. She had known it would be cold. She had stuffed the sweatshirt in her backpack that morning, along with six cans of tuna fish from Miss Sam's cupboard.

But she hadn't brought a can opener, because that had felt like stealing. She was going to have to hit the can with a rock or something. Just as soon as she found a place to sleep.

She had brought something else. Bear. She hoped Mr. Joe wouldn't be too mad that she'd taken him. But Mr. Joe had told her that the mandolin was all fixed. She thought that maybe he wouldn't care because she wasn't going to be living there anymore, anyway. She had Bear, the cans, what was left of her lunch and her sweatshirt. She had even brought a can of root beer, but she had already drunk that.

She was thirsty again, and hungry. She remembered that Miss Sam had said she was going to make fried chicken for dinner. The thought made her sad. She had left Miss Sam a note in the kitchen, right before she went to school that morning. She didn't want her to worry.

She heard dogs barking somewhere in the distance, and she wondered if there was a farm with a barn nearby. Once Miss Sam had read her a book about children who lived in an old boxcar. They didn't have any parents, but they had been so smart they had known just what to do. They had never gotten hungry or cold. She was going to be just the same. She was going to find a warm place to stay and make a little home for the night. Then she and Bear could wait until morning and start walking again. The tuna fish would last a long time. If she needed more food she even had some money Miss Sam had given her to buy Christmas presents.

She wished she had bought Miss Sam a Christmas present and left it behind. She even wished she had bought something for Mr. Joe. She thought about the way he had messed up her hair that morning, and the funny way he called her Brown Eyes. Whenever she thought about her father, she thought maybe he looked like Mr. Joe. Maybe someday her father would call her Brown Eyes, too.

She stopped for a moment. Her cheeks felt wet, even though it wasn't raining anymore. She was tired, and it was getting darker every minute. She took off her backpack and unzipped it to take out Bear. Then, holding him tightly, she trudged on.

"Dinah, she was on the bus going there. We know that much. Nobody remembers seeing her after that." Joe gripped the telephone tighter. "Yeah. I've already called the police. They're organizing a search party to fan out from the factory." He listened. Sam watched the distracted way he brushed his hair back from his forehead. "Yeah, I've told them she's a foster child. They know to contact you when she's found."

He said a few parting words and hung up. Sam wanted to go to him to offer comfort, but she was fast growing numb.

"That wasn't the talk I'd planned to have with Dinah," he said.

She went to him then, and slipped her arms around his waist. They were alone for the moment. The principal had lent them her office to make the call to Dinah. "Where could she be?"

"I'm going out with the cops. Harlan's coming, too, and somebody's calling my faculty to see if they'll volunteer. Dinah suggested you go home and wait. It's possible Corey will call there or even find her way home."

"I want to search, too." Sam moved away from him.

"I know. But you need to go home and wait."

"No!"

"Please go home first and check around really well. Then if you can find somebody to stay by the telephone, you can come. Please?"

He was making sense, even though she wanted nothing more than to start searching. "All right."

He clutched her to him again. "We're going to find her."

"It's cold out there, and wet. How is she going to manage? What if some maniac took her?"

"It's not likely somebody took her from the factory parking lot with all those people around. It looks as if she's run away."

"But why?"

"We'll find out when we find her."

"When?"

"I'm not coming home until she's found."

She could feel tears starting. She fought them. "I feel so helpless."

"See if you can get some women to come to the house to make sandwiches and coffee. Then you can bring them when you join us. The search team's going to need refueling."

She pulled away again. "What if she heard us talking last night? What if she doesn't want to live with us forever, and that's why she left?"

"You can't second-guess a child, Sam. You know that."

"I couldn't get through this if I didn't have you."

He touched her cheek. His voice was rough. "You've got me. And so does she. We'll find her. We'll get through this."

Chaos reigned outside the closed doors of the principal's office. Four teachers volunteered to go home with Sam to begin making sandwiches and jugs of coffee. Polly planned to come over as soon as one of her older children arrived home to stay with Mary Nell. A small search party had already formed in the hall. The police were working on another, and someone was organizing volunteers at the high school. In only a short time there were nearly fifty people ready to begin the search.

Sam watched Joe drive away, then she started for her car. The other women planned to follow after a stop at the grocery store for bread and lunch meat.

The house seemed unforgivably empty when she walked in. She called Corey's name, expecting no response. The sound echoed off the walls, but there was no answer. Even Tinkerbelle seemed to have gone into seclusion.

She checked upstairs first, going from room to room, checking closets and under beds in case Corey was hiding. Then she started downstairs. She almost missed the note. It was on the memo pad beside the telephone. She picked it up to turn over a fresh sheet so that she could keep track of any calls that might come in from Joe or the police. Printed neatly at the bottom was one sentence. "I gone to find my fahter and I took bear."

Sam held the note to her heart as hot tears spilled down her cheeks. Corey hadn't run away because of unkind words on the bus that morning, or because Miss Simpson still hadn't moved her to the apple reading group. She had run away to find her father. She had planned carefully enough to leave this note.

She was still crying when Joe called to see what she had found. And after she managed to tell him, she thought there were tears at the other end of the line, too.

The search was called off at two in the morning. Fog had rolled in, and visibility was near zero. In the interest of safety, the men and women who had volunteered to comb the woods along the highway were sent home. A fresh shift of police continued to search the outbuildings of farms in the area, but no one expected to find anything until the sun came up the next morning.

"It's still in the high forties," Sam said, repeating the one fact that had given her hope throughout the long night.

"Her jacket's warm." Joe's response was just as familiar. He had tried not to picture the little girl huddled under the bulk of her jacket, shivering and crying. But the image had tormented him all night.

He opened the front door of their house and stepped back to let Sam pass. Most of Sam's co-workers had long since gone home. There were only so many sandwiches that could be made and eaten, so much coffee that could be drunk.

They found Polly asleep beside the telephone. Sam woke her gently and sent her on her way. School would open as usual in the morning, and Polly needed her sleep to cope with the questions of her students.

"We're going to bed," Joe told Sam after Polly had left.

"I'll never sleep."

"We're going to bed. Why don't you take a shower and change into whatever you're planning to wear tomorrow? Then you can get up and get going right away if we get a call or as soon as the sun comes up."

He made the suggestion because he knew it was the only way he could get Sam to sleep. He had agreed to come home for that reason alone. Pale and drawn, she nodded. His heart broke when he looked at her. "We're going to find her," he promised.

"I wanted to keep looking."

"There was no point." Roughly he pulled her to him, clutching her tightly. Then he pushed her away. "Go get in the shower. I'll be right behind you."

"I wish it was me out there."

"Sam, please..."

She started up the stairs. He wandered the house looking for—what? For clues? That was a joke. The letter had been clue enough. Corey had gone to find her father. And she had taken nothing with her. Sam thought there might be some cans of tuna fish missing, but she wasn't sure. Other than tuna and one missing bear, it was as if the little girl hadn't wanted anything he and Sam had given her.

He heard the shower running. In the kitchen he flopped down beside the telephone because he was too tired to stand. He put his head back and closed his eyes. The sound of the telephone edged him awake.

Groggily he lifted the receiver. "Yeah?" He tried to make sense out of where he was and why. Somewhere in the distance he could hear water running. Then he came awake suddenly as the voice on the other end began to speak.

Upstairs he was waiting for Sam when she emerged from the shower. "They found her," he said with no ceremony. "She's fine."

"Oh, my God." Sam's legs buckled, but Joe had foreseen that possibility and he grabbed her.

"When it got dark she found a nice warm spot in some farmer's hayloft. Apparently she told the cop who found her all about some book you read her...."

Sam began to cry.

He hugged her. "It's all right. I'm going to go get her right now."

"You're going to go? *We're* going to go. I just have to get dressed."

She definitely wasn't dressed. She was also wet and shivering. He held on to her, but he didn't know if he was giving strength or seeking it. "I'm going," he said. "This is between me and her."

"What are you talking about?"

"That was Dinah on the phone. The sheriff called her first. She's with Corey at the emergency room."

"Emergency—"

"Standard procedure. Dinah says she seems to be fine but hungry. She's working on a bowl of soup."

"What did you mean when you said this was between you and Corey?" Sam grabbed a towel and began to wind it around her.

He watched her glowing skin disappear under the folds of the towel. Suddenly he had enough adrenaline pumping through his bloodstream to wish he had the time to unwind it again. "She told Dinah I didn't want her, Sam. She thought maybe she'd have better luck persuading her real father to take her."

"Oh, no."

"Between that and what you told Dinah yesterday, now

Dinah's trying to decide what to do with her. She's afraid if she sends her back here, Corey will just run away again."

"No. Joe…"

"I'm going to persuade her otherwise."

"But we can do that together."

"No. This one's on me. I'm the reason Corey left. I have to be the reason she comes back. Trust me on this."

Sam stared at him. Then she nodded. "Yes. Go on. Do it."

He smiled, his battle half won. "Get her bed ready. I think she'll be one tired little girl."

"I will."

He hesitated. "Wish me luck."

"I don't think I need to. It's going to be all right."

He kissed her hard and made plans to unwrap the towel—or whatever was equivalent—as soon as Corey was safely at home asleep in her own bed. He left the bathroom, and quickly, the house.

The hospital where Corey had been taken was at the border of the next county. On the telephone Dinah had said that the deputy who found the little girl estimated that she had walked nearly ten miles.

Joe's little girl was a real trouper.

He made the trip as fast as he safely could in the fog, glad that he had succumbed to Killer's lure. At the first opportunity he planned to trade the sports car in for something larger, like a minivan, but in the meantime he appreciated the way Killer covered the miles. He parked in a doctor's private parking space and took the yards to the emergency room at a jog.

Inside, Dinah Ryan was waiting near the cubicle where a nurse told him an exhausted Corey lay sleeping. As he approached, Dinah stationed herself in front of the curtains that separated the little girl from the rest of the noisy room. "We have to talk first, Joe," she said.

He was impatient, but he understood paperwork and details.

"Shoot." He crossed his arms.

"She doesn't want to go home with you."

"Did she say why?"

"She says you don't want her."

"She's wrong."

Dinah's expression softened. "I understand what you've been through tonight. You've been out of your mind with worry. You're a good man. You like kids and you don't want to see one hurt. But that's not the same as wanting to keep her forever. Sam told me yesterday how you feel about adoption."

"Sam was wrong. And I called on and off most of the day to tell you so. Long before I knew Corey had disappeared."

"Be that as it may, you haven't convinced Corey you want her."

"We only found out yesterday that her father was out of the picture, Dinah! For Pete's sake, you couldn't expect us to tell Corey we were going to keep her last night, before we'd had a chance to discuss everything with you. We were afraid Sam had given you second thoughts about me. We didn't want to take any chances you'd say no."

"She heard me talking about her father yesterday."

Joe's anger drained away. "Poor little kid. Does she understand?"

"As well as any kid can. It's not like she ever knew him. I think I've convinced her that he's out of the picture for good."

"And what's in the picture?"

"I guess that will be up to you. And Corey."

Joe saw the curtains parting. An inch at a time. He saw a small hand with plastic rings on every finger peek out from between them. He wanted to grab that small hand, enclose it in his, but he didn't move. He was as still as he had ever been in his life. He pulled his gaze back to Dinah's face.

"I love Corey." He heard what he'd said and knew it was true. He was shaken by his own announcement. Yesterday he had realized he wanted Corey as his daughter, but he hadn't come this far. He and Sam had needed a child; Corey had needed parents. Sam already loved Corey. For the first time in almost a year everything had seemed simple and right. Now it wasn't simple at all.

He loved Corey and probably had for some time. If he couldn't convince her to come home with him, he was going to lose her forever.

He swallowed, but his voice still sounded suspiciously husky. "I love her because she likes bright colors and puzzles and bears better than dolls."

Dinah frowned.

He was picking up speed now and couldn't stop to reassure Dinah. "And because she has trouble with cursive, but her printing's great. And because she likes to read and she remembers everything that's on the pages." He spoke a little faster, determined to get it all in. "See, Dinah, I love Corey because she sneaks into my study sometimes when she's not supposed to, just so she can look at the pictures in my encyclopedia. I know she does it, because she doesn't always put them back in the right place."

"What are you talking about, Joe?" Dinah looked puzzled.

"And she's a kid who knows how to call a lake a lake, never a pond."

"A lake? Joe, are you all right?"

"And I love her because she eats fried chicken like a veteran. And because when she's sick, she doesn't want to bother anybody."

The curtains parted, and a little face squinted out at him. "Well, you woke up anyway that time I was sick!"

"That's because nobody should have to be sick alone." He squatted slowly so that they were eye to eye. But he didn't move toward her. At the periphery of his vision he saw Dinah step aside. "And I love Corey because she has brown eyes like mine and blond hair like Sam's. Of course, I'd love her if she came in shades of purple, too."

"Purple?" She stuck her finger in her mouth.

"And I love her because even when things get really bad, she's brave and she tries not to lie and she tries to think about how other people will feel. I love her for about a million other reasons." His voice caught. "But that's a start."

She dragged her foot on the ground in front of her. He didn't move, and neither did she.

"And because I wrecked your car and burned the fort and broke your mandolin?" she asked at last.

"Those wouldn't be my best reasons."

She frowned. "As much as you love Miss Sam?"

"Different."

She nodded. That seemed to make sense to her. "Like Mr. Harlan loves Mary Nell?"

"Exactly."

"And you want to take me home again?"

"I want to be your father. Your forever father. Will you let me?"

"Does Miss Sam know?"

"Yeah. She says it's okay if I'm your father as long as she gets to be your mother."

Corey looked up from the ground. There was a space between them that seemed like a million miles. "I heard your voice. You woke me up."

"I'm glad."

"And I hoped...maybe you liked me after all."

He opened his arms. She took one step and she was enveloped in a bear hug.

Joe wrapped his arms tightly around her. Corey's arms threatened to choke off his air supply, but he didn't care. He stood and looked straight at Dinah. "You ever heard the expression that possession is nine-tenths of the law?"

She was wiping her eyes. "Go ahead, take her home."

"You'll start the paperwork tomorrow?"

"First thing in the morning."

He turned before she could change her mind. Ten yards across the floor he saw Sam waiting in the doorway. He thought that when he was an old man he would remember her exactly that way. Blond hair loose on her shoulders, a brilliant smile and tears running unchecked down her cheeks. She crossed the room at a run and embraced both of them in a tearful hug.

Joe stood with Corey in his arms and Sam's warm arms around them. And he knew he was a man who lacked nothing.

He was a man who had it all.

Epilogue

Sam listened from the dining room as Joe talked on the kitchen telephone.

"Sure, I understand you're having a problem with Corey. And I'm telling you what you can do about it. First of all, you've got to throw away all the busy work. Then you've got to find something challenging for her to do instead."

Sam chuckled softly. She could almost see Connie Antonio's face as Joe outlined his plan for keeping his fourth-grade daughter out of trouble. He had outlined it to Corey's third-grade teacher last year, at about this same time in the fall. She suspected that there would be a string of these conversations in the years to come.

A purple blur with flopping blond pigtails raced past. "Don't go too far," she called after Corey. "Dinner's early tonight. P.T.A. open house. Remember?"

Tennis shoes screeched against the old pine floors. "What're we having?"

"Chicken."

"Fried?"

"Yep."

"Josh!" Corey shouted.

Sam watched her daughter poised on the brink of flight.

Corey had Joe's awesome energy, and she was just learning how to control it. Joe gave her frequent pointers.

Corey was two years taller and two years healthier than she had been when they adopted her. She smiled often, and her brown eyes sparkled. Her face was alive with intelligence and curiosity, and her petite body was tanned and fit. She was a Camp Fire Girl with a talent for gymnastics and a passion for horseback riding, which she shared with Mary Nell, who was still her best friend. Corey didn't know it yet, but she was going to get her heart's desire for Christmas. A horse of her own.

"Josh!" Corey shouted again.

"You'll bring the house down," Sam scolded.

"Sure. Sure." She said the words just as Joe might have.

A dark-haired little boy came limping into the room. He was a head shorter than Corey, still pale from too many months in a hospital room. Sam's heart turned over at the sight of him, just as it had every day since Josh had come to stay.

"Come on, Josh," Corey said, hands on lavender hips. "You've got to learn to catch me. I'm going to beat you to the lake."

She took off and the door slammed behind her. From the window Sam could see just how slowly she was moving.

Joe came into the room, and Josh gave him a heartbreaking grin before he limped after his sister. Sam went to the door to watch his progress.

"He's moving faster," she said. "I've got to give Corey credit. Josh is definitely moving faster."

Joe came to her and put his arms around her waist. "You look tired."

"This mother stuff is hard work. I'm glad I'm on leave for a while."

"Josh isn't favoring his leg as much. He's looking stronger."

"Corey makes sure he does his exercises. She says that's what big sisters do."

"He's in danger of being mothered to death."

"He needed a mother. Now he's got two."

"And a dad."

"Who he adores."

"Dinah called right before Connie."

Sam leaned back. Joe's arms were warm and strong, arms that could hold a thousand burdens. She closed her eyes and luxuriated in the feel of his body against hers. She thought wicked thoughts. "Was she checking on Josh?"

"Not exactly."

When he didn't elaborate she opened her eyes. "Joe, don't tell me..."

"Okay."

"Another child?"

"You said not to tell you."

"You're right. Don't tell me now. Take me to bed tonight. Make perfect love to me. Then you can tell me."

She felt his hand in her hair. Stroking, soothing. He tucked one long, silky lock behind her ear. His lips were warm against her earlobe. "Twins," he whispered.

Corey threw dog food into the lake. Attila honked in protest, then started for the opposite shore. "See, Josh? The catfish are coming right up to the edge to eat it."

"How come you feed catfish dog food?"

"I don't know. Maybe it's made with worms and stuff fish like." She stared out to the middle of the lake where her father had built a raft. She could swim all the way out and back by herself. Of course, a grown-up had to be watching.

"Did you always live here?" Josh asked.

Corey thought about his question. Josh asked a lot of

questions. "I lived somewhere else once, but I don't remember much about it."

"I don't remember much about the hospital."

"I remember when I was in the hospital once, and Daddy came and got me."

"And he took you home?"

"When we went outside he kissed me and told me I was his little girl." She threw another handful of dog food in the water. "'Course, I wasn't big then."

"I like living here."

Corey thought about all the things she liked. Warm hugs and cold swims in the lake. The new fort sitting back among the trees. Mom teaching her to do cartwheels and Daddy coaching her soccer team. The funny shadows dancing on her ceiling at night when the moon was full. The silly stuffed bear who slept on her pillow. Grandma Rose. Even Grandma Kathryn and Grandpa Fischer. She shrugged. "It's just home."

Josh shrugged, too. "Yeah, just home."

They stood watching the catfish feed. Then hand in hand they walked back home together.

New York Times Bestselling Author

REBECCA
BRANDEWYNE

FOR GOOD OR FOR EVIL—
THE INSIDE STORY...

The noble Hampton family, with its legacy of sin and scandal, suffers the ultimate tragedy: the ruthless murder of one of its own.

There are only two people who can unravel the case—

JAKE SERINGO is the cynical cop who grew up on the mean streets of life;

CLAIRE CONNELLY is the beautiful but aloof broadcast journalist.

They'd parted years ago on explosive terms—now they are on the trail of a bizarre and shocking family secret that could topple a dynasty.

GLORY
SEEKERS

The search begins at your favorite
retail outlet in June 1997.

MIRA The brightest star in women's fiction

New York Times Bestselling Authors

JENNIFER BLAKE
JANET DAILEY
ELIZABETH GAGE

Three *New York Times* bestselling authors bring you three very sensuous, contemporary love stories—all centered around one magical night!

It is a warm, spring night and masquerading as legendary lovers, the elite of New Orleans society have come to celebrate the twenty-fifth anniversary of the Duchaise masquerade ball. But amidst the beauty, music and revelry, some of the world's most legendary lovers are in trouble....

Come midnight at this year's Duchaise ball, passion and scandal will be...

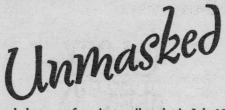

Revealed at your favorite retail outlet in July 1997.

KAREN HARPER

She would risk everything for love....

Brett Benton came to America to claim her inheritance:
one half of Sanborn Shipping. The other half belongs to
Alex Sanborn, a man who awakens the dormant passions
within her—a man committed to a cause that is about to test
his courage, his skill...his very life.

Forced to make a devil's bargain, Brett must betray Alex in
order to protect him. Now, only the hope of love can see them
through to...

DAWN'S EARLY LIGHT

Available in June 1997
at your favorite retail outlet.

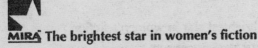

MIRA The brightest star in women's fiction

Look us up on-line at: http://www.romance.net   MKH1

If you fell in love with this
emotional story by award-winning author

EMILIE RICHARDS

Don't miss the opportunity to receive
her other titles, also from MIRA® Books:

#66152	IRON LACE	$5.99 U.S. ☐
		$6.99 CAN. ☐
#66273	RISING TIDES	$5.99 U.S. ☐
		$6.99 CAN. ☐

(limited quantities available)

TOTAL AMOUNT	$
POSTAGE & HANDLING	$
($1.00 for one book, 50¢ for each additional)	
APPLICABLE TAXES*	$ _____
TOTAL PAYABLE	$ _____
(check or money order—please do not send cash)	

To order, complete this form and send it, along with a check or money
order for the total above, payable to MIRA Books, to: **In the U.S.:** 3010
Walden Avenue, P.O. Box 9077, Buffalo, NY 14269-9077; **In Canada:**
P.O. Box 636, Fort Erie, Ontario, L2A 5X3.

Name: _____
Address: _____ City: _____
State/Prov.: _____ Zip/Postal Code: _____

*New York residents remit applicable sales taxes.
Canadian residents remit applicable GST and provincial taxes.

MIRA

Look us up on-line at: http://www.romance.net

MERBL2